Double Dagger Ranch

"You may take what measures are necessary against those that would erect a far worse world than you." Anonymous.

Double Dagger Ranch
&
A Second Chance

By

James Gimpel

2016

James Gimpel asserts his right under the Copyright, Designs and Patents Act 1988 to be identified as the author of this work.

ISBN: 978-0-692-10682-2
Favour, Barlow Press Int.
Library of Congress Control Number: 2018904570

Contents

1) Horse Talk,   p. 1

2) Bad News,   p.11

3) From the Old Rock,   p.23

4) Blood Sport,   p.35

5) Inexplicable Good Luck,   p.44

6) Lovers and Friends,   p.55

7) Cautious Optimism,   p.68

8) Plan It, Work the Plan,   p.77

9) Time Off,   p.87

***

10)   Catch-Up Hell,   p.98

11)   Jaw Breaking Moment,   p.111

12)   Goodbye Old Paint,   p.127

13)   Slow Death by Shame,   p.145

14)   Stolen Cattle & the 2/c,   p.156

15)   CYA,   p.166

16)   Cartel,   p.182

17)   Showdown,   p.194

Epilogue

Dedication

In memory of: Don, Joel, Daryl, Ronnie, Ray, Clarence, Cameron, Uncle Bud and Big Dave.

RIP

1

Horse Talk

Riding out from the headquarters of the Dagger Ranch he turned north along the dirt track road, moved through the gate and down the river bank trail to the low water crossing. In late summer and fall the water level is low enough to wade your horse across. Trout hold in the pool below and Trey can see the circles as they rise to feed on the surface. On the opposite bank, he and his horse climb gradually up for a quarter mile. Then, the snowcapped mountains rise back into view and the table top land above the river spreads out before him.

Trey Blake stopped his horse and stared at the mountain view and the gap in between two long ridges where the trailhead lay. That trail is where roads end and the federally protected Dagger Wilderness Area begins. He thinks of the hunting camp it leads to and feels the old pull of a good ride into the mountains and the hunt.

The sun is well up, there is no wind and it is a bright autumn day that surrounds him. Trey moves on, turning from the mountains. The big chestnut gelding stepped out gladly at an easy trot. The horse moves on a loose rein and with head low is a picture of good quarter horse breeding and training. A light wave of the rein hand moves the horse from the trail east and Trey follows the beaten track the band of mares take down to the river to water.

Trey moves upstream to the river bottom pasture and there the mares look up, first one and then the others. The bell mare speaks her whinny to the visitors and the gelding speaks back. The mares are sleek from good summer grass and bred back again for the next year. The yearlings are off a way, closer to the thick willows along the bank, and the mares turn and horse talk them to come closer for protection.

Trey stops while the mares are still just watching, uncommitted to any action. He is not close enough to see them well but he won't pass through this pasture without checking them. He stops now to allow them to relax and adjust to his interruption of their quiet morning. When they go back to grazing he eases his horse closer and slowly mixes in among them. He visually checks them all, looking at the legs, seeing them clean, void of any cuts or swelling. He looks at their heads, their bright eyes and clear nostrils, all signs of good health. Seeing all accounted for he turns and starts to ride away. Trey is aware of a follower. It is the horse colt, coming over from the willows with flared nostrils and ears straight up. Trey notices with satisfaction the well-formed legs, chest and hip.

The colt moves around to catch the scent and when he catches it squeals and runs off in a great charge through the mares that, though watchful, don't respond to his antics. Trey turns from the mares and moves across the meadow to the back trail that leads to Jay and Ilene's, the ranch foreman's house.

The gelding cues Trey that they are followed with a look back off his right flank but they continue the steady pace while Trey loosens the lariat rope from its latch at the swell of the saddle. He gives the loop three small coils and waits.

The colt charged right up to the gelding's rear, passed him and kicked his heels straight up close to the big horse's head. Then he pranced out in front of them like a dancer. Trey cues his horse, twirls his loop over his head and with a whistling sound, just as the horse colt starts to run, Trey throws with a hard snap of his wrist for the Colt's head and catches it. No longer proud, the horse colt turns in a tight circle to get back to the mares. Trey, forward in the saddle and raising his arm, maintains his mounts speed and lets the loop feed out and does not jerk the slack. The loop opens further, drops to the Colt's shoulder, then his forelegs and the colt gallops free of it. Trey slows his horse easy, stops him, coils the rope and lets his mount blow.

He watches the colt put on his show for the others. It is a victory dance with all of the acrobatics a horse colt can come up with. It's a joy just to watch it. Trey laughs out loud at one hind kick that is so high he could have ridden under it. He tied the coiled rope back in its latch. Always repeating the same lessons with his horse, he tugs on the mane a little and waits until his horse is standing on a loose rein and not fretting to run again. Then, when quiet, he strokes the big Gelding's neck in thanks and rides on.

Trey came up from the river bed to the full section of native prairie land, then he moved toward the only bluff of any real size out there. The house, in the lee of that bluff, faced the river and the small pasture across it. The ranch headquarters sits across the river from the house and you can see the bunkhouse and barn there among the shade of the big cottonwood trees. He rode out onto the dirt road that comes off the old wooden bridge and scattered some chipmunks in the dust. A hawk screeched from the tall trees and the dogs barked as Trey approaches the open gate and rides in.

It's an old house and looks it by the need of paint and a slightly sagging porch roof. It is two stories, with small rooms and one bath, built in the day of fireplace and wood stove heat, when you needed the rooms small for warmth. Jay moved in after he married Ilene. They had raised two children there.

The yard is fenced from left over ranch wire on the back and sides. In front, it has a traditional buck and rail fence like so many Rocky Mountain rural homes and mini-ranches.

The dogs, accustomed to Trey and his visits, begin to quiet. They drop their ears and tails go to wagging. Trey stepped down at the hitch rail and tied up as Ilene came out the front door and said,

"Good morning."

"How is he doing?" Trey asked quietly. He loosened the cinch a little as he spoke.

"It was a rough night." She said, "He's up, still in the back room."

She walked him in and Trey called out as he stepped through the kitchen, then reached in and knocked on the already open bedroom door.

"Come on back Trey," Jay answered. Trey entered and sat down across from him.

"How you feeling?"

Jay smiled a little at Trey's question. His eyes were glassy and sunken looking in his old leathery face, a face now ashen from want of fresh air and sun.

"I am on some solid pain medicine so I don't feel much." Jay looked at his hands and rubbed them together.

"Trey, they called in Hospice."

"Hospice?" Trey repeated before he thought and then said, "Damn." Jay looked straight at Trey and smiled.

"That's exactly what I said. I almost told 'em not to but Ilene said no, let 'em come, that it helps her too. Guess I can see that."

"Sure." Trey said. Ilene came in and asked if they needed anything then went back to the kitchen to get them coffee.

Trey started talking business, and Jay listened carefully. The fall round-up was done. The Cattle are down from the lease lands of summer range, the calf crop, cut out and separated from the cows, now weaning in a different pasture. The trucks would arrive on the coming Monday to ship. The last of the hay is in, bales stored in the two large barns for the coming winter, the hay stacks sit in the large fenced lot in neat rows. As Trey saw that Jay was starting to tire, he stood up to go.

"I am going in to town to see Weismann today. I want to see him before the weekend." Weismann was the ranch accountant and had been for many years.

"Yes," Jay answered. "Give him the head count for shipping Monday. Tell him who you are keeping on this winter. Get commitments for calving season. He forgets the labor needs sometimes."

That was a way off yet, after the first of the year. It was the hardest job on the ranch and the most important one. You needed good cowboys for it. Calving requires all your skills, with cutting a cow out of the herd without disturbing the rest, driving her to the pens or roping her on the spot to pull the calf, maybe deal with a prolapse or a C-section. Skill sets that only the best hands had. The Dagger had that kind of Cowboy, and the good horses they needed to do the work as well.

"What do you hear about the Ranch selling?" Trey asked.

"Nothing. Maybe Weismann will tell you something today."

Trey exhaled loudly, showing his frustration with the topic. It had held a dark cloud over all of them for some time now, first as rumor now as a probable fact.

"Alright." Trey reached for Jay's hand. It was slowly offered back and an awkward moment. They had worked together for many years now and Trey thought he knew how to approach Jay. But, with this dying time, everything was just different. Then as Jay took Trey's hand he firmed up his grip and set up a little, straightening to make eye contact.

"Trey, you go Elk hunting and I'll go too."

"Not," Ilene's voice came from the kitchen.

Ilene, was listening as always, but they didn't mind. She was a part of all of it, all the time, and always had been.

"Maybe find the money plane this year." Jay added.

"Now that would be nice." Ilene said as Trey stepped out into the living room and moved toward the front door. Ilene followed Trey outside to the hitching rail.

"Trey, you tell Clarence to get his butt over here." Her voice was firm and there was an edge to it.

"I will." Trey said as he mounted. "You know how he is."

"Yes, I do. But, it's time now for him to act better." Trey looked down at her from his horse, into her wonderful blue eyes, her tanned face, gray hair pulled back, no makeup ever. It was a face still full of life, and though older it revealed the beauty of her youth. He could easily see why Clarence and Jay had both competed for her.

She gave Trey that confident look and knowing smile of hers. The one that always said the same thing to him. That she trusted him to do what she asked. It made him feel proud he knew her and that she saw him for the man he tried to be. And, without ever hearing the whole story, he knew why Jay had won her. She watched men like she was measuring them and Jay was a man that measured up.

Jay was the most competent man Trey had ever known. Old Clarence was good too, but of a different nature. He could be un-reliable as hell sometimes, like when he was on a drunk. Clarence would duck out now and then and when he returned it was with little explanation. Jay's presence was always felt and never in question.

Trey turned his horse to the road and the old wooden bridge. The dogs did a short bluff of a chase, a couple of yips and barks and then stopped. The water sparkled beneath the bridge with the sunlight reflections. His horse's hooves hit the planks with a loud rhythm and the sound drummed them across.

"I don't know how," he said out loud. His horse's ears snapped back to hear him, and like horseman for eons he spoke to them.

"I don't know how in the hell they have done it, but they have held council with the cancer and are at peace with it somehow." And then the horse's ears pointed forward again.

The dirt road from the bridge rose gently from the river through a cut in the bank. The bank on the left side of the cut offered a steeper climb and Trey leaned forward, grabbed some mane and let his horse lope up it just to feel the strength beneath him. At the top it's a quick fox trot to the barn and horse pens. He rode up, dismounted, tied up and walked into the bunkhouse.

The first thing that hits you when you walk in from the clean mountain air outside is the smell. It smelled of leather, of coffee, of bacon, or whatever was cooking, beans maybe. Now and again you'd smell gun oil, or old spice shaving lotion. Sometimes Clarence's old timey hair oil, or his mentholated sports ointment would hang heavy. Everybody used that. Then there was wood smoke from the stove in winter or the barbeque pit on the porch in summer. Add a good dash of pipe tobacco and the smell of an old school locker room and you'd about have it covered.

The kitchen and quarters are separated by a plank bar, eight feet long with plenty of room around the end of it to walk to and from either room. Just off from the bar the dinner table is near the entry door that opens from the mud room. The mud room is enclosed and adjoins the porch. The table can sit twelve cowhands, which is the number of riders that work cattle at the ranch in peak season, roundup or shipping time. Others could squeeze in at the table or at the plank bar in-between. There are farmhands and irrigation hands too, but they are out in the houses reserved for family men and closer to their fields. When the Cowboys move to other locations they take a bedroll and a tent. It's just too big a country to come back to the bunkhouse every night.

Nobody is there when Trey arrives but the coffee is still warm. He took a cup, filled it and went to his makeshift office in the corner of the living room. As he sat down Clarence came in from outside.

"How is he?" Clarence said.

"They called Hospice in." Trey answered.

Clarence stopped in his tracks and Trey could feel him staring. But he chose to ignore it and stay quiet. He had no words for it anyway, so he picked up a pen and started his shopping list.

Clarence walked into the kitchen and started pulling things out for lunch. He turned on the crockpot to warm the beans and lit the oven to warm the left-over biscuits.

"What you writing?" Clarence said.

"Shopping list." Trey answered.

"For tomorrow?"

"No, today."

"Why today?"

"I need to see Weismann." Trey said. Clarence paused a second then said,

"We usually shop on Saturday. Today is Friday. Weismann's office is closed on Saturdays, ahh, ok, got it. Well, I got a list for you too."

"Don't need it." Trey said and smiled to himself.

"Hell you say. Why not?"

"Because your ass is going with me. And you can buy the groceries."

Clarence stood there and stared at a loaf of bread then he opened the big refrigerator and stared in it for a moment.

"The hell you say." He finally answered.

"Didn't I tell you we do groceries on Saturday?" Clarence continued.

"Can't we change that now and again?"

"Nope, we resist change around here. You should know that by now. Besides, I don't like shopping in the evening and you know that too. I like to be here at the ranch and in the bunkhouse working. Saturday mornings early is my best time to shop."

"Working my ass. Drinking is what you like to do here in the bunkhouse in the evening. How about we go this afternoon and shop and do some drinking in town this time?"

"Nope." Clarence answered.

"Yes" Trey said.

It is an old battle and one that Trey had rarely won, lately anyway. Clarence had a girlfriend now. It caused him to start timing his visits to town around another's schedule that you could never fit into. But this time Trey got up from his chair and grabbed Clarence from behind, pinned his arms and began to walk and half drag Clarence backward toward the door.

"You're going damnit," Trey said. He had Clarence around the middle and started to grope his belly and then released him quickly.

"My God Clarence, you are getting down right puss-gutted." At that moment, Wes and Wiley walked in the door.

"Are we interrupting something?" Wiley asked.

"Naa, come on in. Clarence is getting too fat for his jeans so we are going to town to get him some Dockers." Trey said.

"And what about lunch?" Wiley said.

Wes stepped into the kitchen and smelled the warming beans. He got a plate and checked the oven then pulled out the tinfoil bundle holding the biscuits. The two cowboys fixed their plates and sat down.

"Anybody want a sandwich?" Clarence asked, and all three answered "yes," in unison.

Wiley and Wes, both young and single, were thinking of the weekend coming up and shoving food down. Clarence started looking around at each of them while he chewed. He gave out a long sigh and turned to Wiley.

"You staying on this winter?"

Wiley nodded yes, then turned to Trey and said,

"Are you going to hunt?"

"Yes, think I will."

"I want to go."

"Sure. Anybody else?" Trey said. Wes and Clarence shook their heads.

"Somebody has got to stay here." Clarence said.

"I'll stay here." Wes answered; "I plan to stay on all winter. Ray's coming back for shipping. He wants on all winter too."

"Good," Trey said. Ray was another North Dakota Cowboy, like Wes and the two had served a hitch in the Army together.

"Wiley, if you and Wes will finish chores today you can take tomorrow off early and not worry about being back till Sunday night. Clarence and I will be here. You heard from Roland yet?" Trey said.

"Yeah, he'll be back by Monday. He's shacked up with a new woman back in Idaho."

"Who's putting up the horses?" Wes asked.

"You are!" Both Trey and Wiley said quickly.

"Shit, walked into that one." Wes stood up and stepped out the door. One hour later Clarence and Trey were making the drive into town in Trey's truck and like he usually did, Clarence asked what year it was and what motor it had in it.

"The million-mile motor they call it."

"Yes," Trey said.

"Wonder if anybody ever got that out of one. How many miles on it now?"

"Three hundred thousand and yes, they have." Trey answered.

"Got to take care of it though."

"Of course, you do." Trey said and he laughed at Clarence.

"You ask this stuff every time you get in my truck."

"Ok, well just making conversation." Clarence thought about not saying anything more but since his effort to talk about something else had failed he couldn't help speaking on what had really been bothering all of them.

"You worried about the ranch selling, I can tell it." Clarence said.

"Damn straight."

"Yeah, me too. Hard to find a job at my age. You'll be all right though. You are young enough to start over."

"I hate to have to do it. I went through a lot of jobs before this one held me." And Clarence knew exactly what Trey was saying.

"It's the horses." Clarence said. They were both quiet for a few minutes as they drove and looked at the scenery. The road was clear of traffic now that tourist season was over. Trey slowed when the road took the sharp turns along the river.

"Yes, it is," Trey finally answered, "And the country, the Mountains, all this open space. It just feels right to be in it. Jay mentioned the plane to me this morning. It's been a while since he has spoken of it. It surprised me a little."

"Not me." Clarence said. "Him being sick and living in a company house. Would be a good time to have some money. Besides, what's Ilene to do? When Jay goes the job goes and her employee housing goes with it."

"What do you remember about that plane?" Trey said.

"Well, Tom was flying it. The money story was because that Mexican Contractor from town was on the plane,"

"Yeah, that was Hector Gomez." Trey said.

"And, he was supposed to have a reputation as a drug dealer," Clarence said. "You remember that the papers mentioned it as a theory, to explain why the law got into the hunt for the plane in such a big way. But, I thought it was all just gossip. Mr. Fenwick had Hector doing some honest work for him."

"Yes, his house in town." Trey said.

"It took seven years to find that Forest Service plane." Clarence said. "And then, only when hunters stumbled on it."

"It's almost five years now on Fenwick's plane. Maybe they didn't crash and just took off with the money. But, it's Jay mentioning it again. I think he really does believe it had money on it and I'm prone to respect his opinion." Trey said.

"I'd have to think about that. I didn't know Tom as well as Jay did. I never met Hector but maybe once in my life. Jay had flown on that plane a time or two, looking for lost cattle up in the mountains. Tom flew for the Fenwicks for many years." Clarence said.

"Well, that wilderness is big country. They aren't the first lost up there and they won't be the last." Trey said.

He had ridden in that wilderness many miles and so had Clarence. But you could not live long enough to see it all. They were still talking about it when they pulled up at the grocery store. Trey started to park the truck when Clarence said,

"Just drop me off in front and come back and get me after you see Weismann."

"What if I take longer?" Trey said.

"Don't matter, there's a coffee shop in there. Might see somebody to talk too."

As the truck idled at the front of the grocery Clarence, with his door half opened to get out, hesitated. Trey looked at him with a steady gaze and waited. He had known Clarence a long time and he no longer minded waiting for him to think something through before he spoke it. Most of the time it was worth it.

"Trey, you and me better have a long talk with Jay on those horses. He's the only one that really knows the bloodlines. Some are papered of course but most aren't. Back in the day we had ways of getting our mares bred to good blood without all the fuss they have nowadays. Sort of a poor man's horse market. The deal was that we geld every colt that hit the ground. We just wanted good horseflesh to use every day."

Clarence got out, closed the door of the truck and started inside. He hadn't gone ten steps before somebody came over to say hello to him. Clarence was well known in town as a colorful character and he was a popular one.

Trey drove out of the parking lot and headed for the accountant's office. He was thinking horses. The cavvy, in of itself was quite an accomplishment of Jays. It would be a shame to lose touch with it.

2

Bad News

Mr. Weismann, always cordial when Trey came to see him, offered coffee and a hand shake. In his spacious office, surrounded with western art, the man looked important and Trey made it a point to act that way himself when he was around him. Trey stayed on his feet for a minute or two and looked at the Frederick Remington "Bronco Buster" statue and "The mountain man." Then he turned to the wall with two Charles Russell paintings. One showed cowboys roping a grizzly bear. Weismann waited, moved something on his desk and when Trey turned Weismann pointed to a black leather chair. As Trey set down Weismann spoke.

"You think cowboys ever did that? The bear roping," he said.

"Yeah, tried it at the least." Trey answered. "But, it's the horses getting close enough and on the downwind. That part I'm not so sure of. That would be a bad place to get bucked off. I sure like your office Mr. Weismann, beautiful stuff. Jay help you get that Bull, didn't he?" Trey pointed at the huge Elk rack on the wall behind his desk.

"Yes he did. Jay was a good hunting guide, best I ever had."

"Yeah, he understood that game. He loved it. He ran the hunting camp, didn't he?" Trey said.

"Yes, it was old Mr. Fenwick's passion. Kept it just for himself and friends. It had to have an Outfitter and Jay had the license."

"Could it start operating commercially again?" Trey said.

"Probably, you'd have to go through the Forest Service and see what they would do. And, get your Outfitter's License. They regulate the hell out of that business nowadays." Weismann said.

There was a pause. Weismann held a folder and he handed it to Trey, then opened another one just like it on his desk.

"Take a look Trey, this is all of the ranch's property, livestock and equipment, a complete inventory, at one time anyway." Trey opened his up and began to glance through the pages.

"Don't worry too much about the exact numbers now," Weismann continued. "I do need you to take a pencil and change anything you know to be different. If you will look on page ten you'll see hay and feed inventory. I have the bill for the Alfalfa hay you had delivered for the winter but don't know what you have put up from the ranch's hay meadows. And on page twelve I'll need the exact number of head you are shipping."

"We cut out some replacement heifers." Trey said, "Also, sometime next week, we'll need to ship some dry cows, prolapsed and..."

"Don't worry about that Trey, just put them back in the herd."

"What?" Trey looked up, surprised. They always culled Cows that did not calve or were getting too old or had trouble with calving, like prolapsed, or C-section. There was no profit feeding unproductive animals all winter.

"Trey, there are buyers for the ranch. Fenwick has notified me he is taking the offer. The deal does not include the inventory. The real estate developers will break the ranch up and sell it off in smaller parcels for mini-ranches and development. All the stock and equipment will be auctioned off. The culls will bring a better price mixed in with the herd.

"Shit." Trey said and felt no embarrassment for saying it. The blood involuntarily raced to his head."

"Did you tell Jay?" Trey was on the edge of his seat and leaning well forward now.

"I did not. I will Ilene. She's better to gauge his health and ability to accept this kind of news."

Trey took a deep breath and let it out slow. He thought of a poster he had seen once of a man on a mountain just sitting there. It read, 'Relax, nothing is under control.'

"What happened that made him finally do it?" Trey asked.

"The falling price of oil is a big part of it but the growing price of Real Estate in these small Rocky Mountain towns is a bigger part. It's going through the roof. So much land out here is owned by the Federal Government in the form of National Parks, the US Forest Service, and designated Wilderness Areas. Just not much of it can be developed. Less than ten percent is privately owned in the Two Ocean basin and surrounding valleys. You've seen how the Town has grown. There's the expansion of the Ski Resort and the new airport, both factors as well."

"So, all the cattle, horses," Trey's voice dropped off.

"Gone," Weismann finished for him. "But you have got the

winter yet, and the calving. Then in the spring, after the snows gone, the ranch will go too."

Trey stood and stuck the folders under his arm. They both walked to the door and Weismann stopped and held out his hand. Trey took it firmly.

"I'll help anyway I can." Weismann said, then added, "There might be a way for some of you to stay on. The new owners will need caretakers, people on the property for a while. Look, you really want to take the culls to the sale barn go ahead. No sense letting the Double Dagger sell less than the quality it has always stood for."

And with that brief finality and ringing ears Trey left. But he liked what Weismann had said last. It's what he wanted and Jay would have expected no less. The Double Dagger Ranch had always been about good cattle and horses. Even at a loss, always clean, healthy stock.

Trey laid the folders on the back seat of the truck and drove slowly to the grocery store. He found a spot in front and parked. He got out and walked inside. Clarence was ready. He only had four carts filled to the brim this time. Trey said nothing, did not even look at Clarence but grabbed a loaded cart and pushed it out with Clarence following. In the back of the truck he dropped the tail gate, jumped in and drug the two large ice chests to the end of the truck bed for loading. They put all the frozen goods into the ice chests and closed the lids tight. The bread and lighter bags, stuff that might fly out, he put in the dry box and closed that lid tight. The rest was placed under the tarp in the truck bed and pushed against the tool box and cab wall. All this because a trip to town rarely meant going straight back to the ranch. Goods needed a way to keep for a while. They were headed for the bar.

Trey started talking as soon as they were moving. His voice was flat with little expression. He told Clarence that Weismann had thanked them for all they had done and for taking on the responsibility of finishing the job to the end. Weismann assured him that Fenwick would take care of them. They would receive a good severance and be allowed to stay on the ranch for some un-specified time after the sale to help with anything left to do. And later, as caretakers perhaps. He told him that Fenwick would be coming out in a week or two to meet with the buyers and might need them to help host it.

When they got to the bar, Trey parked and went straight in. Clarence barely kept up with him. Trey ordered a double Bourbon straight up. Clarence did the same. They tossed them both down quickly and ordered two more with beers on the side. The Bar served food, Wes and Wiley would take care of things at the ranch, there was no reason to hurry. They did not want to talk about the news. They were thinking the same thing anyway. They were thinking the Dagger Ranch was a ranching legend and one of the last of a handful that still retained the aura of the old west. Cowboys from all over the country came there to hire on, make a roundup, just to say they had ridden for the Dagger. Most of all they wanted to say they had ridden a string of the Dagger horses for a season, maybe longer. It was a badge of honor and one of the last places you could prove yourself as an authentic, American Cowboy.

"Caretakers?" Clarence said. "He really used that word?"

"Yes, he did," Trey said on the third double bourbon, "and here's to being misjudged once again," he held his glass to Clarence's...

"Wouldn't have it any other way," Clarence said, and that made Trey laugh. For they both understood something. There is a life that some men choose, a seaman, a soldier, a cowboy. It's a way that saves them from a life too easy and too predictable. That's a life with little risk, one of security, pull the shift and the forty-hour week and go home in traffic to a track home near a freeway. That's a life some men can never live. Clarence had all the terms for it from his random reading and knew it in his own, personal way. He held up his glass again and Trey did too,

"To La vie Dan santé," Clarence said, and then they proceeded to get hammered.

Clarence's lady friend, Casey Emmel came in for her shift at the bar. The place was starting to fill up. It was Friday evening and the locals were turning out to enjoy having the town to themselves again after the summer's tourist season had ended. Casey came over to the bar and put her arms around Clarence from the back. She said "Hi" and then seeing his condition and Trey's she said,

"Have you eaten?"

"Not yet," Clarence answered.

"Well, you need to order now before the crowd gets bigger. And before you get too drunk." Clarence looked sheepish, Trey stood there, thought for a second and said,

"You are right. Bring me a baked half-chicken and fries and gravy."

"You?" Casey said to Clarence. When he failed to respond, she said.

"I'll get you the same." She walked into the back, to the kitchen and said to the cook,

"Clarence's drinking on an empty stomach again. Can you put a rush on two Chicken plates and fries?"

Trey and Clarence moved off the bar to grab a table. Clarence was grumbling.

"Don't start, she's right. No good drinking like this. Just feel like hell in the morning." Trey said.

"I guess." Clarence answered and turned and watched Casey out among the tables getting her game on. She was the oldest waitress in town and she knew everybody. Casey was good sized, buxom and strong looking, fifty years old at the least. She was less feminine looking than many men prefer but she suited Clarence. She was always crisp looking in her dress and style and had a graceful balance when she danced or walked. He was getting accustomed to her as she maintained the contact with him over time. She asked little in return. Clarence had started to think he had fallen in love with her but nobody else knew it. He started feeling it now watching her interacting with the customers. She enjoyed her job. She liked people and people liked her. Clarence had not liked it, that she was watching out for him. But that was changing. It just felt good sometimes. Somethings take a while for a man to admit to himself. Clarence had missed many a relationship by courting too slow. That way he could blame circumstance instead of admitting his fear of commitment. It was an old dodge of his.

In a surprisingly short time their plates were set in front of them and both dug in. They chased down their food with whiskey and black coffee. About half-way through Casey came over and sat down. She didn't say anything, she just set and watched them eat. She was grinning from ear to ear.

"What," Clarence finally said, barely looking up.

"Nothing," Casey said. "I like watching hungry men eat. I hadn't seen you lately so I thought I would just see what you looked like."

"Well, how do I look?" Clarence said.

"With that gravy on your handlebar mustache I would say like a Walrus. But a handsome one."

"Well, then." Clarence had to chew and swallow. "That's just fine."

"How you been doing?" she said.

"You saw me last Saturday afternoon, one week ago. That held over till Sunday morning. I am doing practically the same as I was then."

"Well, I'd like to see you more."

"Like when?"

"Like, yesterday and tomorrow."

"My God woman," Clarence shook his head, but he kept eating.

"Here then." She put the check tab on the table. "I'll be out next week to help with shipping. I'll bring a dish." She got up to return to her rounds, still smiling.

When they finished eating Trey picked up the tab and pulled out his wallet. Another girl was at the front cash register when they walked up. Trey turned the ticket over for no particular reason and a note was on the back. It said, "I love you."

"I think this is for you," he said. He handed it to Clarence. Clarence looked at it, "You're right. Put up your money."

Trey did just that and moments later they were in the truck and headed for the ranch. Clarence fell asleep and left Trey to drive, alone with his thoughts. Then, just as they drove through the Ranch's front gate Trey turned the truck down the road to the bridge. Clarence rose up from his slumber and said,

"Are we home?"

Trey pulled into Jay's and said, "Let's see if he's still up."

There was a light on in a couple of rooms. Trey was tired but it wasn't very late. He drove up to the house and before they were out of the truck Ilene was on the porch and shushing the dogs. She spoke to Clarence,

"He is awake but on a lot of medication. Don't be surprised if he drifts off on you."

"Ok," Clarence said. "How you holding up?"

"Oh, you know, hanging in there. Go on in. He's in the bedroom watching TV."

Trey followed Clarence to the bedroom door but when Clarence walked in, Trey stopped and turned back toward the kitchen sink. He was burning with thirst and Jay and Ilene had the best well water in the county. It was a deep spring fed well and cold. Ilene had gone back into her sewing room and when Jay turned off the TV to visit, the purr of her sewing machine could be heard. She was always busy at something. Trey got a large glass from the cabinet and filled it from the faucet. He sat down at the kitchen table and drank the water in the dark and listened to Jay's voice in the other room.

"I still got some of your western movie collection?" Jay said,

"You want some more? I'll bring them over tomorrow."

Nobody likes western movies like a cowhand. Clarence had the best collection of western movies Trey had ever seen. They were the "authentic" ones Clarence always said, meaning ones that had less of a gunfighter story and more of a working man's story. They all had to admit that Clarence, though self-proclaimed, was a good western movie critic and Trey thought that he was spot on when he started talking about them. Clarence was nothing if not authentic himself. He was as real as people get.

"Sorry I ain't been over lately." Clarence said. His thought had been that Jay would come back in for work one morning. But he couldn't say that, not now, not anymore.

"Don't worry about it." Jay said.

"How long we've known each other Jay?" There was quiet and then,

"Near fifty years. The bucking horse sale in Miles City, in or around 1970."

"Yep," Clarence said. "You remember how many horses you bucked out that day? You bucked out eleven head."

"I suppose." Jay answered. "I was trying to figure something out."

"Jay, on all the ranches we worked on, all the rodeos we went to, all the bars we drank in, I never once ran into anybody that ever came close to that number."

"I was feeling pretty punchy that day." Jay said.

"You sure the hell were. The closest I ever heard was seven. Do you remember who did that?"

"I can guess." Jay answered.

"Guess hell, it was me and you know it. And, it was the same day at the same sale."

"That's a lot." Jay said.

"Yes, it is. Unless, of course, you are around. I hurt for a month. I don't know how you got ahead of me like that."

"I know how," Jay answered.

"What then,"

"You started drinking too soon. You thought we had finished and there were more horses in the back pens."

"I guess." Clarence said. "We rode some trails together didn't we? Made all the big roundups." Clarence started naming the list of the big outfits they had ridden for.

"That Oregon country was fine," Jay added. "Don't forget that MB Ranch."

"Yep, what a piece of work. Didn't they have some good horses?"

"Over one hundred head." Jay said.

"I always thought we should have stayed on at that ranch."

"Well, we did better here." Jay answered.

"Yes. You remember the last time I came back after quitting?"

"Which time? You quit more than once. I know you couldn't stand me being the boss. I couldn't just keep kissing your ass to get you to stay. Made me look bad to the other hands." Jay's voice had risen to normal levels now and he sounded to Trey like his old self.

"Well, of course I am talking about the last time I quit and the last time I came back since I haven't left since then and it's been a couple of decades now."

"Ok, I know." Jay said, chuckling under his breath.

"Well, quit being difficult. I have something to say and I'll need your attention for a few minutes." Clarence's tone was turning formal now.

Trey set up to listen closely. He did not want to miss anything. It grew quiet and the sewing machine had stopped. The two old punchers voices were so clearly audible that Trey could hear them breathe.

"That last time, I did not come back to hire on. I was just passing through, riding some of my old back trails. I was at the end of my rope without enough left to tie a knot in. My father had just passed away, my mother gone long before. He died in a line shack in North Dakota. A colt he was riding on a herding job in the badlands had fallen on him. It crushed him inside. He made it back to the line shack but couldn't call anybody. No phones, he crawled on his bunk and died. Jay, this happened when I was way down in Texas and I had just lost a good paying oilfield job. I was trying hard to get another one. Every time I left the ranch life I always fell flat on my face. That time it was no different. It gets humiliating after a while. They expect you to suck up to them out there and the ass biting on those construction jobs they take to new heights. Just doing a good job ain't enough. I drove up to the Dakota's and buried him next to mother. It nearly broke me. The cost of the trip, the fuel, the funeral and I was broke. I had to hock Dad's saddle, his fine old McCall, the one he had made just for himself, and I pawned it. I felt like shit about that and still do. If something had happened to my truck I would have been living under a bridge out of luck and afoot. I watched my folks live and die on some rich man's ranch in a company house with nothing to show and I swore it was not going to happen to me. I just came here and stopped to say good-bye and to apologize to you about how I had been acting."

Trey heard a chair scrape and Clarence's voice grew quieter.

"Jay, all those times before when I had fallen on my face you know what I would tell people? I would tell them I was going 'back to the life,' that's what. But, this last time I did not think I was going back to anything. I thought you and Ilene, well a bridge I had burned is what I thought. I came here to apologize and to say goodbye." Clarence paused and Trey heard him take another deep breath.

"I wondered what was up with you." Jay said.

"I was going to ride off into the sunset, go out to San Francisco and go to the Golden Gate Bridge and jump off it." Clarence's voice was low, his tone solemn.

"Hey," Jay said. "Ain't nothing that bad."

"For you maybe," Clarence answered.

"Why the bridge? I'd figure you for a bullet."

"I use to wonder about it in jump school at Ft. Benning. I decided back then that if my chute didn't open, I was ok with it. I've seen a man after a bullet in the head. It makes your eyes bulge out. With the Bridge, I'd read a story about it once. There's no mess to speak of and they have a patrol boat that picks you up right after and you go straight to cold storage. Buzzards don't get to eat your eyes out before some-body gets to you."

"Yeah, I always hated that part." Jay said. They both laughed and groaned a little at the same time. Old cowhands know the hard facts of dying out on the range by yourself. You cowboy long enough and you'll see it, up close and personal.

"Remember Carl?" Jay continued. "How he covered his head with rocks before he died, up in the Missouri Breaks?"

"Damn right I do. That was a thinking man's cowboy. So, that is why the bridge." Clarence said.

"You couldn't have done it." Jay's voice was matter of fact.

"Jay, there is a time when a man realizes that a ride off into the sunset is his only way home." Clarence said.

Trey listened. He had known these two a long time now and nothing was out of range of their topics and story-telling. But this one was out there a lot further than any he'd heard before. Jay spoke again…

"Cause you hate waiting in line. And, you hate doing what everybody else is doing. You always have to be different. You'd have criticized the other people. If they looked queer or female or hippie or in suits you would not have wanted to do what they were doing. It's just not a proper way for a Cowboy to act." Jay said.

"Well, I'd just take my place in line and wait like everybody else you old smart ass." Clarence spoke now in his dignified voice. The one that you never took seriously.

"You'd have become impatient and gone off to the nearest bar and tortured the bartender and the patrons with your stories until you got over the feeling. That is what you would have done." Jay spoke with conviction.

Trey then heard Clarence distinctly spit out on a held back laugh that came out in a rush of air and Trey had all he could do to hold his laugh in as well. A picture of Clarence, in his high heeled boots, pants tucked into sixteen-inch tops, big Stetson pulled and locked down low on bent ears, like he does it before he gets serious about something, just standing there, waiting in line, as people jumped off the Golden Gate bridge. It was just too ridiculous. Trey grabbed his bandana out of his back pocket and held it against his mouth hard to suppress himself and stay quiet. The pressure put tears in his eyes. He heard a stifled squeal from the sewing room too. Clarence continued,

"Well, I am not going to sit here and argue about it with you. Let me finish. You and Ilene just treated me like the old days, like nothing had ever happened, like a friend." Clarence's voice dropped quiet and changed from the old cowboy bravado that it had taken. Not boisterous, or cocky. Now it was back like he started it, solemn and sincere.

"You put me up in the bunkhouse, told the cook to count me in on meals and told me to rest up and stay as long as I needed. And then, the very next morning you pulled me out after breakfast and down to the corrals and told me to catch a horse, you needed help with something. You kept doing that every day and at the end of the week came out and handed me a paycheck and said you would appreciate my staying on, that you needed the help. I still don't know what for. Trey was your new top hand and good at it and you had full cow crews. You remember what we did? Every day we'd ride around and look at the scenery and talk about whatever came up and life in general. Finally, we'd prowl some cattle, cut one out, maybe doctor it or just practice our old cutting horse game. The one who pushed the cow past the other one wins. A fresh, fine horse every morning, each one better than the day before. It brought me back and the God's truth is it saved me. I had forgotten who I was and you brought me back to the life."

"It always did bring you back. You'd forgotten is all. You are forgetting something else too."

"What's that?"

"You are the best cowhand I ever knew. I know your quality. You're a man to ride the river with, as they used to say. I hated it when you went off to where-ever to do whatever. I knew you wouldn't make it back there in that world. Ilene and I both worried about you. And you never wrote and you did not return my calls, even when you got married."

"I know," Clarence said, "Please don't remind me of that." Clarence had a strong aversion to any mention of him ever being married.

"Clarence, you are a top-hand and I was always proud to ride with you. They don't come any better. Hands we get around here these days, their experience is Dude Wrangling. They can saddle and unsaddle a horse, that's about it. You ride circles around them. And, better still you're a natural born teacher. These kids need that."

"Well, yeah I guess." Clarence sounded humble now.

"Clarence, I was glad to have you, always was. I complained about your drinking is all, never your work. As far as you and Ilene, forget it. You knew her before me. She always cared for you. But she married me and that's the end of it."

Trey heard Clarence's chair scrape back, he heard a murmured something, Clarence then spoke clearly.

"Thanks Jay." Trey heard Clarence cough some, clearing his throat. "God bless you, old friend."

"And you," Jay said, "Thanks for stopping by." Clarence walked out of the bedroom and into the kitchen. He nodded to Trey, who got up too and followed Clarence out the door. Ilene came out as well. On the porch they stopped and turned to her.

"Thanks Clarence," she said. Clarence hugged her and she hugged him back and the warmth of that hug was familiar from the old days. It was a memory that had carried Clarence through many a lonely night in his youth. Trey did not notice it though, as he went to the truck and got in. He did not notice the tears in Clarence's eyes when he got in the truck beside him or the absolute and rare silence between them on the short ride to the bunkhouse. Some things you leave alone. Like moments when feelings are shared without words.

3

From the Old Rock

On Monday morning the cold bite of autumn was in the air. In the first light's stillness the breath of each man and animal were clearly visible. The big semi-trucks had been coming in since mid-night to get the early loads and they were parked and running in a long row on the shoulder of the highway, their stacked pipes sending exhaust straight up into the air.

There were extra hands brought in for the job. Neighbor ranchers to pay back the Dagger hands for coming over to help them. Then a few labor types from town that would take on extra work now and then. Dagger cowboys that had taken off a few days after the round up, had returned. Ray, Wes's Army buddy, and Roland, Wiley's cousin from Idaho, were there. They were mounted in the big pasture moving cows into the first pen. In the last lot, attached to the truck loading chute Clarence and Trey were horseback. Three men handled the shipping cattle quietly along the length of the chute to keep them moving, keeping the weight losing stress to a minimum, but always moving. The front compartment of the truck's trailer held seven head and seven head were cut out in the pen behind them and moved up to the pen where Trey and Clarence sent them up the chute. Once in that compartment, that gate was shut. The next two loads, one over and one under, were twenty-four head each and that number was cut out in the pen behind Trey. Ilene, on a medium bay and Jay's best horse, Cricket, brought them in and they moved twenty-four up the chute, shut that compartment off then twenty-four again and up the chute. Then the last compartment on the rear of the trailer held six and six, already counted and sorted, moved to the chute and into the truck. Then, as the rhythm of the work settled into place each of the pens, in series, already held the right number all the way back to the large lot that held the bulk of the herd. Today they were ready to ship one thousand head in twelve trucks. Over the next five days the truckers drove back late at night, lined up along the side of the highway and the drivers curled up in their sleepers for the night. They would get out and come to the bunkhouse for breakfast and then it all started again. The hands worked twelve plus hour days until it was done.

On the sixth day Trey and Clarence sat on their horses and watched the last truck pull out. As the pens in the back had emptied, first Wiley and Wes came forward with Ray and Roland, riding forward too. Then the next pen, with Ilene horseback and two local ranchers that had been mounted on Jay's best cutting horses, rode forward and they sat on their horses and talked to each other and watched as this last truck pulled away. It was the end of a year's worth of work. It was the only paycheck the ranch received. The tally was a good one. With good weight on the cattle it put the ranch in the black in the last year of its operation.

In every year this was a celebrating time. Rancher's wives, people from town, girlfriends of Wes and Wiley, Clarence's Casey, Trey's lady friend Jen, all were there at the bunkhouse with food and plenty of beer and drinks.

Mr. Weismann had come out and worked at the scales and with the State Brand Inspector to record the count and tally up. Over the years he had always done it. He sometimes made the spring and fall round-ups as well. Today he felt he needed to be there this one last time. It was more than a courtesy. A friendship had been formed and he was always welcome.

"Hey, cheer up, it's party time." Ilene said as she rode forward. They looked at each other but smiles sometimes can't be faked. Later, at the bunkhouse, the four that best knew the Ranches fate stood in the kitchen and drank a toast to Jay, to the ranch and to the days that were long gone by.

The party began to break up. Ilene left to get home to Jay. Trey walked Jen, his lady friend out. Ranchers, hired hands, wives, kids, friends and girlfriends, made their way to pick-up trucks and the day and another season ended on the old Double Dagger Ranch of Wyoming.

***

One week later at an early hour, Ilene stepped in to find that Jay was dead. She sat on the bed beside him for some agonizing minutes. The long vigil was over. The pain of losing her partner and best friend had been with her during her long watch and now her cry of pain was just too deep within to express. Her husband of near fifty years suffered no more. The hole it left in her heart would be a daunting one to heal and she already suspected that it never would. But, she was Wyoming's daughter, a rancher's daughter and a rancher's wife. She knew how to keep going. She would start doing that the minute she got up from the bed. She would start first with the details of the funeral, then what Jay wanted to pass to Trey and to Clarence and friends.

She looked at his face. He looked peaceful enough but there was this subtle expression of his that she knew well. That one that he had shown her in their hardest times. It was not meant to be unkind, just a slight hint of contempt. Not so much for people or her, it was for hardship. That expression was the way he always met it. When she was young and they were first married she thought that look was meant for her but long ago learned that was not it, not if she stiffened her spine. His contempt was for weakness and it did not matter where he saw it. Even if in himself. But she did not want to think about that now. It was Jay's look, that's all. He was a good man, good husband and good father. They had almost split up a couple of times. She sat there and knew she was glad that they hadn't done that because now enough time had passed that the growing apart they had done back then had slowly come back around, like the finishing of a circle and for some years now they had been very close. They had the history together and that is what proved the marriage out. They could trust each other not to quit. Ilene was glad she had stayed around to see that come to pass because it justified her life with him and his with her.

***

When it was time for the funeral the crew dressed in their Sunday best and went together in a pick-up truck convoy to the funeral home in town. They were all early, Clarence had seen to that. Trey and Clarence were pallbearers along with Weismann, Wiley, Wes, and Jay's son-in-law, a young man none of them had gotten to know. Their two daughters hung on both sides of Ilene who though obviously grieved stood and moved as she always had, straight and tall.

After the service they carried Jay out and loaded him into the hearse, then got in the pickup trucks, pulled into line and followed the hearse to the cemetery. The service wound up quickly and when it was over Trey and Clarence escorted Ilene, her daughters and her son-in-law to their car. Trey shut the door and watched the car pull off. He turned to see the funeral home people and the grave crew preparing to lower the coffin. Then he felt Clarence tug at his sleeve and without speaking, motioned him over to Wiley's pick-up truck. Wiley and Wes were standing beside it waiting. Clarence spoke to Wiley who then presented a bottle of good Irish whiskey and they passed it around. Without saying anything, Clarence walked back, dropped Wiley's tail gate and pulled out the shovels. Wiley and Wes each got one. Clarence held one out to Trey and they all turned and walked back to the open grave. The coffin was in the hole and the cover was gone from the dirt pile. Clarence grabbed a handful of dirt and they all followed suit. Clarence then dropped his in the hole and said,

"Goodbye old friend." They all did the same. Clarence then stood straight up with his shovel as if at attention with a rifle. They all stood with their own tool imitating Clarence like soldiers. Clarence removed his hat and placed it over his heart. They all did the same. Clarence looked around at each of them approvingly. Then he said,

"Unto Almighty God we commend the soul of our brother departed, and we commit his body to the ground. Earth to earth, ashes to ashes, dust to dust, Amen."

Clarence put his hat back on and pulled it down low on his brow. He then bent and dug into the pile of dirt with his spade. He swung around and let it fall on the coffin. Wiley and Wes did the same with a scoop each and it was the sound of the dirt hitting the lid that brought Trey out of his trance. So, they were all going to bury their old boss together. It would not be left to strangers to do. The sound of metal in the gravely hill-top soil was sharp and raspy as they started to dig. Trey pulled his own hat down too and turned his shovel to the pile and began to dig, lift, turn and drop and the sounds of the dirt on the coffin, with the wind ruffling in the golden Aspens that surrounded them, it made all ahead seem small enough. The emotion Trey had been holding seemed to fade a little. The physical work provided the release of tension that he was feeling.

The grave was half full of dirt before he even looked at the others. No one was slacking up, just occasional stops to straighten for a second.

"Get it down the sides boys, no unfilled gaps when the hands of the Dagger Ranch do a job, eh?" Clarence said.

"Right," someone answered. Wes knelt with the long bar used at the ranch for a tamping tool when setting fencepost and they waited as he packed the dirt around the sides of the coffin, then the head and the foot of it. With the fill dirt now, level with the coffin lid, it went fast and then they were finished. They rounded the mound up nicely and padded it down with their shovels. Then they stopped and just looked at it.

"Well, ok then." Clarence said. "Let's get back to the house and eat. Ilene said there was plenty but she'd hold some for us if she needed to." And that was that. A long and strong life had ended. A good man passed quietly without complaint or sign of regret and those friends that really knew him had nothing but respect to show for him.

Some days later, Ilene came down to the bunkhouse and she, Trey and Clarence, sat down to go over the horse records. They shuffled paper, drank coffee and kept it up till late. At midnight they had all the horses still living on the ranch matched up to brands and history and to their breeding as near as it was known. Then Ilene left. They would see her again early the next day.

As part of the ranch preparations for winter they pulled shoes off of most of the using horses and turned them out to winter pasture. Fewer were needed for winter work. It was a good time to go over each horse and double check the paperwork. It was necessary for the sale as brand records were kept by state law, but it made a difference to horse buyers, not just for registered horses but those without papers as well. It would matter in the spring when the horses were sold to Ranchers and Cowhands and local folk. They liked to say what their horses came out of and be proud of that even without papers. Trey and Clarence and Ilene would see that they could do that.

Wiley and Wes had gotten out early on the morning wrangle and brought the cavvy into the corrals. As they began to catch horses Clarence set out the shoeing boxes that held the tools they needed.

Trey backed the ranch truck to the high rail fence and dropped the tail gate. He set up a lawn chair in the back so that Ilene could have a seat up high where she could see. She carried a clipboard and the stack of brand inspection papers in a box. Clarence and Trey began to walk among the horses that were still circling a little nervously in the pen. Some they knew immediately and were checked off. Others they caught, haltered and walked out the gate to tie at the hitch rail. This gave Ilene time to shuffle the papers as they called out markings and brands to her.

There are one hundred and sixty-nine horses to go through. That is horses that work cattle and have the training and experience to do it. They are in varying stages of age and experience. Any horse, age seven or older that had not learned his trade had been sold off. Still, the cavvy had gotten a little top heavy with retired horses too aged and battered to keep riding. They were turned back out with each gathering, after getting their feet trimmed, then wormed, and anything else they needed.

It was common to throw the hula-hand when catching horses but Clarence started with the older ones that would step toward him to avoid the catch rope and dip their nose to the halter. The first he caught was in his own string, a big line-backed dun standing near 17 hands and probably weighing fourteen hundred lbs.

"Yellow boy, out of a Texas ranch in the Panhandle, probably 12-year-old. He's got some cold-blood in him. If you need to rope a herd bull this is the horse." Clarence said as he looked up at Ilene.

"Yep, got him. Four black stockings, dark tail and mane, star and a snip."

Clarence opened the big horse's mouth and saw quickly the extended upper and lower teeth with little cusp left, and said,

"Twelve if a day." Then he took the horse to the rail and tied him. Trey came out with one from his string. He said,

"Bangles here, been riding him for three or four years." Trey pulled back from the horse. It was a dark bay sixteen hands with a good long shoulder dropping from a high wither.

"He's from New Mexico breeding, has old Cowboy lineage, unregistered"

"And came from a mare out of Peter McCue,' Ilene added.

"Nine-year-old." Trey said and Ilene answered "Yes."

They stopped for lunch at the bunk house then went right back out and by quitting time had shoes pulled off of thirty head and well-trimmed hooves to finish. They would keep twenty-five head up for the winter and the rest would be turned out in the North pasture and fed good hay, salt and minerals. They had wind shelter on the river bank, under the bluffs and did good there. Then, in the spring it all started over, except this time.

This time it would not start over again. And that knowledge hung over the work, a job that in the past they had enjoyed. Not too easy a day, but easy to gauge your progress as you said goodbye to your string for the season. These beasts of burden, you had close working relationships with, spending more time with them then with people. Yes, you say goodbye.

"Well, least Jay won't have to see it." Clarence said, out of the blue and to no-one in particular.

"You got that right," Trey answered. "I don't think I want to be here to see it either."

"Oh man," Clarence said. "Don't start that talk." And then they went silent again.

Horses that were done went to one pen and those that were not, back where they came. Trey watched from the let-out gate. Bangles bent his knees down right outside it and rolled like he had a hard day and wanted to get the human off. Trey laughed at him as the dust swirled up and a few of the other horses rolled too. The big horse shook and looked back over his left shoulder at Trey, looking right at him, eye to eye. And then he trotted away, ears and tail up high.

Trey turned just in time to keep from being run over by another loose horse wanting the gate. His mind had begun to drift lately and that was a sign of it. Like he was already leaving the ranch, like he was already gone. He did not like the feeling but it wasn't unfamiliar to him. His way to deal with a problem was always to drift. First with his mind and then with his feet. He had always ridden on to what was next as quietly and purposely as any man could and did not look back. Not too often anyway. The difference now that he was older was he had begun to see more behind him than forward.

Each time you start over you start at the bottom of somebodies pecking order. You get enough experience and you know how to do a job and you can end up under someone that doesn't know as much as you do. So, you move on again. New challenges can become confrontations as well. The Cowboy way said a man can always start over. But now, with the years passing and prospects for starting over diminished, even perhaps impossible in regards to replacing the likes of the Double Dagger Ranch, it seemed like his old way would not suffice.

Few things challenged your self-respect like job hunting but he still needed to start acting on this, contact people, and start checking the help wanted ads in Stockman's magazines and papers. He'd be riding the grub line like Cowboys had done forever. He knew that a big part of his trouble was the dreading of it. He had the winter, then what? Caretaker? Jesus Christ.

Trey stopped in his tracks and got out his little shirt pocket notebook. He stood puzzled, thinking. Clarence and Wiley were wrapping things up to stop for the day. They looked at him.

"What then?" Clarence said.

"Which horses did Jay use for pack animals? I can barely remember," Trey asked.

"Well, he always took the grey mare. She's your bell mare. They all think she's their mother. She's nearing twenty I'd say. She helps hold the stock in the Mountains. Your string won't leave you and head for the trailhead if you hobble her and keep her in feed. Jay always said she stayed near camp even when a blizzard hit. And, she's bomb proof for whatever you want to pack on her." Clarence studied a minute and continued...

"That old zebra stripe dun of his always went too. Jay liked him to ride and hunt off of because when you take him out by his-self he stays quiet and doesn't whinny or cry out for other horses. Not even when other horses go by. That means a lot close to Elk. And, he can damn near climb a tree if you ask him too. Then there was Petey, who's dead, and Sherman. He's still here and he's big and will pack anything. I know we brought out a bear on him and he never complained much. So, you going?"

"Yes, I am going, I need to get out of here, clear my head."

"You still going Wiley?" Clarence asked,

"If I can."

"You can." Trey said. "We finish up the horses tomorrow, re-shoe the ones we need and we go day after."

"We got to find out when Fenwick and the buyers are coming in." Clarence said,

"I know, I will." Ilene answered. "Weismann said get the big house open, but they also told him to get the house open in town. Oh, and Trey your lady friend Jennifer's Real Estate office is handling the deal. Maybe you should call her."

"I talked to her at the shipping party but she didn't tell me that." Trey said,

"Well, she told me. She also said you hadn't called in a while and ask me how you were doing. I thought that was strange, you standing right there and all."

"She needed cooling off." Trey said.

"You mean like a horse." Clarence added. Clarence looked at Trey for a response but Trey ignored him.

"Listen Trey, if you need someone to talk to I'm here for you." Clarence continued. His tone sounded, on purpose, phony. Clarence went through the gate to the truck to help Ilene who was passing the lawn chair down and about to crawl over the side.

Trey, knowing Clarence was trying to make light of things, also knew well enough that he'd be the last man to go to with woman problems. Clarence's advice on women had been distilled down over the years till there was not much left for him to say. 'Hard to live with them and hard to live without them,' was about all he could come up with.

"You mean you'll go chase strange women with me?" Trey asked,

"That too, that too." Clarence answered. "But, that Jen is one good looking gal. Rich too, ain't she?"

Trey did not answer that even though the truth was partly there. She and he were fine as long as they were in the bar and dancehall. But, everywhere else, her house for example, he felt as out of place as he would have with the Queen of some foreign country. The woman had financial success head and shoulders above him and strove for more of it like she was driven. She told him once about her inheritance and it was a large number, but she wanted more. The real estate market in the Rocky Mountains was the perfect place for her. She even implied he get into it with her. God, how little she understood him. So, he let their love affair cool and he did not think he would go back. Better to just wait for summer, like the old days, with all the tourist women coming to Two Ocean, Wyoming on vacation. It was an easy solution to a man's needs and no-way permanent. Those women rarely stayed two weekends back to back. He had relied on it for years.

Ilene followed Clarence into the bunkhouse. She had eaten there with the crew many times over the years and to accept the invitation was as normal as anything she ever did. She would say later that she had not finished grieving yet, that the bunkhouse just brought back so many memories. At first her eyes welled up and she simply could not see. Clarence did not seem to notice this but Trey noticed and took her arm as quiet and natural as if he did it every day. She followed him easily as he led her into the common living space. He put her in his chair. She protested, said she would help and Trey said,

"No. You just sit and take it in as you need too. I'll help Clarence in the kitchen."

And so, she sat and she was thankful for the time to gain her composure and just feel at home. She closed her eyes, breathed slow and gradually got control of her emotions. She sipped the water Trey brought and smiled when he sat the jigger of whiskey down on the table beside her. Jay had done that when she was upset and Trey knew it. She drank it down like any cowhand and it put down the rising sob she felt. When she felt the lump in her throat dissolve she called for another.

When Trey stepped back into the kitchen Clarence gave him a questioning look. Trey shook him off as sure as a baseball pitcher shakes off a signal from the catcher. Clarence understood immediately. He was getting ready to cook and so he did what had saved him from an emotional disaster many times before. He just concentrated on what the hell he was doing.

When they ate Ilene was her old self again. The whole crew watched her and listened to her talk. She talked about horses first, things she remembered hearing from the ranch hands in the old days. Jay had picked her out a horse, told her about it from head to tail then left her to it. Her woman's method, her way he left her alone to work through. She'd grown up horseback and knew a lot already. She loved that about Jay. He respected what he saw as her turf. But she could not think about that, not now. She pushed back the memory and changed the subject.

She talked then about the people that had worked on the ranch, old friends with stories of their own and those she was still in touch with. There was the crew when Jay's dad took over, the old guys that Cowboy-ed in the late forties and fifties. These were the generation Jay learned from and rode with from his youth and these guys were good at what they did. There were lots of stories and they flowed into each other easily. Clarence contributed, added, subtracted, grunted and nodded, and finally just listened. Nobody got up to clear the table or do dishes. It was Ilene's night and she glowed with so much energy and natural beauty that Trey would later say that every damn one of them fell in love with her. Her best story left them laughing with her.

The story was about her first night alone in the wilderness hunting Camp. This back before children and many other things. She was a young bride and Jay, for reasons she did not remember, left her alone in camp until the next morning while he rode back out to the trailhead.

"I was scared to sleep in the wall tent by myself because the Grizzly bear had been around. I decided to sleep up in the tree, in the Cache. I was going to come back down early so Jay wouldn't know I was up there. I drug all my bedding out of the tent and over to the tree. I had to put the ladder up and drag my stuff up there and make a bed. When I raised up from my wallowed-out space I remembered the gun Jay had left me for protection and it was in my tent. I climbed back down to get it and while I was down, damn if the bear didn't show up. It was pitch dark and I needed my flashlight bad. But I had taken it up to the Cache with my bedding and left it." She paused for a breath and continued.

"The damn bear went straight up the ladder like he'd been trained in a Circus. He started throwing everything out and tearing it up. I saw my sleeping bag feathers flying everywhere. I thought it was snowing. It was damn cold by the way. I hovered in the tent shivering in the dark with a 12-guage shotgun loaded with buckshot until I heard him, sounded like he had come down sliding on the tree trunk. Then he went in the kitchen tent. When I was sure that's where he was going to spend some time, I ran for my life and that ladder. I climbed up it and kicked it down fast. 'Ha' I yelled, 'got you now you SOB.'

"What happened then?" Wiley said

"I had forgotten the gun again, probably a good thing. Otherwise I would have shot the damn thing. I had no sleeping bag, no blanket. Then it really did start to snow. I had to pee really bad too. That was probably the hardest part, to pee off the end of the deck holding on to a rope with both hands. God, it was cold. Getting down again was not an option for a while. The bear wrecked the cook tent, came back to the ladder on the ground and sniffed it and rose up to look at me. Then he wandered off growling and groaning like they do when they are disappointed and mad about it. It was one hell of a wet, cold night. Somewhere near morning I knew I was going to have to get back on the ground, swing down and drop somehow. That's a high up, ass Cache. But, I couldn't let Jay find me up there."

"Over fifteen feet," Clarence said.

"What a mess, all was on the ground" Then with a sudden shift in her thoughts Ilene stopped, looked up at Clarence and said,

"Wouldn't it be something to have all those people back here again for some kind of re-union? You know, before the ranch is sold off?"

Clarence's head snapped up from his plate like a bird dog going on point.

"Ilene, that's a fine idea. We invite them to the round-up this spring."

"Yes," Ilene said, and nodded her head and looked across the table at her oldest friend left in the world, sitting there with that big old grin on his face. Suddenly she was feeling good and it had been a long time since she had felt that way.

"Ok," she said. "We got all winter to work on it."

Her eyes gleamed with the thought. Trey watched her and then looked at Clarence who got up, grabbed the bottle and circled the table. He poured them all another drink.

"Finish the bear story," he said.

And so, it was underway. Something that had been dreaded could now be seen in a better light. They could even look forward to it. If the ranch was going, if the horses, cattle and people were going to be scattered to the four winds, let it be out with a bang, Western style.

"Well, I swung down without hurting myself. I looked at the mess on the ground and damn near cried. I started cleaning up like I was possessed. I put that heavy ladder up and hauled things on my shoulder as I climbed. I pulled barrels up with ropes, I jerked and pulled and made that Cache look near right again. The groceries for hunting season were not up there yet, thank God. They were still in the bear-proofs and hanging from the meat pole for good measure. For about a week after, at the first sign of anybody wanting to go to the Cache, I jumped to the ladder first and went up. I acted like I loved it up there. And the damn thing is Jay never knew. I had it all right again." She paused for breath.

"The kitchen was a different problem and he saw that. The bear had not gotten anything to eat. I had the kitchen back operational pretty quick but canvas was torn. I made it look like I had put my bed in the kitchen tent because I wanted the stove to stay warm by. You know, to explain my bedroll wrecked. I said it was drug out, to explain the feathers. I let it get wet in the snow. We didn't have a stove in the bed tent yet. Whatever he thought, I wanted to make sure he knew that I had not left the ladder up on that Cache. He'd lectured me on that one already, and more than once. I would have been mortified to hear it again."

4

Blood Sport

As the Ranch crew settled in for the night, Wiley and Trey Blake packed for the hunt. Trey's revolver, in its holster, hung handy on the coat rack. The pair of hunting knives hung with it in the double scabbard he made for them. He pulled out his war bag, a small grip bag and dumped it out on the bed. It held the bugle, the cow calls, extra rifle and pistol ammo and the old box cutter knife he used for capeing. He checked the handle for extra blades. He got out his Ouachita Stone, then the short-handled axe he used for quartering the kill. It came out from under his bunk with a homemade leather case to cover the blade and tie to the saddle. He had just picked up the Bugle when Wiley walked in.

"Do you think the rut is over?" Wiley said.

"No, the cows that didn't breed in the first go-around will come back in heat." Trey said without looking up. He took the bugle's mouth piece and peeled off the old reed.

"Wiley, get the shortwave radio on for the weather." Trey said.

The weather report said rain in the valley. That meant sleet on the way up and snow on top, at least to somebody going up a mountain. They would get to set up camp in the wet. But, that was ok. When a storm broke hunting was always good. Clarence walked in.

"I got the food packed, its frozen left-over beef stew. It's on top in Tupperware. Another Tupperware has chili froze, one with cornbread and rolls. It's all marked. You want to make sandwiches tonight?"

"No, in the morning." Trey said.

"Well, I will say goodnight then."

"Ok, thanks Clarence."

As Trey lay on his bunk waiting for sleep he refused thoughts of the meeting with Weismann, and the news. His window for hunting was closing. The big snow would come soon and block the trails off for the year. The hunting season closing dates were coming soon as well. He felt the need to get up high in the mountains one more time before leaving the area. He needed to move quiet in the deep black timber with his nose in the wind. It was that natural feeling of unhurried presence he craved now. He needed it and hunting provided it.

***

Trey kept a steady pace from the start. He led four pack horses in single file, tied to each other from the back of each pack saddle. Wiley rode behind leading three more. He kept an eye on the loads in front of him and his string bringing up the rear as well. Now, it was just a long gradual climb up the drainage trail to top out at 11,000-foot elevation. Then they could make good time crossing the moonscape top. It was a wilderness hunter's paradise after that. Forty miles from the trailhead they came in on and fifty miles north and east before any other mark of civilization would be met. That isolation kept many hunters away. No light came from the overcast sky, drizzle rolled off their hats and soon the horse's heat came up under the rider's slickers and steam rose from the necks and rumps of the horses they rode and led. All was quiet but the sound of horseshoes on rocks.

***

Clarence had a slow morning so he stopped off at the hay barn to see if the farm hands were feeding. The long, flatbed trailer and the tractor were gone. He drove slowly through a pasture to check cattle. Then, nearing lunch time, he went back to the bunkhouse to put some food out. He put soup on to ward off a cold wet day. He set the table. He put out bread, a jar of pickles and one of olives. He set out warm beans and a pitcher of tea. He sliced some lemons and he sliced some onion and tomatoes. He took note that the sugar, salt and pepper were out on the table. He put down the big hot pad to set the soup pot on and placed a dipper beside it and the bowls. The left-over brisket he left cold and sliced on a long plate. As he was doing these last things he heard Wes come in and stop in the mud room. Wes pulled off his coat and boots there, then he walked in and went in the kitchen for some coffee. He set down with a cup and began putting a sandwich together.

"Nasty day to ride up in the mountains," Wes said.

Clarence nodded his head in agreement and sat down too. But, he did not answer. Wes spoke again,

"I never got back into hunting, after the Army," Wes said.

"Did you hunt much before?"

"Yes, I did. Went out with my uncle and cousins every year. My dad was always working on a job somewhere."

"Let me ask you, you think your hunting back then helped you in the Army?" Clarence said.

"Probably saved my life." Wes answered.

"Yeah, me too. Nature is the mother of all teachers. You know as many times as I have gone to hunting camp with Jay I never hunted that much myself. I wrangled and pulled a pack string mostly. But growing up I hunted. We were always living on a ranch somewhere with lots of game around. The meat was needed at home. We never had much money."

"Those mules you told me about?" Wes asked.

"Yep."

"What happened to them?"

"Jay sold 'em to an Outfitter up in Montana."

"I never worked with mules," Wes said. "I heard they were hard to handle and would lay in wait to get you off guard and hurt you. I heard that if you got on the wrong side of a mule you had an enemy forever."

"True enough. But, the thing is that if you make friends with a mule, then you got a friend forever." Clarence said.

"Who'd want a mule for a friend?" Wes said.

Clarence stopped chewing his food and looked at Wes. Wes looked back and had a little curl to his lips like he did when he thought he had you on something.

"Well, when you work with someone, or a mule, it's not so much just a friendship. It's more like an alliance. An alliance is like a trust and you need that when you are way up in those mountains with nothing but grizzly bears and mountain lions and a couple of million acres of wilderness. Everybody needs to do his or its job and to cooperate with each other, you see."

Clarence exhaled, put a mouthful of food in and waited for a response. Wes continued with his eating. Clarence could never really tell when Wes was happy but he could damn sure tell when he wasn't.

"I've had friends I could not work with." Clarence said, "They just weren't good at doing stuff. Men that were spoiled somehow and never learned to make a hand. Then again, I've had men that were never close friends with me because of one thing or another, over a woman or politics, religion maybe. I would pick them to work with anytime though, because I know they can and would hold with me in a tight spot. You can work with a man like that. You may not always like him but you can respect him. I'll take that anytime over just goofing off with somebody." Clarence said.

"Like your Army buddies, I see it. Why'd he sell 'em then?" Wes said.

"Jay got burned out on the outfitting and didn't need them for anything else. They brought him and Ilene some good money at the time and they were raising a family."

"Well, fuck it then." Wes said. Clarence looked up surprised.

"What's eating' you son?"

"Like, they really will sell our horses?" Wes answered. And there it was.

The horses in Wes's string he considered his and they were his as long as he rode for the ranch. Nobody, not the manager or the owners, or fellow Cowhands, screw around with another man's string of horses. Each horse was in a level of training that only the man that rode them regularly could know. They need consistency. It gets to be sort of personal and adhered to for a reason, it worked.

Clarence did not have a response. He left the food out and went to his room, pulled his boots off and flopped down on his bunk. He looked at his watch and it was one p.m. Forty winks, he thought and closed his eyes. When he opened them back up he looked at his watch again and it said one forty p.m. He loved it when he could do that. It had taken a while to develop. He eased up to sitting real slow and swung his feet to the floor. It didn't pay to jump up quick. His old back liked to be warned before he did something that required it.

Clarence stepped to the window that faced west and looked out. He could see a storm coming. It was building up high behind the Mountains. The thought that it was the last winter on the ranch gave him a longing to slow it down. The ranch had been more than a home, it was a refuge. Now the gates were opening, human wolves were coming in and he could not stop it. Clarence thought of something Casey had said to him not long ago. She had said that she felt 'vulnerable.' She said it after they had dated a while and after they made love. He did not have a clue then what she meant but, he did now.

"Oh my," he said to himself, as he pulled on his boots. "It's going to be a long winter if I keep thinking like this."

***

Wiley watched the Pack Horse loads to his front and rear. In moments, as they moved through the timber and the switchbacks, a partial profile of Trey would appear up ahead. He'd be bent forward in the saddle, left hand lifted on the rein, right hand on the lead horses' rope, the big Buckskin stepping strong and the pack horses settling into their work behind him. Wiley noticed the man's concentration. Trey looked like he was deep in thought about something, somewhere else even.

Wiley knew he wanted to be like Trey Blake. As hard as the work could be the man backed his ears and just went with it. He stayed deeply tangled in the effort, hands on all the way. You really need to be around the right people to learn things like that. You need to see it in action and then see the results. Wiley had realized that this kind were here, on the Dagger Ranch soon after he started work. It was a fit for him. Wiley liked to work, he liked seeing the results of strong effort and he was blessed with the body and stamina for it. He'd found a home.

After a steep section of the canyon trail Trey stopped to let the horses blow. Nothing would tell him to move again until he heard the horses breathing slow to a normal rate. He looked back and saw Wiley slip from his saddle and tighten his own cinch and then remount. There was no snow on this lower section yet but it was wet. The black, silt mud was slick for a man to stand or walk on but good for a well shod horse.

They rode on in the hush of the trees, the smell of the lodge pole and ponderosa pine, up past hillsides of golden Aspen, doing their wonderful dance in the wind. Then higher to the larger Spruce and Cedar, some with intermittent rivulets of water running in shallow trenches across the trail, to drop down to the creek below. The series of waterfalls could be heard down in the canyon.

On one stop for the horses Trey twisted around to his saddle bag and got out a sandwich. He looked back at Wiley and held it up and Wiley nodded and reached for his. When he had it he looked again to see if they would stop there to eat but Trey, with a mouthful, turned and started his horse back up the trail. They would eat as they rode and get it done. Just what Wiley expected.

The string of horses snaked on, moving over and around down timber and boulders in the trail, sounding the strike of horse shoes on stone. This, surrounded by the hard beauty of the mountains and the twisting like moves of the pack-train, this was the life Wiley had chosen and he was loving it.

They topped out. Elevation now was eleven-thousand feet. The trees had thinned as they climbed and now all but dis-appeared. The Cairns showed the trail location now. They would be important on a heavy downcast day, with snow blowing across, when you had no vis-ual reference, no sun, no moon, no stars to guide you. This top trail was three miles across. The view that surrounded this section of the trip would catch your full attention on a clear day. It was high enough that you could see three mountain ranges in three different directions. But not today. Today storm clouds lay heavy in the sky and were mov-ing over them in the color of slate grey. But, the camp was close now. Just as they were back in timber Trey pulled onto a little used trail to the East and rode the short distance to it.

They had daylight left. They dropped the loads, hobbled the horses, strapped the bell on the mare and turned them loose. Wiley's horse too. Trey kept his tied, to be fed from the feed bag later when the rest of the stock was involved with the grass. It's a rule, always keep a wrangle horse up. It's a long walk home if you don't.

They drug a ridge pole out from the cache stack in the timber and tied it hat level, between the two trees that were the right width apart. Then the Baker tent was set up quickly with the back-slant wall staked first and then the fly over the ridge pole, with poles pulled out and roped off at the corners. The tents backside faced the west to block the prevailing winds. They cut some Spruce boughs to sweep the thin layer of snow away from what was now the tent floor. The extra tarp went down and the cowboy bedrolls rolled out on top of it, still in their tarped covers as well.

Trey left the cook fire to Wiley and took his horse to the creek below camp to water. When he came back Wiley had the fire going and had started arranging the grill and skillet.

They went back to the rail-cache and got the heavy saddle rack pole drug out. They put it up in its designated spot. They put their saddles and pack-saddles on the rail. They hung halters, lash ropes and bridles on the saddle horns and made sure all the leather, cinches, britchens and breast collars were off the ground. They put the saddle pads over the saddles and covered all with the mantie tarps.

Trey opened a feed sack and fed his horse. While it was eating they carried the sacks to the meat pole, threw a lash rope over it, tied the sacks, and hoisted them the required height off the ground. It's the law in the wilderness. Don't let the bear get in reach of your food and feed.

There was plenty of squaw wood around so the fire blazed high in front of the baker tent and felt great against the growing chill of the night air. From the Cache a stout grill was pulled out, put over the fire and two pre-baked potatoes wrapped in tinfoil placed at the fireside to be turned and heated. When the coals were right the two big Steaks were placed on. They sizzled nicely on contact and Trey seared both sides first then raked some of the coals to the cool end of the grill and slid the steaks over there to slow cook. He opened a can of beans and put it on the grill still in the can. They rolled over the log stools and sat down close to the heat. Trey put his metal plate on a rock in the fire ring to warm it and took a snort from his flask. He passed it to Wiley. Seeing the darkness drop around them sent both for their gear bags and headlamps.

When they finished eating and looked up from the fire it was pitch-black and no stars in the overcast sky. The sound of the wind in the trees was clearly audible and the logs in the fired popped and fussed with the pine knot contribution. As Trey banked the fire and bedded down it started spitting snow. Their hunting rifles were in the tent with them, and pistols, un-holstered, were in the bedroll. Any bear aggressive enough to drag one of them out of the tent would have to face 44.mag and 357, caliber revolvers. Trey and Wiley fell asleep listening to snow hit the tent fly and the night sounds, a horse crunching feed, the faint clank of the bell from the meadow below and the wind in the trees. It was the first deep sleep Trey had in days.

***

When he opened his eyes, he was still beneath the bed tarp he had pulled over his head in the night. He did not want to get up but his bladder was insisting. He was facing east and in a Baker Tent there is a wide-open view from your bed. It was getting light all-right. He could just see the curl of sunrise light reflecting under the clouds, low over the horizon. Wiley was deep in slumber and breathing quiet. Trey listened for the bell mare and looked to see if his wrangle horse was still at the hitch-pole. He grabbed his hat, slipped on his camp shoe moccasins and blanket lined coat, then stepped out onto the snow-covered ground to take care of his morning business. He shivered from the cold, heard an Elk bugle in the distance and smiled to himself just for being there. There were signs in the western sky of clearing, the mare's bell sounded close and the pile of squaw wood from the night before was adequate to build the fire back up, warm them, make coffee and cook breakfast. His horse whinnied to him from the hitch pole.

"All-right, give me a minute," Trey said.

Once dressed, Trey pulled the coffee pot off the fire, table spooned the grounds in, stirred it well and placed it off center on the grill to slow down the boil. Wiley got up, dressed, and walked to the meat pole. He let the feed sacks down for the wrangle horse, then he let the grocery pannier down and got eggs, bacon, a potato and bread. When he got to the fire pit, Trey started the bacon, used the grease to stir fry chopped potato and onion, pulled the coffee pot off and poured cold water in to settle the grounds. Trey fed his wrangle horse and he and Wiley sat and ate, talked a little and took their time with the morning.

By late morning they wrangled the stock, saddled up and rode out to scout around. The Elk sign was everywhere. They spent the day checking old trails and riding a big half circle around the camp. In the lower meadows they saw some Moose grazing. The trail that went all the way down to the bottom of Cradle creek, they bypassed. It lead to a professional Outfitters Camp, several miles below them. At noon they stopped and ate the last of the sandwiches left over from the day before. They checked a bear den inside a tree's huge base among the roots. It was empty yet and would stay that way until winter was well on the mountain.

They rode to Two Ocean Pass, where the water shed on the continental divide split, one stream headed for the Atlantic and one stream headed for the Pacific. It's where the first Fenwick turned back in a wagon ages ago. They were headed for Oregon and an early autumn snow turned them back. They wintered in the Two Ocean Basin and the next year filed a claim there, the first settlers in the area. The high Mountain Pass that sent them back became the namesake of the town.

Before sunset the hunters were back in camp. They gathered and chopped firewood, stacked it near the fire pit and weighted a piece of tarp over it to keep it dry.

They had a slow evening. They ate, drank a little and planned the next day's hunt. With occasional breaks in topic they passed the evening that way, like hunters have done for ages, reliving past hunts and keeping alive the blood sport culture passed down to them from the beginnings of time.

5

Inexplicable Good Luck

On the morning of the second day they were ready to ride by five a.m. They planned to get above the Elk early and save a ride following them up as the herd left the lower meadows and headed to the high timbered ridges to bed down for the day. Riding in the dark they passed Elk and heard Bugling, but Trey knew where he wanted to go and stuck to his plan. Under the dark gray sky there is little to see by. This part you leave to the horses. They could see fine and were content to follow an obvious trail. Besides he was riding Jay's old Buckskin. If anybody knew these trails it was him. All Trey could see were dark shapes that his horse made frequent snorts at and shied with side steps.

By the time they met the trail he wanted to take up to the ridge there was enough light for Trey to see and the logs and stumps that looked so ominous now took their real form and his horse moved with confidence past them. Once they were up above timberline they stopped to listen. A Bull bugled not far below them. The ridge they were on was open for two or three hundred yards across and how many miles long, Trey did not remember. They dismounted and tied up in an ideal clump of isolated trees and waited for the Elk herd to move up. They faced the growing light. Wiley chambered a round. Trey did the same. Leaning close Trey said,

"You take first shot."

Wiley did not answer. No more words were needed. No cow call or bugle were needed either. When the bull started chuckling at his cows to follow him it came from directly below them. He would come out on his own. Just let it happen.

They were facing East but the bull's talking revealed it was on a cross trail below that would take it behind them. The two hunters moved in their little circle of cover and within minutes the bull stepped out. His rack was silhouetted against the brightening morning sky and it was a big one. The Bull sped up and trotted over past the center of the ridge line moving north as Wiley searched to get the scope cross-hair on him. Then it began quartering away from them, more to the north at a fast walk. The clean broadside opportunity was gone. Trey saw the bull out only two hundred yards at first and now at near two fifty. Neither of them paid attention to the gathering cows on the edge of the timber. The cows had stopped and were staring right at them. The Bull, not understanding the cow's hesitation, stopped, looked back over his left shoulder and bellowed at them. Wiley squeezed the trigger.

There was no second shot opportunity. The Bull disappeared over the ridge. A few cows followed in the bull's direction, moving quickly across. Nothing else came out. They waited.

"You hit him" Trey said.

"Yes,"

"Where?"

"I was aiming low behind the shoulder."

"Hard angle."

"All I had."

Trey looked at Wiley. He had a sheepish look and blood was oozing just above the bridge of the nose and right eye.

"Scope get you?"

Wiley touched it and looked at the blood on his fingers.

"I guess," he answered.

Trey drank some water while Wiley blotted the blood with his bandanna. Trey checked that the horses were well tied and said,

"You ready, we'll go look." They started walking over the ridge both hoping that they would see the bull right there but it wasn't and the careful circling for a blood trail began. Wiley found it first. It was a small spot and all he could see before the tracks showed the rim trail angling steeply down. They both glassed the open area of the slope across and below them but they did not see anything. They started to work themselves deeper down the ridge and found more blood about half-way down. The tree line of thickening timber was only yards away.

"What do you think?" Wiley said.

"This is a black timber canyon if I ever saw it." Trey said.

"I'll walk it down." Wiley said.

"I'll go back for the Ax and then follow you." Trey answered.

It was a winding, twist of switchbacks to get down. Every few yards Wiley had to move off the game trail due to the down timber and move around it. He continued to find blood. Finally, all the way in the bottom Wiley saw the bull. It was on its side with one branch of his Antlers up. The silver tipped royal gave it away, there among the branches of trees and down timber. He heard Trey's steps on crunching snow coming up behind him.

Wiley started to arrange his kill for butchering. Trey lifted up a fore leg and Wiley stuck a rock under the shoulder. Trey pulled the top hind leg wide giving Wiley room to open up the stomach cavity. Once gutted they drug the pile away. They kicked pine straw and dirt over the blood by the carcass to help keep their footing and stopped for a breather.

"You probably should cape it." Trey said.

"Really?"

"Wiley, this is a Boone and Crockett kind of bull."

"I don't have that kind of money."

"Let's Cape it anyway. You can sell the Cape to a taxidermist in town if you don't use it. There's room in the freezer to store it and a big sack of salt in the cache at camp."

"Never caped one. Never shot anything but a cow and a couple of rag horns."

"I have, you'll find out why I bring a box knife."

They went to work. They easily fell back on the old rule that said If you aren't skinning hold a leg. Trey did the work at the base of the horns with his box knife and the tricky part to the eyes and scent glands. Wiley did the long work up from the forelegs, shoulder and neck. With the Capeing finished and set aside, it was time for the Ax. Trey split the chest cavity with it and then quartered the Elk. They cut the hooves off and dragged the quarters in four different directions placing them hair side down and off the ground on downed timber. They covered each quarter with pine and cedar boughs to keep the flies down if it warmed up. Then they walked further away and hung the rack up high as they could reach in a spruce tree, placing it over a limb. They put the Cape with the horns to make it less susceptible to predator bears and scavengers. The last thing Wiley did was cut and knock out the Elk ivories and put them in his pocket.

They gathered up their gear and the backstrap for camp meat and looked for a better trail out. Going down the drainage a way they found a place with a more open slope and began to climb it. When they topped out and were back to the horses more than half the day was gone and the sky to the west threatened more snow. They could feel it and smell it in the air.

"We packing it out today?" Wiley said.

"No, let's go back to camp and we'll get your Elk out in the morning. You can pack him to the ranch from here. I'll hunt for my trophy while you're gone.

"Yeah," Wiley said. "I think I got lucky."

"Yes," Trey answered. "Guys hunt their whole lives and never get a bull like that one. We can score him at the Ranch. Clarence knows how."

They pulled on their slickers and rode as the snow started to fall. Trey thought about thin sliced Elk Tenderloin rolled in flour, salt and pepper, sizzling in the pan. The horses knew they were headed for camp and stepped out with purpose.

The next morning, they rode at daylight and Wiley was on his way with his Elk before noon. He led two pack horses. One had a forequarter on each side topped with the cape and the horns over all. The second just the two hindquarters hanging low on the sides of the horse. Trey took a picture of Wiley riding out along the ridge. The snow had stopped falling and a sliver of light shone through the low clouds. Wiley looked back in time to show his handsome young face in the photo, grinning with pride and red cheeked from the exertion and the cold.

Trey ate his lunch sitting on the ground on his slicker. He had the wind blocked a little with the large log he leaned against. Try as he might to ignore it he was starting to think of Jen. His resolve was weakening and it was pure physical desire that was doing it to him. Like it or not that woman's face, auburn hair, lips, the whole package was getting harder to stay away from. Besides that, it was a long Wyoming winter ahead. He sat quietly thinking about it and fell asleep. When he woke the bulge in his pants was painful.

He got up and put the slicker back on to stay dry while riding. The snow had stopped but low hanging tree boughs would shed the wet flakes in his lap as he brushed by them. He rode further away from camp and then turned his horse up a game trail. He followed it to a bench of level ground. There he could see a series of clearings that ran up to two bare peaks, known locally as the Witch's Peaks. Trey had not been up to them in many years but it was known to hold Elk. Trey tied his horse up, loosened the cinch, and pulled his rifle from the saddle scabbard. He walked across the first meadow and into some trees. The next meadow was one hundred yards wide and twice as long. On the far side of it there was a wall of thick timber. Trey found a spot where he was and faced the open meadow beyond. He decided against bu-gling and used the cow-call every so often. It was less intrusive in the snow covered quiet and fit his mood.

When the evening sky began to darken and long shadows crossed the meadow the grey shapes began to appear. First the calves moved out and did some plucky jumps and hops to stretch after bedding down all day. Then cautious cows followed, watchful. A thermal breeze brought their scent to him. He glassed the edge of the trees looking hard at the large, dark shape within. It was a much bigger animal there but he could not make out the horns in the dwindling light. He thought the bull would not come out in time and as the final light disappeared from the meadow Trey did too.

When he rode into camp he grabbed another horse from the pen and tied it, then un-saddled his, hobbled it and let it and the remainder of the stock out for the night to graze. In a short time, he had his fire going and water on to wash. He stripped, took the limited camp bath and washed the blood from his hands, still there from handling Wiley's kill. He dressed in clean long johns and another pair of pants and car-ried the bloody clothes to the creek nearby. He put the clothes in the cold water and weighted them with rocks and left them there to soak the blood out. He finished his evening with supper, whiskey and water. When he was done he knocked snow off of the tent fly, banked his fire and crawled into his bedroll for a good sleep.

The light snow stopped falling. It was quiet enough to hear the soft sound of a snow owl's wings as it flew over the meadow beside the camp. Trey slept with no thought of the ranch being sold or the Bull Elk he would shoot. He just thought of Jen and the sensuous ways she had to get his attention. He had resisted that the last time he saw her, at the shipping party. Now, he was kicking himself for it. He would not resist her again.

***

After dinner Clarence cleaned the kitchen up and moved toward an early bed time. He had his shots of bourbon but kept it down to just two. At a little after ten p.m. he heard Wiley drive in and park. With flashlight, overshoes and coat, Clarence walked out in the cold night air and looked at Wiley's Trophy bull rack.

"Oh man, you or Trey get that one."

"I did, what you think it will score?"

"Three seventy, eighty." Clarence's practiced eye took it in.

"Boone and Crockett?" Wiley said.

"Maybe, I'll score it tomorrow for you."

Wes came out and helped Wiley hang the quarters in the ranch meat locker. Clarence went back in and pulled some leftovers out of the fridge and set them out. Then he went to his room and shut the door.

In the morning Wiley loaded up and drove back to the trailhead. He cracked the ice on the water trough and put out some feed and hay for the horses. He brushed their backs while they ate the grain in the trough. Then he haltered and brought each of them out to the rail, saddled them and set the feed loads on the pack saddles. He tarped the loads and threw a single diamond hitch over each. Then he mounted and rode out. He was riding by nine a.m. The clouds hung low but no snow fell as his horse dug in and started the long climb up the canyon.

***

Trey saw a little sunlight break out to the east as he rode. He had a plan to ride to that distant meadow again and he did that. In the early morning light he found himself looking at a series of higher meadows just across from the shallow drainage where he'd stopped before. He followed a game trail he found there for an hour or more, always climbing. Then he was up in territory he had never been in. In this place behind the Witches Peaks Trey took his horn and blew it loud. The Bull Elk answered clearly. Trey followed the sound. The Bull moved further away. After a short time, still horseback, he was bushwhacking for lack of trail.

When he came out in another small meadow he reconnected with a game trail on a steepening slope down, but it was washed out. The tracks showed the Elk had just dropped off and down, mountain goat style. Trey sat and stared down at a rocky, scree filled drainage, then looked up again and saw a fine Bull Elk emerge across the canyon and going away, climbing that steep grade. The shot was six hundred yards and hardly reliable. Still mounted he eased his horse back to level ground and tied it up in the trees. He pulled his rifle from the scabbard and started down to cross the rocky drainage on foot. When he had crossed, he moved very carefully up to the next ridge and then got down on all fours to avoid spooking any game on the other side. He laid down the rifle, got his field glass up and then carefully raised his head and glassed the wide, grassy hill before him.

The Bull Elk was there, under three hundred yards out and trying to mount a reluctant cow. The rack on the bull was high, wide and thickly branched. A dozen or more cows and a couple of rag horn bulls walked about and grazed nervously nearby. Trey eased back out of sight behind the ridge and put his binoculars down. He picked up his rifle and checked the dial on the scope then set it for the estimated distance. The sun was coming out and played on the ridge where he sat. He turned and looked through his Scope at the Elk and the bull was now behind a cow and offered no clear shot. Trey waited.

He felt perfectly relaxed. The shot, with the 338-caliber rifle, was well within reach. He looked through the scope again and waited for a clean shot. He looked behind him for something to steady his rifle on, a log or rock maybe. Then something caught his eye. Down the slide, behind him and well below where he had crossed, he saw shining metal, large, upright and glinting in the sun. It was clearly out of place in this wilderness setting where no such signs of civilization should be.

He tried to turn his attention back to the hunt but he couldn't do it. He started scoping down, looking at the metal, starting to see the shape of the thing. He could see that it was a part of a plane. He stood up and put the safety back on the rifle. He slung it and forgetting about the Elk, picked up his binoculars and started down and across the rock. When he got to the wreckage, he unslung the rifle and placed it carefully down. There were broken up treetops coming out of the rocks and sticking out horizontally just above the Tailfin. The fallen trees had protected the rear of the plane from the sliding rock and kept it from being completely crushed. He could see down through the tree trunks along the left side of the plane.

It wasn't hard to imagine how it happened. You could see it. They had flown up the canyon and crashed near the top of it. Then a slide had started and covered most of the plane with rock and broken tree tops. He felt certain that this plane had not been reported found. It's a small town and he would have heard about it. He stuck his head down in between the rocks and broken tree limbs. There was ample room and he laid on his stomach for a closer look. A large hole was open in the fuselage between the tail and the left wing. It was the plane's door location. But there was no door there now.

He got up, picked up his rifle and started back across the slide to the slope and slowly walked up to where he had tied his horse. He placed the rifle, hung by its sling, on the sharp point of a broken off limb. He stepped to his horse, opened the saddle bag on the near side, pulled out his headlamp and put it on over his winter hat. He got a drink of water from the canteen still hanging off the saddle horn and took his time to enjoy the moment of suspense and discovery. It was a shame about the plane but that was done. He was alone and his thoughts were that there was nobody to ask and nobody to deny. He was going into the plane if he could get in there.

He walked back down to the crash site, scrambled over the boulders, stopped and set the straps tight on the headlamp. He turned it on. He pulled his coat off and put his gloves on for sharp metal. The sun was out on the rock and it was warming up but as he crawled down into the opening he felt the cold of a black hole. With belly on the rock, dragging his feet in the narrow space and with arm strength alone pulled himself into the hole that had once been the rear fuselage of the Dagger Ranch's lost plane. He flashed the headlamp straight ahead and saw it was clear to pull himself the rest of the way in. He looked left, up the cabin toward the front of the plane. It was severely collapsed in tangled metal. Wires were evident in clusters there, and lots of debris.

The passenger seats behind the pilot cabin were only partially crushed and the seats behind that were upright and in place. There was no sign of fire, just luggage, some boxes and camping and fishing gear that Tom, the Fenwick's pilot, always had in his plane. Trey got a look into the pilot's cabin with his light and saw the remains of two bodies crushed in the seats. He saw a three-ring binder on what was left of the floor beneath them but he could not reach it. Moving back to the empty passenger seats he started checking luggage. There were three suitcases. He pulled them out one at a time.

The first two contained clothing and nothing more. The third had large plastic bundles about the size of a football secured with duct tape. The bundles looked exactly like something a Federal Agent would hold up for a picture on a TV broadcast, after a drug bust. Sometimes there is truth to rumors, he thought. He closed the suitcase and set it aside. He moved to the rear, to a cargo net that held cardboard boxes against the far wall of the plane. As soon as he reached in and touched one, the cardboard, damp and fragile, came apart in his hands and he could not lift it out of the net in one piece. Inside the box was something solid and Trey pulled his knife out, cut the cargo net and let them all fall out.

The first box held a typical business man's briefcase. He tried to open it but he couldn't. He crawled back out of the plane, pushing the briefcase in front of him. Back out on the rocks in the warming sun Trey took his Leatherman out of its sheath at his side and began fooling with the latches. Just before he popped them one latch flew open with all zeros showing on the combination. He put the other one the same and it sprang open as well. He pulled the lid up and stared in, took a deep breath and let it out in a rush of air.

"Oh…man," he said out loud.

He took one of the wrapped stack of bills out and thumbed through it. It was all one-hundred-dollar bills and the case was full of the same, all wrapped and tightly packed. He looked around as if he felt someone was watching him. He thought about the other boxes in the plane. He closed the briefcase, set it down and crawled back in. When he was sure there were only three more cases to be found he crawled out with them. There in the light of day he opened them one by one and each, like the first one, contained cash money.

He put his coat back on and carried the cases, one in each hand, and one under each arm. He climbed out and up to his horse and set the brief's down. He took the scrap pieces of rope he always had in his saddle bags and tied the case handles together, two each and left enough to make a sling in-between as well. He took his rifle down and put it in the saddle scabbard. He tightened his cinch, untied his horse, retrieved the cases and with the rope sling across his lap he let the cases hang on each side of his legs. He fixed his slicker over the cases to partially cover them and started to ride.

It was awkward, but doable. The horse questioned the bumping cases as they started up the trail but stayed to his work and perked up his pace like he always did when heading back to whatever is home at the time. Trey's worry was running into somebody and it was easily possible in hunting season. A rider would notice the bulk under his slicker. He rode all the way into camp without seeing a soul.

The best hiding spot he came up with was a tree off in a thicket beside the camp. He looked back into one of the cases and kneeling down did a quick estimate of what was in it. He stopped counting at $750,000.00 and realized it would be closer to a million dollars, in just the one case. He closed it and hung it deep in the Spruce boughs, making sure they were all out of site in the thick branches. He walked back to his horse, pulled the bridle and tied him with the halter on. He loosened the cinch and went to the tent.

He felt exhilarated. With little sleep and lots of adrenaline he was feeling a natural high. He built the fire back and heated some food. After taking a shot of whiskey and eating a little, he pulled off his boots, covered them with a tarp and laid down on his bedroll. He stuck his feet in the sleeping bag. He pulled the bed tarp over his shoulder and still in his clothes, lay back and went straight to sleep. By the time Wiley rode in it was dark out. Trey had risen and hung a lantern. It was lit at the hitch pole and supper in the Dutch oven was hot and ready.

Trey had decided not to say anything to Wiley. That was going to be hard but he needed time to work through this find and all its implications. Wiley was an honest kind of young man, so why tempt it. They hobbled horses and turned them out with the bell mare. Trey kept a mount at the rail and fed it. Then they hung the feed sacks Wiley had brought on the meat pole. As they went about the chores Trey repeatedly glanced at the hiding place in the Spruce branches. He just could not help it.

Even though the cases were out of sight, the spot was hard for him to ignore. Wiley's conversation was about his trophy and Trey listened and tried to stay interested. But, there was a whole new game afoot now. He knew the implications and was already feeling a change coming over him. He thought of possessions he always wanted and never had. He thought about paying his truck off. He dreamed of a new horse trailer, the kind with sleeping quarters up front. He dreamed with relish of owning a string of the ranch's horses. And then he actually thought about his own ranch. That was a dream from way back in time.

It didn't seem odd that the old memory would intrude just now. Money was the connection. The family had owned a farm and ranch in Nebraska when Trey was a kid. Grandpa went into debt in the recession of the early seventies, when the bottom fell out of the cattle market. Ten years later, with Trey's father helping, they'd begun to pull out of the debt and were nearly clear when the early eighties recession hit. All over the country family farms went on the auction block. The highest suicide rate in the nation for several years running occurred in America's farm belt. Trey's folks lost the home place and they lost Grandpa too. The stress was too much for the old man. For all the years after his grandmother never stopped praying for God to release her of the hate she held for bankers, lawyers, politicians and the whole bunch she saw as those that caused it. She told Trey before she died that false hopes and dreams were for children. He was a man now and he had to keep his feet on the ground. She said,

"Son, don't expect anybody to care that wasn't there. They won't because they can't. Just take care of yourself and your own ones."

"Don't farm, don't ranch," she said. "They'll take it and leave you with nothing. It ain't legal to kill them so you might as well join 'em. Just get a job and hold too it." And so, Trey had.

He woke well before dawn with those thoughts still in his head. His watch said four am. He stirred the coals, put on fire wood and the coffee pot too. Then he crawled back in the sack. He just laid there awake and let the dream fade away. In a little while he was smiling at the campfire. When he saw the steam spit from the mouth of the coffee pot, he grabbed the pad, took the pot off the fire and stirred in the grounds. The smell was wonderful. He put the pot back on to return to a boil and waited. He was still smiling when he poured his first cup.

"You awake?" he said to Wiley. A muffled "yes" came back from the sleeping bag. "Coffee's ready." Trey said.

6

Lovers & Friends

Clarence stood in the bunkhouse and looked at his watch. It was three pm and he was holding a shot of straight bourbon whiskey. Usually he held off his drinking till five pm or later. But he was losing the struggle and the time had been moving up on him. He tossed it down and went to the fridge and grabbed a beer. He drank that beer so fast it reminded him of younger days. Without a pause he did the bourbon a second and then a third time. Then the drinking was on him and when that happened he always quit counting. He put on the music and wondered what day it was. It was a weekday; the weekend was close. Was it Thursday or Friday? He was not going to be able to justify this without knowing the day so he just dropped the question. He called Ilene. They talked for an hour. Before they hung up she said,

"Hey old friend, take it easy on that stuff." It made the tears well up in his eyes.

Clarence went to his pipe and tobacco. He loaded it, lit up and cursed the cost of a high-taxed, good smoke. It was a poor man's tax and he hated it. Still he paid it and smoked it. In defense of that he once said it was like high dollar whiskey, it's worth it.

He paced and stirred with some music. He had put on George Jones, and then Willie, and it was not right. He put on the Chieftains and that Celtic sound, was right. The sound of the ancient fathers. Clarence was ready to go way back to the depths of his folk, his people as far as he could go. He listened and felt the pain and longing he heard in the Bagpipes. There was no music that felt the mountains early morning mist or evening clouds like this music. Sometimes there was just a place you knew just from the sound it made. It was a music for the outdoors, and a panoramic scene surrounding you. Deep down the emotion pulled him. Then he decided to go to town. He left a note for Wes. It said,

"Gone to town. TV dinners are a foot deep in the freezer, pick one or two."

***

Casey knew that Clarence was drinking when he called. It was a brief conversation but she'd not considered saying no. She thought about feeding him and put on some left-over stew. She did a bread mix and put it in the oven. She went to the bathroom and freshened up. She rejected the thought that came to her, that Clarence was drinking and wouldn't notice how she looked anyway. She went back to the kitchen cabinet and took her bottle of bourbon and set it out. She set out ice and a pitcher of water. She checked her beer and there was enough for her to have one and she did. She even poured a shot of whiskey for herself and took it straight up. Clarence needed her, she needed him. She no longer felt used, she felt grateful. She needed a love and he was it. Casey was a full out western woman now, in a place where men were still men and the women were supposed to like it that way. Clarence would show up at her door with a drunken smile, an appetite for whiskey, then food and finally for her. That is just the way it was.

***

Clarence's eyes popped open at daylight coming through the window. He set up and saw the glass of water on the bedtable. He knew Casey had put it there for him. He was always thirsty after a drunk. He guzzled it like he did his beer the night before and went straight in to her shower. He was not feeling good but when you had been drinking as long as he had you learned you'd get passed it.

Casey had breakfast going when Clarence stepped out into the kitchen. He was mostly dressed but carrying his boots and looking for his hat. Neither of them said anything. She put his plate out and poured the fresh coffee. Clarence had always been able to eat, drunk or sober and he had no trouble now. Casey ate with him, pushing things to him, salt, pepper, butter, jam, toast. It was all there. He finished first and then watched her finishing up. She looked so fresh to him and he felt so damn sour,

"What day is this," he asked quietly.

"It's Saturday."

"Good,"

"For what?" Casey said.

"I don't like to get drunk during the work week." Clarence said.

Casey laughed out loud. Her laugh made him feel better. She kept chuckling and shaking her head as she stood and took their plates to the sink.

"Well, you are just a responsible kind of man aren't you," she said.

"That's correct."

"You going back out to the ranch?" Casey asked.

"Got too, Trey and Wiley are in the Mountains. Got range to cover. When do you go in to work?"

"Not till eleven. I'm off at eight tonight..." Casey raised her eyebrows as if anticipating something and Clarence knew what. She reached in her cabinet and pulled out a go cup, filled it with coffee, put the top on tight and set it on the table in front of him.

"Ok, I will call you later." He said.

"Well ok then." As she answered, he rose, stepped to her at the counter and gave her a good hug and a kiss on the forehead. She knew it was all she could expect. Mouth kissing was for nighttime stuff to Clarence and in the daytime, you kept your distance. She was used to it and at their age, she once admitted, he had a point.

***

Clarence had prowled cattle with a pickup truck before, when he was in a hurry. But, in general he frowned upon it. When he saw the cow limping with a piece of wire around her leg it reminded him of why. He tried to raise Wes on the truck radio but there was no answer. Now he had to drive back to Headquarters, hookup a trailer, catch a horse, saddle and go back to the pasture and find the cow again.

When Clarence drove up at the corral he was relieved to see Wes there. He had the ranch truck and a trailer already hooked up for a cow he'd found. He had a horse saddled and tied to the fence. All Clarence needed was a horse for himself. Wes had him one in no time, caught and ready to saddle.

While driving out to catch the cow Wes gobbled a sandwich and coffee from the thermos. They bounced with the truck but Clarence drove slowly on the wet and muddy, dirt road. He had his window open and was feeling better in the cold damp air. He started to forget about his hangover.

The rest of the day would be lost to him now. By the time they caught the cow and doctored it, it was going to be late and on Saturday they liked to quit early. He kicked himself for going in to town and knew he'd call Casey when they got back and cancel going in again.

When they got back to the headquarters they put the limping cow in the hospital pen. They had removed the wire in the pasture with her stretched out, headed and heeled, but the cut would need some watching and time to heal, before putting her out again. Clarence got a syringe and Antibiotic from the fridge in the barn and put the cow in the chute for 40 ccs against infection. With horses put up and fed and a quick check with the farm hands at the barn, they were back at the bunkhouse soon enough. Clarence had Wes fire the grill. He pulled steaks out to thaw and he did the rest of the supper in the kitchen. They were drinking beer and night was setting in when Wiley and Trey drove in. Trey had his Elk. When Clarence saw it he said,

"About a two fifty score I'd guess, but respectable."

It was a quick thing to grill more meat for them while Trey and Wiley put the horses up and hung the Elk quarters in the meat locker. Everybody was tired and even though it was a Saturday night they all moved off to the TV room and showers, and finally their bunks and sleep.

***

The next morning Trey was moving early and Clarence followed him to the kitchen and the coffee

"Going back into the camp," Trey said.

"Wiley going?" Clarence asked.

"No, I can get it."

Clarence waited for Trey to ask about the pastures checked and the hay and other chores, but he didn't and Clarence decided not to bring anything up. He made him breakfast and Trey made himself five sandwiches with thick pieces of meat on each.

"I'm gone," Trey said. "I'll get into camp tonight and should be back by dark tomorrow."

"No hurry, I got the fort."

Trey looked at Clarence for a few seconds. It was as if he wanted to say something and seeing it Clarence waited, but nothing was said and Trey drove out as the first clear sunrise in a week broke through with that low autumn light of a Rocky Mountain morning. Trey was driving out when Wiley came into the kitchen.

"I don't know why we didn't bring everything back with us yesterday." Wiley said.

"You were short two pack horses with Trey's meat." Clarence

said.

"True, but we still had room."

"With mules ok, but you are packing good cow ponies and it ain't right to overload them. One-hundred fifty pounds per horse we always say."

"They can carry more than that," Wiley said, "I weigh a hundred and seventy."

"Not when its dead weight. Dead weight is different." Clarence said.

***

The trailhead had quite a few more trucks and horse trailers parked there. But the spot, beside Jays old Outfitter corrals, was clear and still respected behind the single poled gate and faded sign. The camps were all around the wooded area surrounding the trailhead. The local, weekend hunters were off work, trying to get their Elk before winter set in. Most of these hunters would peel off the Canyon trail at one of the many side trails that you could take to meadows and Elk feeding lower down. Trey parked and pulled his three horses out of the pens and saddled up.

There was pressure for the chore ahead of him. He'd left the money hidden at camp not wanting to reveal it to Wiley. Now, with a moment of truth approaching, when each step he took moved him closer to the act of taking that money home with him, he had the strong feeling that he would keep it. He would not think it a crime. It seemed to him the crime had already been committed. Still, there might be consequences, he knew that too.

Before he rode out he stuffed a good load of hay in the rack for Wiley's horse. As he moved out with his pack string he took a dip of Snuff and felt the burn. He turned and heard Wiley's horse's cry out at being left alone.

"It's all right boy, we'll be back." He yelled to it. Then he turned and started out. Jay always said it was worth it to any serious Big Game Hunter, this long ride into the deep wilderness. There were times Trey had questioned that, but not now. This time it was damn sure worth more than any long ride he had ever made, doing the big circle on the ranch's range or going in to this wilderness hunting camp. He was feeling justified somehow, and in a way he had never quite felt before.

***

On the following day, after dark, Trey drove into the ranch. He had the briefcases locked in his tool box behind the cab of his pickup. The pack gear and his saddle were in the truck bed. He opened the gate to the corrals and without backing up to it he simply swung the trailer gate open, walked in the trailer and one at a time dropped the halters that were tied to the trailer rail and let the four horses back out on their own. They went straight into the corral gate and headed for the hay the boys had left waiting in the bins.

He closed the gate, got back in the truck and backed the trailer into its spot. He unhooked it and drove over to the bunk house and parked. He walked in the door carrying his small bag of personals. Clarence had made a pot roast and it was still warm in the oven. Trey picked up a plate, filled it and carried it into the TV room and sat in his chair. They were all there watching a movie, all in their half stages of undress and stretched out in the usual places.

Trey ate with his gear on. His hat was pulled down, his coat collar pulled up. His chaps, muddy boots and spurs stuck out on crossed legs, on the rug. The only thing he had removed were his gloves.

Clarence looked over at him and could not see his face for the hat and his hands and his plate. You could smell the wood smoke and outside air coming off him and a whiff from the floor draft brought up the odor of horse shit. Clarence thought Trey was just staring at the TV screen but Trey saw Clarence looking at his muddy boots on the rug.

"I'll clean it up, don't worry about it." Trey said. He took another mouthful,

"What you watching?"

"It's, ahh, ahhh," Clarence stuttered, not quite remembering.

"Good one," Trey said. Then he got up and stood there with the empty plate.

"That actress plays her part well." Trey said to nobody in particular.

"I fall in love with her every time I watch it." Clarence answered.

Trey went back into the kitchen, set his plate down, went to the cabinet for whiskey and poured a shot. He wanted to go into town, he wanted to see someone really bad, but he held himself to thoughts of the drink, the shower, and the bed. Sometimes you surprise a woman and it works, but odds are she could resent it after too long an absence. He had been thinking about odds all the way out of the mountains. All he had come up with was to start playing any odds in his favor, no matter what they were.

The refrigerator light was the only light on in the kitchen and it glowed like a campfire against his weathered face. Clarence could see him from where he sat and he could not help but see it as a fine shot for a western movie. Trey was a handsome man even to Clarence and when he looked back at the TV screen he thought Trey could hold his own with any of the actors on it just in his looks. And, anything else for that matter. The fridge door slammed hard. Trey stuck his head in the TV room.

"Screw it, I'll see you in the morning," he said, then turned and walked out the front door. Clarence heard his truck start up and peel out gravel from the bunkhouse parking lot.

"Where's he going?" Wes said.

"Bet I know," Clarence answered.

"Damned right," Wiley said.

"He didn't even clean up." Wes said.

Clarence thought about how Trey had sat and ate so stiff like and hadn't even removed his coat or chaps. The man had been horseback in the cold mountains for about thirty-six hours. That would be twenty-four or so riding, leave about eleven hours for taking care of the horses, breaking camp, then packing and loading it. Loading and unloading the trailer and driving from the ranch to the trailhead and back again. Sleep and eat had to play in there somewhere.

"Sometimes it's hard to take your armor off when you come from a fight like he just has." Clarence said. Wes set up from his chair and looked at Wiley and said,

"What fight?" Wiley looked at Clarence and smiled,

"You come up with some good shit sometimes, Clarence." He said.

***

Trey picked up his truck phone before he was out the gate and set it to dial Jen's number and then waited. He wanted to be on the town side of the canyon when he called. That would be closer to her house and he'd have a good signal. He wanted it to sound casual like he'd stopped by in passing. He knew she'd know better but it kept up a bit of protocol. Then the thought turned dark. She might be with someone. Think again, that didn't matter. That was something he needed to know anyway.

***

Jen turned off the TV when she saw Trey's number come up on her ringing phone. She was alone with her dog, already dressed for bed, and it was getting late. Trey said he wanted to stop by, she said sure and then he asked her if she would open up the garage door. He said he wasn't dressed to come in the house. She had seen him after work before and with the wet slush and mud she understood. She had a mud room in her entry but it never got dirty. It was as neat as the rest of her house.

Trey pulled in the drive and her garage door was open. He stepped out of his truck and into the light. Jen stepped into the garage and looked at him. He was a sight. She could smell the wood smoke right away. He was unshaven, there was the slight jingle of his spurs on the pavement, his hat was back on his head in a relaxed way. His big hands were coming out of his pockets as he reached for her then bent down to kiss her. She did not resist and the smell of whiskey and tobacco was not offensive to her, not here in the cold, clean night air of the garage. The pungency of it excited her.

"I'm too dirty to come in the house."

"Yes, you are, unless…"

"They kissed again, slower and longer.

"I took them off here." He finished her thought. "I have been thinking about you hard. In the mountains I felt you, your presence somehow."

Jen knew what he meant at a deep physical level. In fact, she knew that feeling very well. She gave a throaty chuckle as she looked at him, as she looked into his eyes. Trey unbuckled his chaps. She put her hands on his waist and turned him and pulled the zippers down on the back of his shotgun leggings. He undid the buckle and stepped out of the stiff leather. The chaps stood like stove pipe, on their own for a moment, and then crumbled to the floor. They both laughed as they watched it happen. Trey sat on a short bench by the door and pulled off his boots, spurs still on, and Jen handed him a garage rag to wipe the mud from his hands. Even his thick socks looked sexy to her. He looked at her as he wiped his hands, then set the rag down as she pushed the button on the wall that lowered the door. They were kissing hard before the door bottomed out. She pressed full against him and she could feel his body press against her strong.

They stepped into the house and they both pulled off his big coat. She took his hat and hung it on her hallway rack. She had put it there when she first started seeing him. He stepped into the washroom in the hall and washed his face and hands. She stood right up against the open-door jam and watched him do it. She was not thinking now, she was just waiting for him. He said something about taking a shower and she might have shaken her head no. His smell was of musk, pine, whiskey, and campfire, 'fresh from the fight,' she thought. She didn't want it washed off. She wanted to crawl inside it. He pulled her close and started kissing her neck. His hands slid down to the small of her back and then to the front and slipped inside the robe and then between her legs. Only her flannel pajamas were between his hand and her and he squeezed and pressed his palm there.

"You're wet" he said, softly in her ear. Her voice bubbled, and her knees sank her weight onto his hand.

"I was wet before I hung up the phone," she said.

All that they were doing moved to the moment in her room when she was spread out on the bed and she lifted her hips as he pulled down the pajama pants and tossed them to the side. He eased on top and entered her. They were both in a moment that only a real natural desire can get you to if you let it happen. They made love with a connection that was deep and natural. Neither would remember detail, length of time or method. It was the intensity that would be remembered. They were still making love when Jen's alarm clock went off.

***

It was late morning when Trey pulled into the ranch headquarters. Nobody was there. He went inside, stripped, took a long hot shower and put on a clean set of work clothes. Then he went to the ranch radio and put out a call for Clarence.

Trey realized when he woke up at Jen's that he needed to tell somebody about what he'd found. He almost told her. But he kept his secret. He needed advice he trusted. Wiley was young and Trey knew as well as anyone how careless a young man can be. Clarence was the man he trusted with something like this. In minutes the old Cowboy's voice crackled over the radio.

"What" was Clarence's response

"Where are you?"

"I'm at Jay's feeding the dogs. Ilene's gone to her sisters for a week."

"Stay there, I'll be right over."

"I'll be back at the office in a minute."

"Stay there!" Trey said firmly. He moved out quick to his truck, cranked it and drove over, crossed the bridge and pulled into the drive-way. He turned his truck around and backed up under Jay's carport. That put the truck under cover and out of the wind.

Clarence was leaning on his truck out in the yard with his arms crossed over his big old Sheepskin coat. He had on his winter cap with the earflaps down. The dogs were quiet, busy with their feeding. Trey sat in his truck and kept it running with the heater on. He waved Clarence over and pointed for him to get in. Clarence walked over, got in and closed the door. He looked at Trey and said,

"You aren't going to tell me you're getting married, are you?"

"No, but it's damn near as scary."

"Nothing is as scary as that." Clarence's look and tone of voice was so matter of fact that Trey started laughing. He had a hard time stopping. He'd just gotten rich and laid and he was starting to feel damn good."

"You had a good night, didn't you?" Clarence said.

"Oh yeah."

"Well, I'm happy for you. Jen's a good gal. I always liked her and she's about as sexy as they come."

Trey smiled and nodded his head. He had a funny buzz going on inside him. It was like his body was humming.

"So, what is it then?" Clarence said. "You heard something else about the ranch?"

"No." Trey looked away when he spoke, "I found the plane."

Clarence sat in stunned silence. He was looking harder at Trey now, his bushy eyebrows lifted, his voice rose as he spoke,

"Fenwick's plane, the Ranch's plane, you found it, where?"

Trey pointed at the Mountains.

"I figured that much, where up there? have you reported it?" Trey shook his head in silence.

"Why not?"

Trey looked at Clarence now with a telling expression on his face, a gleam in his eye and a sly smile to go with it. It was a look that suggested Clarence might already know and Clarence read it dead on.

"Oh shit, where is it?" Clarence's face started to spread with a grin as Trey nodded toward the back of his truck. As soon as he did Clarence was out the door and headed for the tailgate. Trey shut the truck off and pulled the keys that held the one to the tool box. They both climbed into the bed. Trey opened the tool box, pulled the top case out and went down on one knee to open it in the truck bed. Clarence's mouth fell wide open when he saw what the briefcase contained.

"Holy shit, I always thought it, Jay knew it, and you found it. Holy shit,"

Clarence flopped down on his haunches beside the briefcase and leaned back against the wheel weld of the truck bed and simply stared. Trey knelt there without moving, just smiling. After a long pause he said,

"And there's three more."

"All the same?" Clarence said,

"Yep, all the same."

"Holy shit."

"That's exactly what I said."

"I wish Jay was here." Clarence said.

"Me too. But, we still got Ilene."

"Damn right," Clarence said, "Keep it in the family." Trey looked at Clarence and considered what he had just said.

"We got to be careful. I don't think I know the rules here."

Clarence pulled his hat off and started scratching his bald spot. He had a look as intense as any expression Trey had ever seen on him.

"What are you thinking now?" Clarence asked.

Trey started closing the case, then stopped and looked up at Clarence.

"You need any money?"

"Don't tempt me. Let me think."

Trey closed the case, put it in the toolbox and locked it down. Then they climbed off the bed, closed the tailgate and walked back to the truck cab. Trey started the truck and got the heater going again. Clarence climbed in beside him.

"Trey, the first thing that comes to mind is you need to know the law on this. It don't matter if you follow it or not, not to me anyway. A poor man has a right to be rich as anybody else. I've read that behind every fortune there's a crime. There may be a law being broken, just by not reporting the plane. Anybody see you up there?" Trey shook his head.

"Wiley?" Clarence added. Trey shook his head, again.

"You going to tell him?"

"No, and I hate it. But, for now, no."

"Ok, here is what comes to mind. The only Lawyer we know is Weismann. I think I trust him. Do you?"

"I guess so Clarence. If you do. I know Jay did, so yes."

"How about I go and see him. Just me. I get his assurance of confidence and tell him a what if story, then asked him what he would do. No names, no facts. I'll see if you can hire him as your attorney. That way we know he's working for you and he has to keep it confidential and such."

"We hire him," Trey corrected. "You and me. I want you in on this."

Clarence could see the concern on his friend's face and hear it in his voice. Clarence realized Trey might decide to report the plane and turn in the money. He was an honest man, the kind that deep down never felt like he should have anything that he had not earned himself. Clarence knew this about all of them. Wiley, Wes, the farm hands, the part-time roundup hands, the irrigation hands in the summer. He knew because it was in him too. It's played up like humility as a badge of honor. But as Clarence aged and gained life's hard-won experience his thinking changed. Now, to Clarence, any man that ignored opportunity just simply did not get something about life. That being the fact of good timing and inexplicable good luck and pushing an opportunity. It had been a problem of Clarence's his entire life. He had kicked himself in his later years for the good things he'd let slip by.

But, that did not have to be Trey Blake. When that man was on point he got things done. He had all the quality of a man that deserved better then to just drive off in the Sunset with his pick-up, an old horse trailer, some clothes and tack and one or two horses in the back. Trey was a man that had stepped into a big job on a big ranch, one who had easily won the attention of a beautiful and successful young woman, one who had the respect and admiration of everyone that really knew him and the jealousy of all the want to-be Cowboys in the county. In their world that was as good as it got. Till now anyway. Clarence reached his hand over and Trey shook it.

"I'm with you." Clarence said, then opened the truck door and got out. He looked back in before he closed the door and said,

"I'll go talk to Weismann. I'll not mention any names or details. I don't believe the man will do anything to hurt us. I just don't believe that."

"Ok," Trey said.

Trey felt the relief. He'd shared the burden. He knew he needed the man's savvy at a time like this. Trey considered Clarence a Cowboy philosopher and the man had surprised him many times with his general run of knowledge on plenty of subjects. Let Clarence Colton get his meter running on a problem and it was a problem that was about to find a solution. It was Clarence's way and he was a natural at it.

7

Cautious Optimism

Weismann looked at Clarence from across the desk and tried to understand what the old puncher wanted from him.

"I have to know more about what you are concerned with, before I can give you advice. I can't tell you that I would represent you without it. It may not be in my line of practice."

"But, you are a lawyer?"

"Yes, Tax Attorney. I handle business accounts like Fenwick's, as well as large business and Real Estate transactions. I don't handle divorces for example. I am not a criminal defense counselor either."

"Yes, but in your capacity, you keep Mr. Fenwick out of trouble by keeping his business transactions legal, stuff like that." Clarence said, and made sure he didn't blink.

"Yes, you could put it that way."

"And, if he has a legal problem you'd help him survive it, and he has your full confidence in keeping his business just between you and him, right?"

Weismann could see that Clarence was set on some kind of tactic. As an attorney Weismann was accustomed to controlling a conversation like this. Still, he did not want to lean on Clarence. He liked him too much and he knew Clarence was his own man anyway. So what use would it be?

"That is called 'client, attorney privilege,'" Weismann said. "So yes, everything is in confidence."

"Well ok. I want to hire you right now and then we'll go from there." Clarence said.

"I would give a consultation for free but if you insist give me five dollars and then I will officially be your attorney. But, just for now. Until I know more."

Clarence jumped up out of his seat, pulled his billfold out and laid five dollars on the desk. Then he reached and shook Weismann's hand.

"It's a deal then. I have hired you and all I am about to tell is just between you and me." Clarence looked down at the five-dollar bill and back at Weismann and said,

"There is plenty more where that came from."

Weismann could not help laughing. Clarence had a mischievous grin when he spoke. The laugh eased the strain that, coming to this conclusion, had brought on. Clarence sat back down and pulled his chair up closer to the desk and started to speak, quietly.

"Ok, once upon a time, maybe, there was an honest man who found some not so honest money. This money had been lost. The men that had it were lost with it. But, the money was not stolen. It's just gained illegally and the guy that finds it wants to keep it, wants to use it without drawing suspicion on himself, to live a better life, to spend it. What would you advise him to do?"

Weismann's smile was fading fast, his expression showed full attention.

"The men that were lost, were they murdered?" Wiseman said,

"No, accident."

"What kind of accident?"

"Ahh, I don't know, plane crash maybe," Clarence tried not to say that and cringed when it came out anyway.

"How much money did he find?" Weismann asked.

"A lot…"

"How much?"

"Maybe like a million dollars, maybe more."

Clarence could see that Weismann's face flushed a little, his head went down and ducked like he was about to butt against something. But, Weismann checked himself. He knew he had shown too much of a reaction. He would not push on the dollar amount of the find. He knew instantly what had happened and he already knew how much money there was. But, he could not tell Clarence that.

Clarence waited for a response. He feared Weismann would offer up some serious objection of some kind, something responsible, law abiding, like give it back, give it to the authorities, whatever. But Weismann did not do that. He simply sat there and stared. His game face was on, Clarence thought. He watched as Weismann leaned back in his chair, took a deep breath and looked down at nothing. Then he raised his head and said,

"Clarence did you find the Ranch's airplane?" Clarence nodded his head yes and said nothing.

"Ok, who else is in on this?"

"Trey Blake."

"No one else?"

Clarence shook his head, no. Weismann rubbed his neck and then stood up and walked around the desk. He began to pace in the open area.

"Mr. Weismann, I ah," Clarence started to speak but Weismann stopped him.

"Call me Charles. We have known each other a long time and we are getting ready to know each other a lot better."

Clarence exhaled in relief. Weismann was saying he would help, would represent them. But, he had to ask...

"So, you'll take us as clients?"

"Yes, I will. Look Clarence, neither of you have done anything that I can't get you out of, so far anyway. So, don't worry. I want to see you and Trey in a few days. I'll call you. But remember, if either of you start talking, break silence, throw the money around in public, I won't be able to help. Is that clear?"

Clarence nodded quietly as he stood up slow. He shook hands with Weismann then turned and while walking to the door he said,

"I'll tell Trey and we'll look forward to hearing from you. Thank you." And Clarence walked out.

Weismann went back to his desk and sat down. He spun the chair around and pulled the curtain back on his window that faced the street. He watched Clarence cross and get into the ranch pickup truck and drive away.

Weismann thought about this news. After five years lost, someone had finally found the plane. He had often dreaded it. He and Fenwick had both dreaded it. The circumstantial evidence, the fact that this was a company plane and company pilot, all of that would have put them through a lot of legal scrutiny. He had prepared himself then to respond when it happened. Weismann still had the outline he had made of effective legal responses should there be an investigation of The Ranch. It was in his file. Then the search was called off and over time it slipped down the list of priorities and the possibility of the plane not having crashed at all, but simply stolen and flown somewhere else, was the thought. The file that he had prepared for their defense was still in his safe, two hard copies, one of which he would have to pull out and review again, now that this had happened.

He continued staring out the window after Clarence had pulled out and driven away. He thought about what was in his favor, how to turn the difficulty to their benefit. The fact that Trey and Clarence had found the plane was a good thing. The fact that they had not reported it was excellent, and the fact they had come to him was better still. If he had every doubted these were sensible men they were proving to be that now.

Fenwick had another plane that crashed on the run-way at the Aspen Colorado Airport, many years before. They had slipped by that one since the plane had burned. It was not carrying anything much anyway. They had delivered and were going back for another load. The cash had been brought to Weismann by a courier who had driven it up in a rental car.

Weismann laundered the money through the ranch expenses. He got twenty percent for doing it. Some years there was more money than expected. The ranch had made profits and the drug business in the Rocky Mountain region was booming. When this happened, they sent the excess cash to another source, somewhere. Weismann did not always know where and did not want to know. This, the money Clarence and Trey had found, resulted from too good a year, three years in a row and made the cash impossible to hide in the Ranch's books.

No one had given Fenwick a hard time about the loss of this money or Weismann either. The plane's loss and subsequent search had made the news and that, though bad for the bottom line, was understood by the Cartel. They lost product and money often enough to accept it as the cost of doing business. The volume of sales combined with a huge markup, that was how they made up losses. Fenwick had said this more than once to ease Weismann's mind about a late-night visit from some shadowy character. Now, Clarence and Trey had the drug money. And, to beat all of Weismann's expectations, they were thinking about keeping it. He would have never thought they had it in them. He started laughing about it to himself. Three and one-half million dollars, that's what they had. Weismann had counted it out to the Pilot and the Mexican Contractor the very morning of the flight, right there in his office.

If the plane was found now, by others, it would be nothing but good that the money was not on it. If nothing else were on the plane to point to drug smuggling, that would be truly perfect.

Fenwick had quit the drug business and the loss of this plane served as a good reason. Weismann had advised it for both of them.

Others that were involved understood this. The finding of the plane would open a drag net that could expose them all. So, all agreed. At Dagger Ranch they stopped moving the money and waited until this day, the day the plane would be found. One way or another it was back in his lap now and Weisman had to deal with it.

Here we go again, he thought, here we go again. He was going to do the best thing he could do and that is trust these two cowhands and convince them they could trust him. Then school them, guide and manage them and tell not one damn soul. Not even Fenwick. When the next person found the plane, Weismann would be as surprised as anybody else. Until that time, he would proceed like he always had. He would make sure these lucky Cowboys understood the price. It was their silence and Weismann's twenty percent.

***

On the drive back to the ranch Clarence thought about how quick Weismann had caught on. And, that the plane contained money. It was curious to Clarence but he could see no use in worrying about it. That would do no good in furthering any solution. It was a, work the parts, one at a time kind-of thing. Weismann would help, that was all he needed to know for now. When he pulled up at the bunkhouse Trey was there at the table drinking coffee and waiting.

"Who's here?" Clarence said as he walked in.

"Nobody,"

"Well, come on then,"

"Where?"

"Just get your coat." Clarence said. "I don't want anybody to walk in on us. You drive." They walked out and got into Trey's truck.

"Where too?"

"Let's go down to the old headquarters barn." Clarence answered.

It was all on dirt road, all the way past the Ranch airstrip, to the far Southeast corner of the deeded ranch property. Along the way, through the low water crossings, with spinning tires up the gravel hills, they talked and Clarence told Trey of the meeting with Weisman in detail.

Trey listened and did not ask why they were going to the old barn and headquarters. The barn there was a fine one built in the 1890's of virgin pine. It had the standard second story hay loft. The roof was hand hewed cedar shingle now covered with sheet iron, added back in the forties. It was good enough to last a couple of lifetimes. When they approached the barn across the meadow it looked huge and isolated with nothing around it but the shell of old cabins and corrals long since abandoned and left to choke with tumbleweeds.

They drove up and walked to the big double doors and each taking one they swung them open. When they stepped in they felt as reverent as if they were in a church. Inside, covering most of the ground floor space were the last three chuck wagons of the Double Dagger, stored there these many long years. They looked like they were still in good condition, ready for another round-up. The canvas was long gone but the arched boughs that once held it in place rose up like the rib cage of an old buffalo carcass out on the plains.

Clarence walked to an inside door and opened it. It led to a set of side rooms within the barn. The center one, with its own door to the outside was the original business office of the ranch. It still had the furniture, the roll topped desk, the barrel chairs, the lanterns, the big pot-bellied wood stove. Tally books were still on the shelves. It was a room full of the ranches history from the very beginning. They both looked at the old black and white photos on the wall. Faces of tough men in a rough country stared back at them. Clarence knew who some of them were and some were lost to memory.

"Ilene could name some of them," Clarence said.

"Been awhile since we were out here," Trey said.

"Yeah, well looky here," Clarence pulled back the curtain that hung across the closet in place of a door. It was the ranch safe. A large, heavy, antique of a thing that nobody in their right mind would try to move anywhere.

"I can see where you are going with this Clarence." Trey sat in the barrel chair at the desk and Clarence went over and pulled the curtains on the windows to let in some light. The curtains were made from old tow sacks, once used for feed.

"They never brought electricity out here?" Trey said. Clarence shook his head as he sat down.

"No, as I recall old man Fenwick didn't want highline poles crossing the pastures. Said it was an eyesore."

"So, the new headquarters ended up where it is now, where the electricity didn't have far to go off the highway." Trey said.

"Yep, and we got privacy here. Anyone comes up we'll hear them way off."

"Less they are horseback."

"Less they are horseback," Clarence agreed.

"Some of the boys will ask questions."

"We'll tell 'em we are inventorying down here is all. And there is plenty of stuff to put on the auction block with the rest of the ranch, that's here. Can't ignore that."

"They'd expect to help," Trey said.

"Tell 'em it's woman's work. Somebody has to stay with the cattle anyhow." Clarence said.

"You got it figured. " Trey said. "All-right. Let's give it a quick clean up. Later, we can get some kerosene for the lanterns, firewood for the stove…can you open that thing?" Trey pointed at the safe.

Clarence went over, squatted down in front of it and began twisting the dial. He turned the handle and opened it easily. It was empty.

"How the hell did you do that?" Trey said.

Clarence pointed to the wall behind the safe. The combination was written there plain for anyone to see.

"Those old timers were some kind of characters. They would protect whatever was in the safe with their guns and their lives but damned if they were going to memorize a bunch of numbers." Clarence said, chuckling under his breath.

"Yes, they were," Trey spoke approvingly as he looked at the photos again.

"You may have been given a chance to be just like them." Clarence said.

"How's that?"

"Well, you know the history and the men that built lives out here, men that civilized this country. What kind of grit it took to claim something as your own and hang on to it and build it up. You might have the means now to do that yourself."

Clarence looked at Trey's face closely and he could see a realization of what was said working on his old friend. It was there, just a look in Trey's eyes that a man only got when he saw the possibilities of a thing.

They closed the barn back up as they went out. It had not been locked. It was far out on ranch property, a corner surrounded by BLM land on three sides. It was not a place that anyone could see from the highway. They'd see it only if they were crossing the ranch for some reason. Even so Trey thought about getting locks.

"There's chain in the shop, are there any locks with keys around?" Trey asked.

"Yes, there's a box in the shop with some we aren't using. When we went to the master lock system it left them over."

They climbed in the pickup and Clarence talked as they drove. The early season snow was melting and it was muddy. The first big freeze of winter had not come to the valley yet. As the truck fishtailed and bumped along Clarence said,

"Trey, let's get Weismann to come out here. He can park at the headquarters and we can drive him out to the barn. You hadn't counted it all have you?" Clarence asked.

"No, not yet."

"Let's put it in the safe. Get it out and away from the headquarters."

"Yeah, it can't stay in my tool box. The bunkhouse either."

"Maybe I should stay out of it now." Clarence said.

"Don't think that way Clarence. This is between friends and you are already proving your worth. I'm cutting you in full partner. We need to see what Weismann thinks. I am going to need you all the way through. This ain't over by far."

"Charles will figure it out." Clarence said.

"Charles? You guys on first name basis now?" Trey asked.

"I expect so. The money and all. When a man becomes a thousand-aire he moves up in the world, don't you know."

"I thought you already were a thousand-aire,"

"Well, now I am a two thousand-aire. You'll give me that much won't you?"

"Jesus Clarence, all these years you only saved a thousand dollars?"

"Little more than that. Not much more. When the Ranch goes I won't last six months out on the road looking for work."

"Shit," Trey said. And his own heart sank a little thinking about the ranch selling again. He had forgotten about it for a little while. His numbers wouldn't hold him long either. Paying for housing again, buying your own food and fuel out on the road. His savings wouldn't last very long at all.

When they got back to the ranch Weismann had called, but he left no message. Clarence called him back and they agreed to meet the next morning. Clarence told him straight out that he needed to come to the ranch and Weismann agreed. Clarence stood, and went back into Trey's room and told him what was said.

"Ok, let's load some firewood in my truck. Is there kerosene at the shop still?" Trey said.

"Yes, I'll run down. I'll get the chain and some locks. Anything else?"

"Just some cleaning stuff. I'll get what's in the kitchen closet. We'll back up to the wood pile before we leave."

***

As darkness fell Wiley and Wes drove up pulling a trailer, parked at the corral gate and unloaded their horses and two sick cows. They put them in the pens and fed them, then put the horses up and fed them. Both Trey and Clarence were drinking together when the crew came in the door. They stopped talking as soon as the boys walked in. The smell of food cooking filled the kitchen.

Wiley got a glass, sat down and held it expectantly toward Clarence. Clarence poured him a drink.

"What's up?" Wiley said.

"You are," Clarence answered, "What have you been doing?"

"I'd rather not say," Wiley said.

"Oh?" Trey said. He sat looking sideways at Wiley, with his chin resting on his hand, his elbow on the table.

"I don't want to re-hash it." Wiley said. "We had a slow day, we got stuck, truck and trailer. We went too far before we un-loaded the horses. Went all the way to the axles. We had to get the farm hands to bring over a tractor and pull us out." It just took up too much time and we didn't get the pastures all checked."

"That's ok Wiley," Trey said. "It's not like its calving season."

"Yeah, guess so."

"You just keep doing much as you can and Clarence and I will ride with you soon as we can."

"Tomorrow?" Wes asked.

"No, we meet with Weisman tomorrow, he's coming out. Just do what you can."

"Ok, so what's for supper?"

"It's hot, it's brown and there's plenty of it." Clarence said.

"That sounds really good." Wes answered with a growl.

8

Plan the Work, Work the Plan

The following morning broke bright and clear with a heavy frost on the ground. Trey drove to the old headquarters a little fast. The mud was still frozen from the night before and he pushed it to make time and get the money out of the truck and someplace safe. Clarence waited back at the bunkhouse to meet Weismann and drive him out as soon as he arrived. Trey pulled up at the barn and parked close to the side door that opened into the office. He walked in with an armload of kindling and started a fire in the stove, then he opened the flue to let it blaze up for a good draw. He stepped back outside and walked away from the barn until he could see the stove pipe on the roof. He half expected it to be clogged with bird nest after all this time but it was probably still screened up there and the smoke was just right. It rose straight up into the clear blue sky.

He did not feel concerned about what was about to take place. Clarence's clarity and good sense had helped make that happen. Now, with legal advice coming, he felt confident in the moves that would be made going forward. He would count on nothing like luck now; the luck had already happened. Now it was time to focus and work it out.

He took a look around outside. There was nothing to see but empty space and the isolation of it was reassuring. He dropped his tailgate, climbed up into the truck bed, took out his key and opened his toolbox. The briefcases were just as he had left them. He took them out and stacked all four on the tailgate, jumped down and carried them in and set them on the long table against the wall. He went out and got cleaning supplies from the truck and came back in. He built the stove fire up some more, set the flue half-way and by the time he had the table and the desk wiped off he had to remove his coat. A warm stove would be a nice touch to the meeting and Trey wanted it comfortable so that they could take their time.

When Clarence and Weismann drove up Trey was standing outside with his coat back on. Weismann shook Trey's hand and followed him inside and after many long years the hat rack had coats and hats hanging on it again. A lantern was lit and the old place, the original headquarters of the Dagger Ranch, sprang back to life.

Weismann ask to see the money and they opened the cases one by one. They emptied the cases and all three took a pile and the counting started. One of the cases had bills of smaller denominations and a quick count of it was made. When done they had a firm total of three million, three hundred thousand dollars.

Weismann knew two hundred thousand was missing. But he did not comment on that. If the pilot and passenger took it, it might still be on the plane, stuffed in their personal luggage. Weismann said,

"As I'm sure Clarence told you, you can't spend it. Not much of it anyway. You cannot suddenly arrive in town with a lot of unexplained money and expect it not to be noticed. If you put as little as fifteen thousand cash at one time in your bank account you could draw attention from a Federal Agent. If you travel and the highway patrol pulls you over and they search your vehicle, they can confiscate cash and will. What we use to call drug dogs are now trained to smell out cash money instead."

"Never heard of that." Trey said.

"If you can't explain the money they take it and they keep it. Hell will freeze over before you get it back."

"Bastards." Clarence said.

"Tell me about it," Weismann said in agreement.

Clarence asked them to sit down. He had brought a thermos full of coffee and a bag of homemade doughnuts and he set it out. He poured from his big thermos into paper cups. He put more wood in the stove as Weisman talked. His talk was so full of useful information that both Clarence and Trey would hash it over many times in the coming winter days. All in all, it went something like this...

Weismann told them that this kind of money had to be laundered through legitimate businesses. He said he would set up an LLC, a Limited Liability partnership that would contain a list of investors and would require a list of officers. The LLC would be a business and ranching was a good one to use. A big Ranch was a business that could absorb a lot of cash and plenty of ranchers, feed lot operators, sale barn and auction houses would still deal in cash. The LLC would buy Cattle and horses and the money they received when they sold the stock would be the money they could spend, in other words the money that was laundered. He told them that there are so many LLC's started each year that they cannot all be closely monitored. On paper each investor puts up an amount that would not draw much attention and the accumulative amount, though large for an individual, would not be large for an entire Company. Everything that Clarence or Trey had or bought would not be owned by them but by the LLC. So, if anyone asked them how, they could afford a new truck, for example, they would say and the paperwork would confirm, it belonged to the LLC. This should be enough to defer anybody's curiosity. And, since they were known in the area as Cowboy and Ranch manager types, they would be able to hide in plain sight. They would be able to draw good salaries and pay taxes on it just like any other legal income. A couple of good seasons go by and they could start putting money away as their own, to buy out the LLC themselves if they wanted too.

When he finished Trey and Clarence sat and looked at him for a long moment. They were visibly impressed.

"You've done this before, haven't you?" Clarence said.

A smile crept into the corners of Weismann's mouth. He shrugged his shoulders and did not answer.

"This is not the kind of money that can buy a large ranch and stock it too," Clarence said.

"Right, you'll have to lease land to carry the livestock. All of the Ranch leases will be up for grabs after we sell out. Words not out everywhere yet, that the Ranch is being sold. I can have you first in line. I pay those lease fees for the Ranch. You tell me which ones you want and I will pay them up and sign them over to the LLC. This way you can get well ahead of any ranchers waiting in line for some more grazing land. I don't think anybody would as much as make a peep about it."

"How do I get people money that I want to help out?" Trey said.

"Like who?" Weismann said.

"Like Ilene."

"You could give her small amounts at a time but that would make her suspicious and the less anyone else knows the better." Weismann said. Then he held up his hand,

"She asked me, since Jay died, if the Hunting Camp was worth anything. You know those Permits were once in the Ranch's Name. Later Jay's was the only name on them. A good, economically viable, hunting camp in that area could be worth a couple of hundred thousand, maybe more depending on marketing, equipment and live-stock."

"And Fenwick?" Clarence said.

"He's never mentioned that camp to me in all these years it's been inactive. Still, I keet paying the fees. My guess is you get Ilene to go down and renew the permits in her name. Play the sympathy card, widow, no money, she inherited it, whatever. The Forest Service might do it. I'll write a letter of release from the ranch to her, to show them. Even give them a call. Trey, you get the Outfitters license and run the Camp for her. Get it up and going and buy her out. She doesn't have to do a thing for the money and you've got another business to launder through. It can be a cash business too and that means a cash cow to anybody with an ounce of greed in their belly. When we sell out in the spring, I will fail to list it as a ranch asset. Of course, this could never be discussed with anyone outside of this circle."

Weismann was speaking to them with a conviction grown by long experience. Neither Trey or Clarence had any thought of complaint or contradiction. That would be stupid against a man talking facts to you.

"There is more. I am taking a risk. The going rate is twenty percent. I am going to have you sign a lot of paperwork that absolves me of everything the law allows, but it is still twenty-percent."

"Ok," Trey said. "Do I give you all the money now or what?"

"Yes, the sooner the better. I need to get the LLC started, then open its bank account. You Trey, I'll put on the account as manager of operations. Then you can sign checks. I can also put you and Clarence down as shareholders. I'll mention Sweat Equity as a major part of your contribution to cover you later, if needed. Sweat Equity will equal cash money when you sell out, if you ever do. It gives you another layer of protection. We time it with the Ranch's spring sale and you can pick up things you might need at a good price. The LLC will be just another buyer among many. Put cattle on the leases for the summer. Just run a yearling operation like Dagger has done in the past. We made money as I recall."

Trey stood up and went to the table. He picked up one of the brief cases and opened it. He counted money out and did not stop until he had one-hundred thousand dollars on the table. He sat it aside on the roll top desk.

"I'm keeping that out. I'll be careful how I use it." He said.

Weismann moved to the case, did a quick count and took out five of the stacks of cash.

"This will be a down payment on my percentage. I get paid money to manage money and I need to know you are all-right with that and I need to know now, before I leave."

Clarence noticed Trey's hesitation. Trey was looking at Weismann like he was a little surprised. Then, he nodded his head in agreement and smiled at his own thoughts...

"I'm getting a feeling this money is going to go through us like shit through a goose." He said. Clarence and Weismann laughed out loud and if there was any tension in the room, it dissipated.

"Well, yes that can happen." Weismann said. "But, if you manage what you purchase and if you have a couple of good years in the cattle market, it'll start to come back to you clean and legal. That's the best you can hope for. If you think about it that way it'll help you to be patient with the process."

"About the investors, and officers of the LLC, how does that work?" Clarence said.

"Let me work that out. I can be an officer and so can both of you. As far as the investors are concerned what I can tell you is that you will never hear from them or have to give them any money." Weismann said.

"And, there is one more thing. Was there anything else on the plane? Anything illegal?" he asked.

"Yes, there was a suitcase that contained bundles, looked like drugs to me." Trey answered.

"Did you leave it there?" Weismann said.

"Yes."

"You need to go back and get rid of it." Weismann said. He thought about the missing two hundred thousand but decided against mentioning it.

"Get rid of it, how?" Trey said.

"Just get it away from the plane, destroy it, burn it, whatever. The main thing is, no criminal activity need be associated with the plane when and if someone else finds it. It will be suspected, already has been, but no hard evidence. So, don't leave them anything to find. Are we good then?" Weismann finished.

"Yes, we are." Trey answered. Weismann reached for Trey's hand and they shook. Then he shook Clarence's hand and their agreement was sealed that old-fashioned way. And, that was good enough. It might not hold in some circles but to Cowhands and to Weismann it would hold. They moved to the coat rack. Clarence followed, helped him on with his coat, pulled his own coat on and they both picked up the briefcases and walked out the door. They climbed in the truck and drove away.

Trey went to his cash and took a thousand out, folded it, then stopped and stared at the money that was left. He was thinking small still. It was time to change that. He counted out nine more thousand and put the money into his coat pocket. He'd give Clarence half of it just for grins. He put the rest in the safe and locked it up. He wrote the combination down on a piece of paper and put that in his billfold. Then he rubbed the numbers off the wall.

Trey walked outside to his truck. He got the chains and padlocks and started locking up the doors. At the last he closed the flue to the stove to starve the fire. It was just coals now. He blew out the lanterns, closed the curtains on the small windows and then stood for a minute and stared at the photos on the wall. He thought about what those old characters would think, what they would have done in his place. And, as he looked he knew the answer. They would have stepped up to the opportunity just like he had. He felt sure of it. Those men, in that time, understood the root hog or die realities in life as well as any free men could.

When Trey got back to the bunkhouse he walked in and went to Clarence's room. The door was open and Clarence was lying on the bed with his hat and boots off, head propped up on a pillow. Trey sat down in the old Cowhand's reading chair and looked around the small room. On every wall there was a bookcase and on every inch of shelf space there was a book. There were some stacked on the floor as well. Trey nodded toward the pile.

"That where you get all your savvy?" Trey asked.

"Yes. Then, when it all checks out with my experience I hang on to it."

"You sure figured this out right. Most people would have been scared to death to do what we are doing."

"Yes," Clarence answered, "They would. You could still back out."

"How were you sure of Weismann?" Trey said, ignoring the comment.

"Back in the day, before you came on, things happened. Hands hired on and quit, stole things. Sometimes the end of a year's tally did not come up right. A group of illegals over in that Eagle Claw Valley took twenty-five head of cattle right under our nose one year. Turned out our herder scared out and rode off and never told us. But, those Mexicans must have known he was gone." Clarence took a breath, then continued...

"Charles Weismann always had Jay's back. Those things never got to Fenwick, he never knew." Clarence paused and kept staring up at the ceiling...

"I don't know what Jay figured out exactly but he knew Weismann would pad or change the books sometimes."

"So, it was like a conspiracy?" Trey said.

"No, I wouldn't put it that way. They never sat down and planned it as far as I know. Jay never profited anything extra. If it was a conspiracy it was a conspiracy of mutual silence. No more than that. Jay was an honest man. Over time Jay and Weismann began to trust each other. They both wanted to keep their jobs and had made decisions to protect those jobs. They could do that better if they were working together."

Trey sank deeper into the reading chair and closed his eyes. He suddenly felt very tired. His thought was that he had never really done anything to protect his job, besides going to work every day and just doing it. A couple of times that wasn't enough and he had to move on. But, you should learn to watch your back. Maybe that's what Jay had learned. Now, maybe Trey Blake would too.

Trey didn't feel up to going back into the mountains. Nights would be real cold up there now and the first big snow of winter could come any day. He opened his eyes and looked back at the book shelves.

"So, what do these books teach you about right and wrong, like keeping what really ain't yours?" Trey said.

"If it's not yours whose is it?" Clarence answered.

"I guess I don't know." Trey said. Clarence rose up and swung his feet down to the floor.

"Trey, years ago my mother and dad had gold coins. I don't know how many but it was a sack full. About that time the federal government outlawed Americans from having gold. Said anybody that had any to turn it in. They'd get paid paper dollar for gold dollar. My dad hit the roof. He'd got that gold from his dad and was told to just hold on to it for a rainy day. Well, my mother had just found Jesus. She was a real holy roller in church. She convinced my dad to turn the gold coins in to the United States Government because it was the only honest thing he could do, obey the law. Can you imagine? In today's world thinking that it was not just ok but a good and right thing to do, to let the government take what is yours, hell, not even take, just give it to them? My dad was a young man then. When he got older, he hated himself for doing that. Many a time he mentioned it. Gold became legal again, those coins worth more than a thousand dollars an ounce today. Probably a hundred thousand dollars in gold in today's prices, my daddy gave to the US government because it was the right thing to do. So, I ask you, whose gold was that?" Clarence paused for breath...

"Trey, it was not the right thing to do. It was a dumber than a fence post thing to do. Those books teach me about morality but, how to think something through as well, that is, question it. Napoleon, when about to appoint a new General in his Army would ask if the man was 'lucky.' What he meant by that is, is the man ready. Is the man ready for his destiny? Good luck, opportunity, none of that matters if you are not ready for it." Trey stayed quiet and listened. It was kind of fun to get Clarence really going on something. If you could keep up with his thinking anyway, how he saw a thing.

"The books teach me what I can figure from rational thought. The closest thing to religion for me these days is a philosophy book or two. They question just about everything and they give a good account for intuition and good old common sense. What those books teach me is that as I grow older I am supposed to grow wiser. Otherwise there's no point. And, my wisdom teaches me that you get a chance to pull yourself up and better your situation and you don't have to hurt no innocent person, then do it and to hell with anybody that would lay a guilt trip on poor folks when we get a chance to better ourselves."

Clarence's voice had risen with more than a little emotion. Trey heard annoyance loud and clear. Clarence pulled on his boots with an anger like thrust and slammed his feet down on the plank boards. It made a point and Trey had nothing he could think of to reply. Clarence got up and said,

"Trey, every man out there worth his salt should be fighting for his share. Why not you? You take a kid like Wes, he's got nothing but this job and he's helpless to do anything about losing it. He's trying to figure out if it's his fault somehow. The kid's whole world is horses, cows, weather and big country. We used to be like him. Weismann's advice tells you all you need to know. I gotta' put out some lunch." Clarence got up and left the room.

Trey stayed seated for a minute. He did a mental check of what Clarence had said and did not find fault in any of it. He wondered what he had been thinking to bring Clarence to a boil. Then again, maybe he had not been thinking, more like feeling. It was like a fear he was feeling, was that it? Not right or wrong, just fear of consequences? But that wasn't all of it. Another warning thought came to him. He was capable of choking back his own sense of enjoyment. It was like he didn't trust being happy about something so If he felt it, he'd shut it off. And what's the deal on that?

"Fear my ass..." he said to himself.

He had faith in Clarence and had shown it, bringing him in on the find. He had faith in Weismann and had shown it the same way. Now he needed more faith in himself. With a deep breath he rose from the chair and straightened up. He stretched, squared his shoulders and stepped out. Hell, this bronc was saddled. Now it was time to ride him and just maybe it was time to pull out the confidence that he could do just that.

The boys were coming in to eat. Trey was the boss. He sat in his chair, at the head of the table. He reached for the sandwich makings. Things were being passed to him. Nobody was talking. Wiley looked at Trey and started to say something but then did not. Trey looked at Clarence. His old face was still red from his outburst. Maybe Trey's was too. Maybe the hands saw it and were staying quiet because of it. When Clarence sat down he looked at Trey again and waited. Trey looked back at him.

"Should I say grace?" Clarence said.

"No, I'm good," Trey answered.

"I wouldn't mind if you did," Wes said.

"Ok, hats off, hats off damn it. Maybe you'd rather hold hands," Clarence said, and it had a tone to it, a don't screw with me tone.

The hats flew toward the hat rack like flying saucers. All fell to the floor and it drew a laugh from everybody. Trey's was still on his head. He eased it off and carefully took the brim and spun it, almost gently toward the hat rack. It landed perfect and hung there. Then, with heads bowed and mouths full of food, the chewing stopped and Clarence said grace.

"Thank you, Lord, for the food and the job, for good horses too.

Please help us all as we move toward a new year and a new future and help us to stomach the sale of this fine old Ranch, all its holdings and livestock, all its history and so much more, so as a bunch of rich bastards can get richer and poor men can get poorer hunting another job."

Trey coughed and looked up at Clarence. Clarence took it to mean, 'shut up'. Clarence glared back and said, "Amen!"

9

Time Off

With fall roundup over the competition between the hands for time off hit its annual peak. Clarence and Trey would hold the fort, as usual. But this time, with their new-found wealth, that was harder to do. They were chomping at a bit too, a bit of cash.

Trey had to ride back in, to the plane. Jay's horse string was ready. Clarence caught Trey the two longest legged, fastest walking horses on the ranch. Jay, being the long-time boss, by tradition was the man that took the big circle at roundup time. That was the longest ride around the perimeter of the range and pasture being gathered. You pushed cattle from that perimeter back toward a centralized point. You get them headed that way and other Cowboys pick them up in an ever-tightening circle. You had to have the right kind of horse for that ride. It is a horse that can cover ground in a smooth trot all day long, up and down, over and across a difficult variety of terrain.

None of them had made a move on Jay's string of horses. Trey had his own big circle types but he didn't say 'no' when Clarence presented these. In truth, Trey had more than once thought about using Jay's string. But, it was too soon and disrespectable somehow. Now he had the chance to saddle them up and approval from Clarence sealed the deal. Clarence stroked them, walked around them and said,

"These two came out of Montana, the 'Big Dry' country. Jay had a friend that got them as colts off the Mackey Ranch. I loved it when Jay did that. He was a man on a mission and I was his sidekick. We'd load up, hook-up the horse trailer and take off. Had a lot of fun on those trips. Jay would be grinning like he would do when he had one of his, "Victories," he called 'em. He loved getting another good horse. You put the pack saddle on either one of them. Then ride one in and the other out. You take the one you like best and I'll take the other when you get back in."

"Ok." Trey said.

"Oh, and if you run into that Scab, Kane, just avoid him. He is as nosey as an old woman and will question you as if he owns that country up there. He is an intimidator and will sure rain on your parade. Don't give him an opening."

"Wiley and I never saw him." Trey said.

"Well, to me it means you probably will this time. I've heard, for a while now, he's been using our hunting Camp. But he won't stay put long. He has to move around to keep the Game Warden and the Forest Service off his ass."

"You'd think he'd get busted." Trey said.

"They are scared of him. All of 'em. He's a notorious bully and has had them intimidated for years. You are one of the few men I know that wouldn't take any shit off him. But, you can't get into anything now, there's too much to lose."

"Right!" Trey said. "Adios, hold down the fort."

"See you tomorrow night." Clarence answered.

It was clear weather for the ride, but it was cold. Trey's one pack horse carried a short-handled snow shovel and some horse feed, along with his bedroll and food. It had snowed since the last trip and he might have to dig himself back into the plane. He hardly noticed the work of getting the horses saddled and ready. He locked his truck, put his coat on, mounted and rode off in the deep thoughts that came with his resolve and his purpose.

It was growing dark when he reached the top and crossed. Some clouds had drifted in, the low light was a pewter gray. When he rode down and approached the hunting Camp he could see a big fire going and a couple of wall tents were up. He immediately turned around. He would go ahead and ride to the plane now. If it was Kane, Trey would do like Clarence said, just stay away from him.

***

Trey had ridden in the growing darkness as near to the crash site as he wanted to be. He stopped for the night. He did it old time, Indian fighter style. He made a cold camp, no fire, dropped the packs, loosened cinches and left the horses saddled. He gave his stock grain and ate cold food himself. Then, only taking his boots, outer coat and chaps off, he rolled up in his bedroll. He slept and was up and at the plane before there was even enough light to see it clearly. He moved down to it and did what he came to do. He crawled in, pulled the one suitcase aside and opened it. He put the drug bundles in his empty day pack and crawled out with it. He slung the backpack with the drug bundles onto his back, picked up the shovel, climbed over the scree and back up out of the ravine. When he reached the top, he turned and looked back across the drainage. He saw a bright, hunter orange jacket through the trees. Somebody was up there.

Trey stuffed the day pack in a pannier, the shovel in the other side, threw a quick squaw hitch over the load, untied, mounted and rode out. His horses were ready for home and they stepped out lively, not missing a beat. He decided to just ride. He would get rid of the drugs later. Seeing the hunter had spooked him and whether they had seen him or not he wanted out of there before they could meet. To risk being ridden up on while burning and destroying the drugs would be unacceptable. That would have to wait. When he was up and crossing the top, he looked to the West and silently wished for a snow storm to cover his tracks around the plane. It was clear sky.

Trey rode into the trailhead parking area and straight to the corrals thinking how fast the trip had gone. He tied up and started his truck and while the Diesel engine warmed he un-loaded the packs and put them in his truck bed. Then he loaded his horses in the trailer. He looked around the parking area but saw no one. There was still enough shooting light to keep the hunters in the woods. He pulled the truck out until the horse trailer was clear of the gate, then went to his toolbox and found one piece of chain and a padlock left-over from the day at the old barn. He closed and locked the gate and added that key to his key ring. Trey was going to buy the camp from Ilene and he was starting to feel a sense of propriety. He needed to send a message to the scab, Kane. That being that the Ranch still claimed the base camp corrals and the wilderness camp.

When Trey got back Clarence had his 'Happy Veteran's Day' sign up and was flying Old Glory off the porch. Late as it was the crew was still at the table eating Clarence's cake and drinking his Whiskey. When Clarence stood to greet Trey, he wobbled a little. Trey, just for the fun of it said,

"Are you sure all of you are veterans?" Every single one of them raised their hands and drunkenly nodded their heads.

"And you too Mr. Trey, thanks for your service." Clarence said.

Trey went to the table and Clarence slid him a shot glass and poured it for him. Trey held his glass up for a toast and they all joined him.

"Some gave all, all gave some. Here's to those that wish us well.

Those that don't can go to hell." They all gave a cheer and drank. It's what they did every Veterans' day. Jay had started it, Clarence kept it going. It's a thing about blue collar working men, they tend to military service for their country and that is worth honoring even if you had to do it yourselves.

***

On Thanksgiving weekend, the first big snow fell in the valley. Snowplows worked overtime on the highway and mountain passes. Snow blowers in driveways and sidewalks were out every morning in town. The farmhands were feeding cattle off of the ranch hay sleds, once pulled by horse teams. Now it was four-wheel drive tractors with tire chains on. Winter hats with earflaps replaced Stetsons, insulated Pack boots replaced Cowboy boots and saddle stirrups were changed out from Ox-bows to the big wide type to accommodate the winter boots. And, for much of the time the Cowhands put down their lariat ropes, broke ice on water troughs and shoveled snow.

Elk started crossing highways headed for the Refuge of lower ground at all hours and Big Horn Sheep would soon graze steep slopes right off the roads. One night late, traveling back to the ranch from Jen's, Trey almost hit the biggest Mule Deer Buck he'd ever seen. All this the signs of huge snowfall in the high country and the wilderness closed for the winter.

Trey and Clarence kept the road to the old headquarters barn open themselves and no-body questioned it since the auction people had been in there doing an inventory before the big storm. With the snowplow mounted on the ranch 4x4 truck and chained up all around, they managed to keep up with the snowfall.

Ilene was coming around every day to help with the inventory. Weismann had gotten her on the payroll and she was the one that often talked on the phone with members of the Fenwick family.

The owner's large house had been shut up for many years. Ilene was sent out to open it. A few of the family had shown up to go through and claim things, furniture, paintings and knick-knacks. They marked them with tape to be mailed and some they took with them. Ilene's job was to sift through what remained and ship it to the ad-dresses she was given. Much of the rest was marked to be separated and shipped to Fenwick and kept by the family from the list he and his wife had sent. Ilene hired a few women friends from town to help her and when they had packed and tagged what was to be shipped she arranged for the mover to come out and load it up. Whatever was left, mainly clothes, she was to donate to good will or some other charitable organization that received such things.

For a time in the ranch's history, after the death of Fenwick's grandfather, the grandmother ran the ranch. This old family matriarch was known throughout the greater Two Ocean Country as a hands-on woman that loved the ranch life as much as any man could. She rarely left it. Her pictures, in frames in much of the hallway and bedroom, showed a lean faced woman with short cropped hair, aristocratic features and a figure that would have complimented any picture frame it was given.

Her time in life was the roaring twenties. In her photograph's, she had the length of leg that any horse woman would envy and her bearing was of one accustomed to high social position. The close-ups revealed her feminine side as well. They showed her with lipstick and eye-shadow, in flirty demure poses as if copying the movie stars of that golden age. In other photos she was often surrounded by a handful of girlfriends, also dressed in the Cowgirl style of the era and then a few with the Cowhands around and Ilene stopped and looked hard at one of those.

She saw him there, Jay, at maybe twelve or thirteen. He was holding the reins of his horse and Ilene knew it was Mott. Jay had talked about him many times. Mott was a small blue roan, cold backed, stubborn, a range bred colt that no-body on the ranch wanted. He was too small and too mean. Jay's dad stood beside him in the photo with some seventeen-hand big circle horse. Both Jay and his dad were looking ready. The two were off center of the photo and they stood, almost apart from nearly ten others, employees, all cowboy types. She sat and stared at her cowboy, Jay, way back then, when he was just a kid and all was before him.

Jay had told Ilene the story. His dad had said, "Son, if you want to cowboy with me and my outfit you show me you can master this horse and I will take you on. If you beat him nobody on this ranch will ever question your deserving to ride with us. If he best you I'll send you to town to pump gas for a living."

It took many long minutes for Ilene to put that photo down. She cried inside to think of that kid and she laughed at the cut of his jaw as he stood in the photo, not smiling but glaring at the photographer.

Ilene knew that the picture was taken after Mott's submission. Ilene knew the story. Long after the hands would say, "If Jay and Mott go after a bunch quitter consider it caught."

Ilene was captivated by the idea of a woman running the ranch. She wanted to know so much more about her. But, there was little information and the drawer full of personal letters seemed off limits to Ilene. She kept the photo with Jay and his dad and Mott. And, though the letters and rest of the photos were not specifically asked for by the family, Ilene packed them carefully to send anyway. Some great grand-daughter should know about this woman and her life on the ranch. Some daughter should know, about the blood in her veins from this classy lady. So, Ilene crafted a note, addressed it to "Whom It May Concern," and put it in on top with the packing. In the note she had written,

"To the female descendants of this grand lady I suggest you study her through these mementos, letters and photos. See what she can teach you. There is a lot here to be proud of and I am sure a lot to learn from her as well. Her reputation on the Double Dagger Ranch is well known to those of us who have lived and worked here as well as the community at large. Her Wyoming, born and bred blood, runs in your veins. Be proud of it."

Clarence came in during these packing days and tried to help. But he got in the way and Ilene, in spite of her appreciation, had pushed him aside. Then he did something that surprised the hell out of her. He opened a door that was at the end of a hall that Ilene thought led outside. And it did lead outside, but only after you walked through a huge walk in and walk through closet complete with dressing room and makeup table, restroom and sink. It had full length mirrors set as well as any high dollar department store. It seemed to be designed to walk into from the hall in the back of the house, in robe and slippers, and walk out the back door dressed and ready for the day. Out that door was a very private porch, one handy to the stables along a good walkway. So, this was where the women guests, seen in all the photos, could be re-attired in western garb and out the door as slick as you pleased.

The room was filled with hat boxes up on high shelves. They held western Cowgirl hats in the style of the period. Black, brown, white, blue, red, all in the old-time twenties style, with wide, flat brims, high crowns and fancy beaded hatbands. There were beautiful silk kerchiefs.

There were racks of women's, pure silk, western shirts and marked of different sizes as clearly as if in a clothing store. Lower shelves held riding boots reaching clear to the knee, with three-inch heels topped with spur counters. They were in all sizes. There were fancy leather leggings with Mexican silver buckles and Sterling Silver, Concho-ed, leather vests. There were jackets and there were beautiful Italian leather and deer skin riding gloves in drawers. Some clothing even had the name of the guest. They were marked for the girlfriends to find easily when they visited the ranch.

They dressed like movie stars of old. And too, in that grand, dude ranch era, movie stars had actually been guests at the ranch. The old autographed photos proved it. Ilene sat down and cried at the beautiful things and Clarence walked in to see what was up and awkwardly stood there beside her with his jaw dropped at the extravagance of it all.

"This ain't going to Good Will," Clarence said.

As Ilene heard Clarence's words she nodded her head up and down and wiped her eyes on her shirtsleeve. Clarence picked up a beautiful silk handkerchief and handed it to her and then she started laughing.

"Not that one" she said. She put it down and pulled out her own cotton handkerchief and blew her nose. Within minutes she was putting on hats and looking in the mirror, then jackets too and laughing like a school girl. Clarence was confused by what he saw, some kind of a woman's mood swing? Still, he stood by and waited.

"Wonder how the poor folks are doing," Clarence said awkwardly and he started to laugh too. Clarence loved many things and one of them was seeing a woman laugh. And, so genuine, from pure honest delight. It warmed his heart. As his face flushed a little and good memories sprang up they began to laugh together.

Ilene brought Clarence aboard to help. Now, he was officially recognized. They had their moment there together and that sealed it. He worked with her, moving this precious cargo to her house. Trey stopped by and could see the friendship between them and wondered a little about it. But, he had come to know that they kept a certain distance. He invited Ilene over for supper. Ilene made a point to tell him to call Casey out for supper as well. Clarence stayed silent and worked at his task. He had his short notice, dinner guest menu already down. Had for years. Thaw some steaks, light the grill, bake some potatoes and warm some beans. The bread would be biscuits. He could do it blindfolded.

It was that night that Ilene spoke of the reason Fenwick had given her for not flying up to sort through the family possessions. He told her that it was just too painful to contemplate. She said it was proof that the family was having a little trouble letting go of so much of their history at the ranch. It was emotional and it was sad. So, he simply deferred.

His instructions were, that Ilene was to call his secretary with questions of what they might want to preserve for the family's history. What they picked would be packaged, marked and shipped to a storage facility. After all these years the ranch and family's once valued belongings, would simply be sold or packed away in boxes. It seemed a shame. But each of them at the table, in their own way understood it. Clarence, with his head down and averted eyes may have said it best,

"What's hard to come by is hard to let go of. I don't blame him for not wanting to put himself through that." And then, in spite of himself Clarence visualized the yard sale, when his x-wife to be, laid out everything they had together and spread it out in the front yard to be sold for pennies on the dollar.

Clarence saw his saddle on the ground that day, with ten dollars marked on it with tape. He had driven up just in time. He began grabbing his stuff out of the yard and throwing it as fast as he could in his truck bed. He sped off with the sound of her screaming at him, yelling that she was calling the police. He hit the highway north and back to the old life. His saddle of all things. It was worth a thousand dollars if it was worth a dime and she'd put ten dollars on it without as much as a word to him. What's the deal on that?

A lot of years had passed and things like this still rose up to spoil his present moments. But, he'd learned something. He had learned that when a woman was done with you, she was done. It was worse than a contempt for you, it was to imagine that you never existed in the first place. He had also learned to keep those thoughts to himself. No-body wanted to hear them, especially another woman.

***

Jen had gone to her family in Denver for the holidays. Wiley took off for his folk's home in Idaho and his cousin Roland went too. That left Clarence, Trey, Raymond and Wes on duty at the ranch. The farm hands all stayed around as well, having their families in houses on ranch property. They fed the cattle, plowed the roads and took care of any maintenance.

In early January, just before calving season began, Weismann called to tell them the LLC was ready to go. He just needed a name. Clarence and Trey had studied on it for some time. On their last evening at the old headquarters barn, when the auction inventory people had left the premises, Trey and Clarence had started drinking there. They stoked up the stove, lit a lantern and sat before the pictures on the wall. Clarence pulled out good cigars and his flask was full of high dollar Kentucky Bourbon. Trey had beer in his truck in a cooler in the bed. No need now to put it on ice. The cooler was there to keep the beer from freezing.

They discussed the famous brands of ranches of the past and how legend told they came to be. On the frosty window Clarence took his finger and drew a couple of signs he had been familiar with. But nothing struck him and he ran out of frost as the room warmed.

"It needs to be simple," Trey said.

"Yes, and I'd hate it if it peeled easy." Clarence answered. He was thinking of brands with letters or numbers or symbols with lines too close to each other.

"The brand should say something of the story of the start of the ranch." Clarence continued,

"I say we try to stay with that tradition." Trey agreed,

"Like the ‡, mark for Double Dagger. You know the story, Old man Fenwick said he'd been stabbed in the back twice. Once by a woman and once by his best friend. Guess he wanted to remember it." Clarence said.

Clarence was sitting down again. His hat was back on his head. The lantern light was hard on his eyes. He took off his reading glasses and tried to rub them clean on a corner of his dirty bandana.

"Money," he murmured.

"What about it?" Trey said.

"This is about the money," Clarence said.

"What isn't" Trey answered. "But, it's about having a chance too."

Clarence reached over and got the yellow pad Trey had been scratching on.

"Somebody'd think we was studying Petroglyphs of ancient peoples they see that." Clarence said as he looked at it.

"Maybe we are. We're a dying breed, aren't we?"

With the pencil Clarence made a 'c' on the sheet, then he drew the number '2' in front of it. Then he put a slash in-between them. He turned the pad around for Trey to see. Trey bent closer and stared at it. It was a 2/c.

"So, what's it saying?" Trey said.

"It says, 'Second Chance,' that's what the money is giving us.". Trey stared at the brand and really did like it. So, they agreed. They'd have to check with the State Brand people, to see if the brand was registered. If not, it was theirs. It told the story, but to them only and that worked.

***

Clarence walked through a dark house. There were people there but not with him. He stepped into the front room and then out the door to a porch. On his left a young couple stood close, facing each other in the night shadows. He knew the young woman and spoke to her. She was beautiful and Clarence felt envious of the guy with her. She smiled at Clarence and turned back to her young man. Clarence walked down steps and there were people in the yard. It was foggy out and there was music. He knew the band and started over to them but something stopped him. He looked to his left and she was standing there, alone with her back to him. Her hair was up in the back and he could see her neck. That figure he knew well. He stepped up close behind her and reached around her waist in an embrace. He pressed her backside against him. He turned her. She looked so beautiful. Her eyes looked up at him but she kept her head down. She kept her hands in the pockets of her short denim jacket. He was taller than she and he had to bend to kiss her. As his face moved close to hers she made no move away or toward him. She did not lift her chin to meet him. With his arms around her he felt her standing stiffly and he knew she was not his. He knew she would never be his again.

He woke up in the cold dark room of the bunk house with a level of emotional emptiness that made him shudder. He looked at the alarm clock. It was two in the morning. That was the time he usually woke up when he drank too much the night before. He felt the headache, the dry mouth and the loneliness. He sat up quietly and drank the water he always set out for nights like this. He drank but it did not quench his thirst and it did not clean his palate. The only relief he would find would be to get up and find something to eat. Either that or take another shot of whiskey. It was at times like this that he knew why he could not ever have the woman he loved. It was the drinking and he knew it as well as he had ever known anything. He would never be able to share with anyone how a moment like this felt. It was like being on the edge of an abyss. The woman was Ilene and though she slept that very night alone, only a half a mile from where he stood, she might as well have been in Paris France. And yet, after all these years he ached for her, just like way back then. Her face in the dream was so young, so beautiful. So many fine years ahead for her, so many broken years ahead for him.

Clarence shivered in the cold room. He put on his robe and slippers. He pulled his knit watch cap down around his ears and shuffled into the kitchen. He poured a glass of milk and found some cookies and like old men everywhere sat in the wee hours alone at a table and ate and drank. Finally, he got up, opened the wood box on the stove and put more stove wood in. He opened the flue a little and shuffled back to bed. Every bone in his body seemed to touch a nerve as he moved. He turned off the light, got back in bed and refused himself the thoughts he had woken up with. If he could not find sleep he could at least rest. After a while he looked for the dream again but it would not come.

The next thing he knew he was listening to boots on the wood plank floor. He sat up, swung his feet down and made a decision. He was going to hire a cook himself. Hell, he had money and cooking for this crew was getting to be too time consuming. He told rather than asked Trey and like the good friend he was Trey nodded in agreement and said,

"Go ahead. What brought this on?"

"I need to get back in shape. I want to be ready for whatever is coming and I need to get outside more to do that."

"Hell yes, do it. I've kind of missed you out there. Ilene's through with the inventory. Want me to ask her?"

"No, I don't. Let me handle it." Clarence said, and then he went to the kitchen to start breakfast.

10

Catch-Up Hell

Benedict Kane stood in his half-empty little house and stared into a mirror. He had been thinking hard about what he had stumbled on in the mountains. He just could not get his mind off of it. The plane had long been a Holy Grail to him. Many nights he had conjured up a vision of finding it with lots of money on board. With enough money he would have his revenge on the people that had passed him by. He could dangle it in front of his x-wife and watch her squirm. She would want to come back to him. He would refuse her. He would rub it in the face of those that despised him. He was a big ugly man but money would make him beautiful. He had been called a bully his entire life but wait until they saw him now. With money you could reach an entirely new level of intimidation. He craved it like a wolf craved blood.

Kane knew that someone had been there before him. When he stumbled onto the plane's tail he saw the tracks and saw that snow had been shoveled out. He crawled in and noticed the cargo net had been cut with a knife. He saw clumps of dirty snow from a boot sole lying frozen and intact inside the door with the tread still showing. He had poked and reached up into the pilot's cabin for whatever he might be able to get to. He found nothing.

He rode back to the camp and finished the hunt he was on. He was so distracted that his two hunters, having paid good money for the trip, were not able to fill their tags. When they packed out and down to the trailhead he saw that a lock was back on the gate to the Dagger Ranch corrals. No one would have done that except, the Ranch hands. Kane went to his truck, drug out his bolt cutters and cut the lock again just for the hell of it. He didn't need the pens but he cut the lock anyway. He was loading up and going home. He just liked to do things like that, when he had a chance, when no one was looking.

So, they were in the area when he was. He could see that someone had used the wilderness camp before he got there. Anyplace you tie horses reveal their presence, even when snow covered it. The manure was fresh and the pawed-up ground still showed. He doubted anyone but the Dagger Ranch hands would use that camp. Only he would do that. He was Benedict Kane and he did what suited him. You just had to be flexible, move in and then move out to somewhere else.

Kane never liked those Ranch hands. Who the hell did they think they were? Big shots, just because they rode for a big outfit? He started to let the demons come back to visit him. The ones he harbored after being slighted. Those men had not shown him respect and he hated them for it. He thought, like always, he would find a way to provoke a fight and then beat the shit out of them. Nobody could take Kane in a fistfight. His weight, his height, his reach was more than normal men. He always relied on it and it always came through for him. He liked to sucker punch a man. Catch him flatfooted and really nail him. Then he would jump on him, on the ground and go to work. It didn't matter how you won, just win. It made other men fear you. But not those Ranch hands. They'd actually laughed at him once. When Kane asked the manager, Jay, to fight him the man had said,

"Sure, I'll fight you. But, it'll be horseback. You and me both mounted, how about that and how about right now? And, the man swung his horse off the trail in a clearing and put his horse through its paces. Quick lope, quick stop, quick turns, back up, turn on a dime, almost show horse stuff. Kane had looked at the fine horseflesh under Jay and the handle the man had on the surefooted, well trained mount and knew he couldn't take him that way. Not on the flea bag he was riding. When he refused, they had laughed at him and when he had called them cowards they told him to learn to ride a horse before they challenged real Cowboys to a contest. Then they simply rode away.

Kane wondered what was found on the plane by whoever was there before him. Would they report it? If not, there could only be one reason. They found something worth keeping their mouths shut about. He could not think anything else. He just knew it. With that in mind he decided he would not report it either. It could be used maybe, like having leverage against them, whoever they were.

The hunter he was guiding that day, he left at noontime to watch a meadow. Then he went off on a scout in the other direction. When he was coming back Kane took a faint trail up a drainage he had not been in before. There was a game trail there and he followed it. Eventually, he was on foot leading his horse over the difficult ground and cussing himself for starting up it in the first place. He started to turn around and the trail was just too narrow, with wall on one side and drop-off on the other. Then he had seen it. It rose like an odd, shiny obelisk with the sunlight of midday full on it. When back with his hunter he said nothing. When back in his camp he said nothing. When he had dumped his hunters off in town he rode back in by himself to study the plane. He took a small car jack he had taken off a little foreign car years ago and tried to get into the pilot cabin with it by jacking up the ceiling a little. It didn't help. He thought about things he needed to do to get in that cabin. Once he had the list in his mind he rode back out. He would get the right tools and pack them back in.

He got home and started putting it together when the storm hit. It really dumped a lot of snow and it was enough to close the mountain trails until spring. Kane sat morose and dejected as he watched it fall and finally hauled his stock to the little pasture he leased South of the town of Two Ocean and dumped his string of mules and horses out for the winter. They would lose a lot of weight there but it was cheap to keep them. When the ranch manager came to the gate and ask for money, Kane gave him a couple of hundred dollars. When the guy looked at the few bills and started to say something Kane gave him a dirty look and lied,

"It's all I got. Try not to starve 'em to death," he said, and he drove off, his empty trailer clanging behind him.

***

Casey was home and about to leave for work when Clarence called. He explained what he needed and she knew exactly where to start looking. She had come to the Town of Two Ocean, "Fresh from the city, needing a change." She liked to say. And she worked any jobs she could get. That was all the jobs that were hard to get people to do. She had waitressed, washed dishes, cleaned houses & motel rooms, cooked, drove delivery for auto parts stores, detailed rich people's cars and shoveled horse shit on the dude ranches. You name it, Casey had done it. All that was before the invasion from Mexico. They had those jobs now.

The old friends that had once done the work with her were all gone now. She had watched them pack-up and drive away one by tearful one as they began to get older and realize they were not going to find mister right or ever get paid above minimum wage. Two Ocean was a tourist town and not much else. There was no industry, never had been. As prices went up for food, housing and gasoline, workers actually saw wages go down. It was a stunning thing for a blue-collar kind of girl to grasp. She would have been long gone herself if it had not been for a small but timely inheritance that allowed her to buy her little one-bedroom town house and pay off a decent vehicle to drive. She squeezed what was left until the eagles were screaming and she kept working hard. But, her place in the life of Two Ocean was still precarious and she felt it every day. It was one thing to be poor in a community of poor folks, but quite another when you lived in a town full of rich people. Then you felt it every day. When she finally got her old Cowboy to notice her at the bar, then to dance with her, then to stay with her, she thought she saw a chance to have someone to share that struggle with.

Clarence was a working cowhand. For him, all it would take was a horse fall to bring him down in some remote pasture out there. He didn't seem to have much to offer. But her risk was larger than that. Her risk was the lonely heartache that came with having no-one and the way that made her feel. That's what she feared now, most of all. It was the loneliness. Every time Clarence called her, anytime he needed her, it gave her hope.

As the Hispanic population grew in the back quarters of Two Ocean's trailer courts, stuck back up narrow, cold canyons out of sight and out of mind, Casey had worked with and gotten to know them. What they had going was their family's willingness to stick together, live in crowded housing and pool their resources. Now, with Clarence's need for cooking and cleaning, they were the only ones she knew to call. The one she knew best was Helena Gomez. Casey called her and they met at the restaurant on a Saturday morning. She told Helena what Clarence needed. He wanted a cleaning crew once a week and a cook every day. That cook had to be a man and he could board at the ranch as part of his pay.

On the following Saturday Helena and her crew met Casey at the restaurant and drove with her out to the ranch. Helena looked the place over and a price was agreed on. The three-woman crew went to work right away, and the cleaning began. Clarence stepped into the kitchen with the Hispanic man that Helena had brought out.

Casey saw an opportunity. She was not on the cleaning crew but she picked up a rag and a spray bottle of cleaner and went into Clarence's room to clean it. She could not help herself. It was a natural call to her. This was the first time she had the opportunity to poke around in the old Cogger's stuff and she wasn't going to miss out on it. She took a last look into the kitchen and saw that the two men had already started cooking together.

She stepped into Clarence's room. Somehow, dusting led to opening dresser drawers. The closet needed looking into as well. Later she was under the bed, just to see if it was dirty. It was, so she pulled out the half full-duffle bag and the old suitcase. She had to move them to clean under the bunk, didn't she? Casey had plans for this Cowboy and if there was anything she needed to know about him she wanted to know it now.

It was late morning. The hands would be coming in for lunch soon. The Hispanic man was middle-aged. He spoke good English and had spent much of his life in the States. Clarence wanted to know if he could fix American food and he said he could. The man's name was Marcos Sanchez.

They started with Clarence's planned lunch of soup and hot sandwiches. Clarence asked Marcos if he could make a Ruben and the man said he could. Clarence had the makings for it. He set the ingredients out on the kitchen counter. There really wasn't time for a good home-made soup but Clarence kept plenty of canned soup around and he pulled out two large of Campbell's potato soup and put it on.

Later, when Clarence showed Marcos the freezer the man responded with sincere admiration. There was plenty of red meat in there and Marcos knew many ways to prepare it. Clarence cautioned him,

"A ranch like this is one of the few places a man can get tired of red-meat." Clarence said. "Mix it up. I do chicken and pork a couple of times a week. Some of the hands will fish and bring home Trout."

Clarence liked the look of the man. He was clean. He told Clarence of his cooking experience and some history behind it. Marcos had spent some time in jail down in Texas. He had done a three-year stint in Huntsville for robbery. There, he had learned to cook. Then, when he got out he had started as a fry cook at a Pancake House and had pretty much stayed with it. He learned to bake too. He started that at a grocery store deli doing their fresh bread and rolls. He did cakes as well. He said he was a cousin of Helena's and he had come up North because there were lots of jobs for cooks in the tourist towns of the Rocky Mountains. The off season made it harder to find work just now and housing was high priced. Marcos was glad to accept this offer.

They agreed on salary and Clarence showed their new cook his corner of the bunkhouse. It had a small bunk bed, a table, a lamp and a stand-alone army surplus wall locker. The man seemed happy with it. After the women were through cleaning, he left with them and went back to town to get his things and move in.

Clarence was tickled pink. Now he had time to get out more and money too. He started spending more time horseback again and going to town. Then, without any notice, he took off to Denver for a little vacation. Marcos was cooking fine. Trey started to slip too.

Trey started missing days at work, some meals and nights at the bunkhouse. He took off a long weekend that turned into nearly a week with Jen when they drove over to the Sundance film festival in Utah. Jen had tickets and she was surprised and delighted when Trey accepted her invitation. It was quite a week. Trey got his Skiing legs back under him and insisted on paying for lift tickets, meals, bar, saying Jen had furnished the rooms and tickets to the films shown. When he bought himself some new ski clothes in this expensive town Jen got curious. She asked him about the money that he was spending at dinner one night. He looked her straight in the eye and without blinking said,

"Don't worry about it. It's mine to spend." He knew he said that with an edge to his voice because she flinched a little and backed off. He ordered some shots of Bourbon while he ate and though she declined, suggested she do the same. Before the night was over they were dancing somewhere, getting close to each other and hit the room hot to trot. Toward the end of the week Trey called the ranch and talked to Wiley. The word he got from him was,

"Where the hell are you?"

At breakfast Trey told Jen to pack and before she knew it they were driving back to Wyoming and Trey was putting the gas pedal of Jen's SUV down pretty hard.

On the drive they talked about the week. He could not believe how good it felt to have gotten away from the ranch like that, with this beautiful woman beside him and money to spend. But, self-indulgence had not been Trey's way in life and as the miles and hours passed he had to fight back a growing sense of guilt. There, in Sundance they were surrounded by people with money and he guessed he wanted to act like he was one of them. Trey heard Weismann's words of caution echoing in his ear. This trip would have to be one time and one time only. Trey Blake had his message from Wiley too. That message was "help," and Trey was driving hard for home. It was time to ride again.

***

Casey knew from Helena, who knew from Marcos, that Clarence had disappeared. She managed to hold out for forty-eight hours. Then, almost completely out of her mind she called the bunkhouse again. No luck. So, she called Ilene. No one answered so she left a message. After another day passed there was no response from her either.

In the afternoon shadows of a lonely day off Casey sank into a very irrational state of mind. She could see Clarence and Ilene in a Motel somewhere getting it on. Casey went to her room and fell face down on her bed. She threw a fit of screaming and crying. When she finished she went to the backdoor for some air and her cat was so frightened it hurt itself trying to get out through the first crack in the door jam. Casey began to cuss the cat for doing that. As it limped off, she yelled,

"You damned, stupid pussy. You are a worthless slut of a cat and no right at all to squeal if I slam a door on your worthless ass. I know men that would shoot you for just walking across their yard like the dumb bitch you are."

Casey could feel herself slipping. Now she was heading for a level of rage that she knew, even as she let it come, that if Clarence ever saw this side of her she would never see him again.

In Clarence's room, the day she cleaned it she had found a letter that had never been mailed. She read it quickly and put it back like she found it. It was a love letter and it wasn't to her. Casey knew a little history on her Cowboy. She knew he was married for a short time. She knew, hoped any way that like her he had no children. That fact helps, with less obstacles and a clearer road ahead for her intentions. Then, there was Ilene. Casey had been around them both and with her radar always on around Clarence, she sensed a strange distance they kept with each other, a distance self-imposed and un-natural it seemed to Casey. She decided that it was faked. Casey decided that they were once lovers. In fact, she knew it. She knew as sure as anything. She had ignored it, she had hoped for the best, she had decided to stay coy and confident, maintain a lady like poise, but who the hell was she kidding?

"My ass," she said out loud and then began to march around her little apartment house and when she reached the kitchen pulled out the whiskey bottle, took a shot and marched some more. After four or five rounds of marching and doing shots she turned on the stereo to play some music. She found her bitch to listen to. It was raw Blues from a woman scorned in love. And, then Casey collapsed face down on her bed again and just as she started thinking some really bad things the phone rang.

"Shit, damnit," Casey said to herself as she went to the phone and without picking it up stood there and listened to the message as the caller spoke it.

"Hi, Casey this is Ilene. I have not heard from Clarence. Its calving season and they will be riding pastures all hours. So, don't worry. That blow of a storm that just came through will trigger calves to drop. It can be hell. Call me."

Then it buzzed and Casey hit the end button. Casey was swooning drunk on her feet and as she listened she felt embarrassed and ashamed. When it was all said and done she was a town girl and what the hell did she know. But, Ilene had returned her call. That meant a lot. Casey swore right then and there to be-friends with this woman. You take things as they come and you take people as they are to you, not to hearsay from anybody else. Casey sat down and cried. She could not have said why. She fell asleep. The phone rang again and it was Clarence that left the message this time.

She turned off the music, then played the message again. She was listening for something and it wasn't words. She listened for tone in his voice, a change in tempo or something that would suggest what he had been up to. Mostly she listened for the sound of guilt. He said,

"The shit has hit the fan out here. I took off on business a couple of days ago. Just got back, Trey gone and the hands are about to mutiny. I'll explain later. Right now, I am covered up." And he hung up.

She heard no guilt in his voice but he was a cagey old bastard. Maybe he just fooled her. So, she decided she would imagine the guilt anyway, damn it. At least until she could face her own meltdown. Besides, who the hell was that love letter to anyway? She could ask, but the fact that she went through his stuff would be obvious. At her age she should know the limits of a woman's prying nature on a single man. It takes years of training to get a man accustomed to that level of meddling. It was just possible that he would not explain anything to her, or worse, that if he did it, out of her wheedling him, then it would be over between them. He would not forgive her for digging into his life, a life he lived far and long before he knew her. Casey went to the bathroom and looked at her face and screamed at herself,

"Shut up you bitch, shut the hell up!" After that she relaxed, drank some more, ate a little and watched TV.

***

Trey and Jen followed the storm east, driving behind it for Two Ocean, Wyoming. Clarence, coming north from Denver had hit it dead on as he drove. He had been in four-wheel drive the whole way and had to drive around the closed road sign at one point. He got a ticket for that but he made it to the Ranch. Clarence didn't say why he had left and his manner did not invite questions. Besides, everyone was whipped out tired and not talking much. All he heard were moans and groans from every little bunk room corner. He was not surprised Trey had left either. It was like they both saw it coming in each other, to break from the routine and find a place to spend some of that money.

Wiley slow walked across the room and pulled on his pack boots by the door. His cousin Roland followed. Marcos handed them their lunch boxes and thermos. They walked out the door like two surly boys going somewhere they didn't want to go. Wes and Ray were still in their bunks. They had pulled the old morning tower and slept in. Clarence dressed warm and gathered his gear. He went to his truck and starting putting his tire chains back on. He had his calving chain in his saddle bags. He had a calf puller he could pick up at the barn. He'd check with the farm crew. He needed to let them know he was back, that they would call him if they saw a cow down when they were feeding. While he was at it Trey's truck drove in and Clarence stopped and went back to the bunkhouse to meet him and see what was up. When he walked in he was surprised to see his friend standing there in the kitchen in what looked like a rock star, ski-suit. It actually had reflection designs on it that glowed.

"My God Trey, get that shit off before somebody sees you." Clarence said.

"I know, I know." Trey stepped into his room and Clarence followed.

"I'm just going out. Taking my truck." Clarence said.

"Wait a minute and I'll go with you. I got a feeling we are going to take some heat from the crew."

"We deserve it." Clarence said.

"Yes, we do, so let's stick together."

They started the drive both framing their excuses to each other.

They pulled under the Diesel fuel farm tank and filled the truck up. The hardened snow crunched under the truck tires as they drove out.

They were feeling guilty but they both agreed that all they could do now was fall in and pick-up the slack. Trey figured to start at the calving barn. When they pulled up to it they were dumb-founded. There was a pile of frozen calves right by the door. There might have been a dozen of them.

"Shake it off," Clarence said. "That was a bad storm you missed. I was driving in it. It closed the highway down to the South." They walked in the barn silent and every heat lamp had one or two calves beneath it. Empty nursing bottles were all over the place. The scene revealed the fight the boys had been in.

In the snow-covered pasture, bordering the back end of the barn, there were over forty head of young cows, some with calves, most without. These would be the mothers of those dead or under a lamp. They were munching the hay that had been put out, then turning and bawling at the barn.

"We got to start pairing up in a big way. There's another storm coming and we'll need the room in the barn." Trey said.

"You want me to radio for Wiley?" Clarence said.

"Yes, but if they are busy, and I expect they are, call Marcos and tell him to wake up Wes and Ray. We got to have help. Tell 'em to come horseback."

Snow had drifted up against the gate to the covered alley along the side of the barn. But, the shovel was there and Trey went straight to it. They used this alley to pair the calves back up with the mothers. It was fifteen feet wide and ran the entire length of the barn. There were five small pens on the other side of the alley and each had a hay bunk and water. When Clarence came back he said Wes and Roland were coming and Wiley had not answered.

"Let's clean the place up some." Trey said.

"Rodger that." Clarence said as he helped push the frozen gate open. They pushed it all the way to the drive fence and hooked the chain that would keep it open. Trey went back to the calves and started picking up the empty bottles and taking them to the barn sink. Trey was ashamed of himself for taking time off. He heard his father's words from way back in time, when he thought his son was slacking off on his chores.

"Who do you think you are?" The voice said and he had felt

embarrassed then just like he did now. To make it worse he could still smell Jen's perfume coming up from the neck of his shirt. That was so out of place in the barn that it annoyed the hell out of him.

Wes and Roland showed up horseback. Trey had them ride out to the big lot and push a few of the young cows up the alley and then sit on their horses to hold the gate. Leaving Roland horseback, Wes tied up and helped as they began the long and laborious task of placing calves in the alley with these, mostly first calf heifers, for signs of pairing up.

The calves were warm and dry now and eager to cooperate. When a cow appeared to take a calf, somebody went afoot and they quietly eased the pair into a side pen and shut that gate. Every so often they would slip in a few more cows and let them settle down and mosey through a few more calves.

Finally, they had all of the calves back with their mothers or one that took them anyway. But, you have to check and double check to make sure they are nursing before you turn them back out to pasture. For now, they left them where they were.

When the cows left with no calf were the same number of the dead calf pile they paused for a break. Trey called Wiley on the radio and told him they didn't need him, but they got no answer. Then, just before dark Trey saw them riding down the fence line horseback with some more cows, heavy with calf, to put by the calving barn for the night.

When Wiley had the cows in the lot, he and Roland rode around the back of the barn to a gate that brought the riders to the front. Their horse's muzzles were covered in ice and in the cold air, their breath was as pure as steam. Wiley looked tired and mad when he dismounted. Clarence, leaving Trey in the barn came out to meet him first and sense his mood.

"These all came from the Broadus Canyon pasture, didn't they?" Clarence said as he nodded at the frozen calf pile.

"Yep," Wiley answered.

"They were piled up along the Southeast corner?" Clarence said it like a statement as much as a question.

"Yep," Wiley answered. "The Storm hit after mid-night. We all just hunkered down. At daylight snow was blowing sideways. The temperature had dropped to thirty below. It was lower than that with the wind chill."

Roland kept quiet as Wiley spoke and just held his horses rein without tying up. He looked behind Clarence at the barn door and Trey was standing there. Clarence turned to Trey and said,

"We should have moved them."

"Nobody told me that," Wiley said.

"I screwed up." Trey said. "It wasn't your fault. Jay warned me about that pasture. When the wind is right and comes down that canyon it comes out like a cyclone and twice as cold as when it went in."

"Why didn't we move them?" Wiley said,

"I don't know," Trey looked down at his feet and shook his head. The truth was he meant to and just didn't do it. Some years the wind never hit that canyon like that. All this shit on his mind, and the money and Jen and what?

"I just screwed up. Sorry guys, wasn't your call or your fault."

"Where were you anyway?" Wiley said.

Trey didn't answer. He just went over and got in the truck and cranked it. Clarence climbed in with him. Trey stuck his head out of the truck window and said,

"Let's go eat supper. It's almost dark. We'll go from there." As they drove off Roland turned to Wiley and said,

"Pussy-whipped." Wiley's head snapped around,

"Don't let him hear you say that." he said. But he laughed when he said it and he felt the relief of having the boss back. Now, they'd get their shit together.

They had always allowed for Wiley's romps in town. Even though Trey rarely did it, he needed allowance too. It was only that it was calving season. It was bad timing and Wiley was surprised at Trey for doing it. Clarence as well for that matter. But, they had too much to do to start a big feud over it now. They'd need focus to keep up with the work. Wiley had been with these men long enough to know something. He turned to Roland and said,

"They'll make up for it."

"They better," Roland said.

"Don't start that. Two bad actors don't make a good one." Wiley answered.

"Now you sound like Clarence." Roland said.

***

Clarence held onto the dash board as Trey drove out a little fast but then he slowed and Clarence relaxed again. He took a deep breath and looked over at Trey.

"Guess we need to get Spring Bear Tags" he said.

"Yeah, we got plenty of bait." Trey answered. He almost laughed but held it back. Clarence was trying to lighten the situation up, Trey knew that.

"Mountain Lion traps too. I bought some new guns in Denver."

"What'd you get?" Trey said and Clarence began to recite a list that was a surprising range of weapons, from historic to assault types and one Elephant gun. Trey said nothing. He just did not have a response for that last one.

"Well, let's carry them out with us tomorrow and do some shooting." Clarence said and looked over at his friend. He could see that his mood was better.

"We need to make this up to Wiley." Trey added.

"You will," Clarence answered, with a confidence that sounded like it was already done. And, maybe it was already done. In Trey's mind anyway. He had decided to get that hunting camp and if Wiley wanted it he was going to give it to him. That had the kind of profit that could give a man serious income if handled right.

One day not far in their future, Trey saw them sitting up in the mountains in that good camp, stoking the coals of the fire on a cold autumn night. That's when he would tell Wiley why he wanted to give him the camp. He owed him something for leaving him out in the first place. Hell, they were riding together.

Wiley had become part of the family that rode for the Ranch. Clarence and Trey had the oldest connection, by far. Hands came and went. All had their reasons. You need to form a core group of buckaroos that were born for it. Wiley was. Besides that, a 'you earned this', kind of moment was called for. Those words, so hard to come by in life, so valuable when it does, Trey knew of that. He would tell Wiley when it was time, how valuable a good hand can be and how much Trey Blake appreciated him.

11

Jaw Breaking Moment

The blow from the loss at Broadus Canyon had been hard to take for the whole crew. It hit no one harder than it did Trey. He went back to work like a much-absorbed man. He was in the prime of his life and his energy and strength were capable of some impressive effort. The hours he put in were brutal. Clarence would find him on a couple of bales of hay in the calving barn in the wee hours sound asleep, his horse in there with him with the bridle off and munching hay. Sometimes he would go to ride a pasture and find Trey in the truck, already out there watching a cow, timing her, giving her the two hours or so of labor to drop it on her own. If not then you pulled it.

When Trey found something he couldn't handle by himself, he called out on the truck radio. He'd ask for help or to bring him a horse. They weren't losing any more calves. A few looked so far gone Clarence would have written them off. Then he'd find Trey in the barn force feeding it and shooting it with vitamins under a heat lamp. At supper in the bunkhouse one night, with Trey living on sandwiches and never there anymore, Wes asked where he was? Clarence answered with a mouthful of food,

"He's probably in the barn resurrecting another calf from the dead."

One evening Clarence stood out on the porch of the bunkhouse and took a deep breath and smelled something. After all the deep cold, when nothing could be sniffed except truck fumes and wood smoke, it was there. It's like the very earth and its musky, birth giving smell was waking up from a long sleep. The day felt almost balmy. It was Spring he was smelling.

All the snow in the Valley meadows suddenly had dimples across the surface. All the snow on the rooftops started sliding off. The trucks started quicker. The hair came off thick on the horse brush as the horses started to shed their winter coat. There were rivulets of water with its noisy trickles everywhere.

When Trey woke up looking tired and haggard that morning, he staggered into the kitchen and Clarence said to him...

"Don't miss it!"

"Miss what?"

"Spring. You got your long winter still weighing you down. Time to put your spring hat on. Get winter out of your head and off your back."

Trey looked across the table at Clarence. Marcos slid out a platter of fried eggs and bacon. Trey tried to think about what Clarence was saying but he could not get the point of it.

"Clarence do you have those numbers?"

"Yes, we are at least eighty percent through it. And the losses are going to be under three percent now. If we are careful we might get it back down to two percent."

"Even with?"

"Even with. So, you can ease up some. I talked to Weisman and he said to tell him what leases we want, they re-new in a few weeks." Clarence said.

Trey started eating, a blank look on his face. He knew they needed to do this but he had to let go of some of the Dagger Ranch work to get his head around the 2/c again. It was going to take a lot of number crunching and he wasn't looking forward to it.

"Ok," Trey said. "Let's meet about ten. That gives me a couple of hours to line everybody out. Marcos, fix us a couple of lunches."

Clarence drove out to the old barn early and lit the stove in the office. He pulled out his files with the notes he had been making. He had all the topo maps of every lease the Dagger Ranch had ever used and he had Jay's note books on each of them. There, he found all of the relevant information he needed. There was the size of the particular lease first, the dates the lease opened and closed and then there was the number of head the government entity allowed to run on each parcel during the summer grazing season.

There was U.S. Forest Service land, Bureau of Land Management land, State of Wyoming land and finally privately held acreage that absentee owners leased out each year. Jay had noted the number of head they had run in the past in a notebook. The leases they had run yearlings on were noted, with average weight gain. That was what Clarence was looking for.

What Trey and Clarence had not decided was how many cattle they intended to run and how much cash they needed to hold over to pay the overhead for that grazing season. Then, they could project a selling price. Clarence pulled out his Livestock weekly and started checking the market on cattle. He heard Trey's truck drive up splashing through the thawing slush. The wet brakes screeched as he pulled to a stop.

Trey walked in, sat down and waited for Clarence to finish his math. When Clarence looked up Trey said,

"Sometimes I just want to take the money and run."

"Well, that's what most men would do. Only natural." Clarence answered.

"I've wondered if we should just buy a piece of good ranchland, one that would carry about 1,500 head of mother cows. Set up house and kick back." Trey said.

"Well, I don't know if a man could set that up with the money we have. Not anymore. There'd be a bank loan in there somewhere. Then, if you have a couple of hard years, you got to go to the Bank for more and now the place is in hock. When that happens it's not yours anymore."

"I've seen that." Trey said, and thought of the family farm in Nebraska, lost now all these years. Clarence pushed back in his chair and got up. He went to the stove and opened it to stoke the fire.

"Trey, we do it this way first and take it year to year. At some point we decide to get out. We don't have to go to the bank, we don't have to be married to it. We can do something else next time.

"What?" Trey said.

"I could think of somethings. Let's just stay with the plan. There's the old Conant Ranch. It's been for sale a long while, maybe still is.

"It won't sell because it's so isolated." Trey said. The area the Conant ranch was located in was long known as the badlands.

"Yes, but the out of state buyers and real estate people don't realize there is some of the best native pasture in the state down in those wide coulees' and good water everywhere you need it to be. We can have those leases that border it too." Clarence said.

Trey did not respond. He was inclined to just listen and think about questions later. Clarence went on,

"You know, it is next to three of our Government leases, Forest Service on the north-west corner and State land on the south west corner. Then off on the north-east there's the Camel Hump drainage. Real good grass there. I've been looking at Jay's notes. The State land had

Indian Rice grass and common Timothy coming up good in April, right up to May and June. There is a long boggy area out there you got to watch. You remember, it isn't fenced off and they go in to graze that Blue Grass and bog down. The Slough Grass is there too and fair forage, cattle like it. So, it stays in grass. It's well worth pulling a few out of bogs for the weight they gain. There is Needle and Thread grass at all points in between and Inland Salt Grass too. All good long as we don't overgraze."

Trey could see Clarence had his Ranch Manager hat on and did not want to interrupt him. Trey listened.

"The Forest Service lease to the North has wheat grass all over the lower slopes." Clarence continued,

"That's good forage and it's plenty there just as the other pastures start to dry up. That's good till August. Up in the timber there is plenty of Fescue grass. It'll graze into fall. We round 'em up in September, ship 'em and we are done. Think of it. No haying, no feeding cattle, no calving. Just off for the winter. But, not just off my friend. We're off with money too." Clarence was smiling with this added little finish to his talk.

"Don't know if I could handle that much time off." Trey said. But, he started smiling with Clarence and the thought of it wasn't bad at all.

"We'll get out and run the roads. Buy horses. Wiley and Wes would be all over that like glue. Let 'em start Team Roping' together maybe. I've always wondered how they'd do on the pro circuit. I sometimes think they missed their calling. It's a great way to advertise a good horse for sale." Clarence paused for a breath.

"We'd be living the dream just like the rich horse folks. The only difference is we'd know what we were doing." Clarence said.

Clarence was still standing up as he talked, with his hands spread out like a preacher making a point. Trey laughed at him and gave a nod of approval. Rich people and horses, Clarence had said what they had always thought.

"I like it. Lot of rich women in the horse business. We'll have the hunting Camp to work in the fall too." Trey said.

"Yep, and how cool is that." Clarence said,

Clarence sat back down and went quiet. He still had to figure up how many head they could run. He reached for the Livestock Weekly and slid it over to Trey.

"We need to figure how many head plus expenses. That would be the costs of horse feed and equipment and salaries and feeding everybody, all that stuff. Give me the futures on September Feeders." Clarence said.

Trey opened the paper. He grabbed the scratch pad and calculator on the desk. "What else?"

"Just reach and get it and go from there." Clarence answered.

"Money can make a lot of paperwork for a man," Trey said quietly, as he took his hat off and put it on the end of the table.

"Only if he wants to keep any of it." Clarence answered.

***

Jen Coffer was closing up her office to head out a little early. Her annual spring vacation was coming up and she had more planning and packing to do at home. Nobody that was anybody stayed in Two Ocean in the spring with the muddy streams and sleet and mess of the spring breakup. She thought of Trey Blake. She had only talked to him a few times since the trip to Sundance and she had not seen him at all. She was feeling all of the frustration she had come to expect from dating him.

She had questions too. When the Dagger Ranch was sold what were his plans? She had asked him this a couple of times and he had responded by saying something was in the works. She had asked what and where, he said he was not sure yet. She had taken that to mean he would likely be moving off somewhere and with the way the Two Ocean Country had become populated in recent years she could expect it to be, way off. The big ranches were all gone in this part of the world and way off was all that was left. That was not going to work for her. She kept telling herself she had to let him go. But, she could not seem to do it. Not yet anyway. Maybe one final little push would do it. His not calling was getting the right momentum up to make that push.

Jen was a modern woman and proud of it. She could drop a man without a lot of emotional effort. Trey Blake was proving harder to do that with but she knew she could manage it. So, she stopped trying to reach him and then he called. She muttered "damn it" to herself when she heard his voice and felt it's tug on her.

She could say no. She could do another man easily enough but when she did and when it left her feeling like a slut, she would have to deal with that again. At her age and with all her experience, that wasn't getting easier to do and sleeping with more than one man at a time was always a "slutty" kind of activity. So, she'd wait. She would wait until she knew she could say 'no' to Trey first.

Driving herself at work was the best way. This Dagger Ranch sale had several realtors and lawyers in and out of state to deal with and she had her part worked out to a tee. And, with the staggering commissions, it put her on a cloud nine of a different kind. She smiled and thought of that young attorney in Texas. Maybe he could get away for a little spring fling. Maybe meet her somewhere. He sure had seemed interested. Jen had a keen nose for that kind of attention. She barely had noticed he was married, with young children. That had never stopped her before. For now, Trey had phoned and he still had first call with her. So, she went with it again and let the rest of her stable wait. In Two Ocean, where the men out numbered the women seven to one, they have a saying…

"You don't lose your girlfriend, you just miss your turn." She always got a laugh out of that one. It helped her feel her power like the money did.

Trey said he was coming to town. He was stopping by. They could go out or they could stay in. She wanted to say let's go out to have him pay for his absence, make him linger around her. But, that was risky. For one thing he drank too much when they went out. When they stayed in he drank little but made love the same way he drank. It was aggressive. She decided they would stay in. Maybe she'd figure more of him out if she could just pay attention around him. Maybe if she could concentrate and stop trying to figure out what he meant by what he was saying and focus on what he was saying she could get closer to knowing what she meant to him. But when they were together alone it was all fuzzy, blurred and fluid. She could not think. Damn it! She picked up her phone. She'd decided. They would go out. The blurred part could wait.

Jen wanted to meet at a restaurant a little south of Two Ocean. Trey had to drive past the housing addition she lived in to get there. She told him not to stop and pick her up. She said she had business to tend to in town first. They would just meet at the Buckhorn Tavern.

When Trey walked in he did what he always did, he walked straight to the bar and got a shot of bourbon and a beer. He had noticed Jen's black SUV in the parking lot but the place was crowded and he did not look around to locate her. He wanted a drink first. He stepped to the bar. On his second round he did look and saw her with one of the town Cowboys and another lady in the corner at a table. Jen was laughing and smiling real big at something the man said. Just as Trey looked he saw another man come up and sit down beside Jen. Her bright smile and beautiful eyes shone like a light as she leaned toward the man. Trey knew him or knew of him at least. He was a mountaineer and local skier. He was tall, athletic and tanned. There was a flicker, a split second in time, but Trey saw it. Jen looked up and straight at him. Trey knew instantly what it said. It said, 'look at me, I do have other options.'

Oh man, he thought. Time to pay up. The price is going to be high. It was going to be jealously and perhaps humiliation thrown in as well. She looked up at him again and waved him over. She asked him to pull up a chair but there wasn't any. The table was small, against the wall with room for only four chairs. A fifth chair would have to be on the end, out in the isle. Trey walked across the room and found one. He carried the chair back and dutifully sat down and pulled up close to the table. He had to lean over each time a waitress wanted to squeeze by and Trey knew he wouldn't last long that way. Being shoved around and allowing it was not in his nature.

The town Cowboy's name was Bob. Trey knew him. He was like many of the locals, no cowhand but dressed like it and during the work week went to their real jobs. Electrician, Plumber, delivery truck driver, whatever. Bob was a good guy. He was always cordial. He introduced the young woman he was sitting with. She was new in town. She had a job in a gift shop. She would work the summer and see how things went. The mountaineer, Carl, was a local from way back. He was single and a hustler of rich ladies. They had crossed trails many times in the years gone by running the tourist women. Trey's read on him was a vain, egotistical type. He was a pretty boy with some real cojones beneath the faked surface. Trey figured that's what it took to climb mountains.

The place was noisy but Trey could make out that Carl was putting together an expedition to climb somewhere. He was looking for sponsors. Would Jen be interested?

"Oh yes, very," she said. Carl had not acknowledged Trey's presence. Trey leaned forward again as a waitress squeezed by him and stood by to take their order. He looked at his watch. It was eight pm. He had not eaten since around eleven am when he took his lunch. That was too long for him and the bourbon was giving him a strong buzz. He stood up and reached down to shake hands with Bob.

"Good to see you Bob and good luck to you," He said to the girl sitting there. He bent across the table and put his hand-on Jen's shoulder and squeezed it a little too hard, and he knew it when he did it. She looked up at him and he said to her,

"Can you step out with me for a second. I need to go and I want to tell you something."

Jen was surprised and he could see that. Carl gave him a look for the first time and it wasn't friendly. They never had been friendly. Some of these mountaineer, local types did not like the Cowboy image of the town. Trey read the man's look. It was a look of contempt and it said to Trey,

"Yes, leave shit kicker. I got business to tend too." Trey knew what business that was and with his own testosterone buildup he knew he needed to leave. He could feel his blood pressure rising from head to toe and all points in-between. Just outside the entrance, off to one side, on the wide-open well-lit deck area, Jen and Trey stopped. He leaned close to her.

"You are setting me up, aren't you?" he said.

"What?" Jen answered. Her nose crinkled up with her lip, in a contemptable snarl.

"You're drunk, aren't you?" she answered,

"This will only work if when I ask a question you answer it and then ask me a question and I will answer that. When you ask a question back without answering mine first it fucks it up. I thought you and I had a date tonight," He said.

"Date, with you? And, don't you use that 'F' word in front of me. You don't know the meaning of the word date. I'm meeting friends for dinner. I just invited you to come along."

"Come along, tag along, that's what I'm doing here?"

She looked angry and just as she started to say something else Carl approached from Trey's left side, a mistake he would come to regret. He put his arm over Trey's shoulder and with his face way too close, said,

"Is there a problem here?" Trey stared for a second. The snooty bastard had wine breath.

Trey Blake had moments in his life that sometimes scared him and this was one of them. He looked at the man now in a very different way than he would normally look at another man. Trey looked at him closely and studied his face. They were both the same height and Trey looked straight at the man's eyes. They were piercing and predatorial. The man's nose was bent off a little to the side with a knot about midway down. It had been broken before. But, the most outstanding feature of his face was his jaw line. It was almost a characterization of a manly jaw. It was the jaw of a proud cut gelding. It was very square, dropping low and level with the chin. It had a well-defined, ninety-degree curve in front of and just below the ear that made a beautiful target and Trey came up with his right fist closed and hit the man's jaw right in that sweet spot. He hit it from underneath as well as across, a bit of a hook thrown in. It is also an easy punch to get your body under to lift it. It gave the contact a torque like power to the fist as it struck and Trey heard the jaw break. Carl never heard a thing. He was unconscious before he hit the deck.

It was a bad thing to do and Trey knew it instantly. He had sucker punched the guy just like Jen sucker punched him with her entire, make you jealous and get you riled up dinner out with a clear message,

"I have another man in the wings now." That was the message.

The sound of the jaw breaking made Jen nauseated. She went pale and almost fell. Trey grabbed her arm to steady her but she jerked it away fast. Trey saw fear in her eyes. She took a deep, gasping breath and shouted to someone nearby.

"Call an ambulance, call the police," she said as she bent down to Carl. Trey backed away and turned. Bob was outside now and looking at him,

"Better go Trey. They are calling the cops." Trey looked at him hard trying to think and Bob threw up his hands, palms outward and said,

"Hey man. I didn't see a thing."

Trey nodded and walked off to his truck. He got in and drove for home. One moment he felt guilty and the next he felt like hitting the guy all over again. Trey talked out loud to himself as he drove, words for Jen that she would never hear because Trey knew she'd never be able to take it.

"You going to climb a mountain all right, climbing Mt. Jen. She has a little furry mountain for you, it's Mount Venus you son of a bitch." And then he wanted to turn the truck around and hit the guy again and again. Maybe crack some ribs too. Hold him up a while, don't let him fall, and dig with those body punches. But he didn't, he forced his mind back on the road. He held to the thought of, get back to the ranch. He needed his friends around. He needed to go over this a few times with somebody. He needed to reason why an action like this was so easy for him. All it took was the right ingredients and he was as predictable to himself as any fool could be. That meant he could have kept from doing it and that was it, that was the place that scared him about himself.

Trey drove east to the ranch in the darkness of the canyon and the night, while his hormones raged inside him. His hands squeezed the steering wheel and his heart pounded in his chest. He was going to have to pay for this. There was only one thing that was different now, than the other times he had gotten into trouble. Different now from past times when he had been drunk and thrown in jail. Now, he had the money to pay to get out of it. That eased his anguish some as he drove. That knowledge was enough to help him start to calm down. By the time he turned off the highway to the Ranch he was coming down hard from the high and feeling very hungry. He stomped into the bunkhouse, went straight to the 'fridge for a beer and dug for left-over food.

The guys were watching TV. The place was quiet. It was a week-night and still not really late. Trey walked into the living room and sat down in his chair. He had two pieces of bread with left over steak between them. Clarence looked over at him and said,

"Didn't expect you home tonight."

"Me neither." Trey said. Clarence waited. He picked up the remote and muted the TV. He looked at Trey. Wes said,

"Hey, I was listening to that."

Trey got up and waved for Clarence to follow. The sound came back on the TV. They went into the kitchen and both sat down at the long plank table. Trey told Clarence what had happened. When he finished Clarence said,

"Where'd that come from?"

"Deep." Trey answered.

"Think he'll press charges?"

"Don't blame him." Trey said. Clarence studied Trey's face. There was nothing apologetic in his manner or expression.

"I don't know. There was a time when men did not sic their lawyers on you for things like this. It's kind of cowardly if you think about it." Clarence said.

"No, they'd just lay for you and bushwhack you on the trail some-where." Trey answered.

"Your thoughts are a little dark Trey," Clarence said. But, he knew Trey had a point. It seemed they ignored how chickenshit some men could be. Then the reminder comes when it's too late to stop it.

Trey did not answer. He got up and went to the cabinet and pulled out the whiskey. Clarence dug a bowl of something out of the fridge and put it on to warm.

"When that's heated, eat it. It'll help you sleep better than the whiskey will." And at that, Clarence went back to the TV room and Trey sat and drank and ate and finally went to bed. His last thoughts as he lay on his bunk were of the moment that Carl had come up and said, 'Everything ok here?' It was the look Trey saw on Jen's face when she answered,

"No, I'm fine, but thank you so much Carl." And she smiled at the man as if she was thrilled with his gallant presence and then looked at Trey and frowned like she was looking at a sleaze ball. There, in that moment Trey could see how it happened. Carl was the honorable gen-tleman protecting Jen from him. Trey was the dis-honorable threat. That was the trigger that got old Carl's jaw cracked for him. Jen had pulled that trigger as sure as Trey had. Then, in split-seconds her ex-pression went from condescension toward him to fear. It was like see-ing an in-experienced person pull the trigger on a gun, then jump at the explosion it brings and stare at it like it was acting on its own. Sometimes that ain't true, even with a man. Sometimes you should look at cause before you judge the crime.

He dozed in a half-dream that pressured his loins and left him in a fitful agony of desire. One thing though, old Carl wasn't humping it either. That thought gave him an intense feeling of satisfaction. That son of a bitch was getting his jaw wired back up instead. It would be a long time before he'd even be able to enjoy a simple kiss.

Trey tossed all night but still rose early. Physically he felt strong. In the coming days Trey would think more on it, to try and reason it out. Now he felt kind of good. Still, he lost that fight. When you sucker punch a man and walk off the field and leave him face down in his own blood that is not an honorable action by any stretch. If you give a man no chance to defend himself you can't really win because there is no honor in it. You lose by foul. If there is a referee, he's going to' throw you out of the ring and give the fight to your opponent. And that is rightfully so.

It seemed natural enough to turn this contempt onto Jen, but that did nothing to quench his physical desire for her. He just felt the desire for her differently. He felt no prerequisite for courtesy or gentleness toward her now. Now it felt only like animal impulse. That changed things. That would increase the disrespect he had occasionally felt toward her. Right or wrong he was going to have to put his relationship with her on the shit list and way down on priorities. It couldn't be helped.

After breakfast the bunkhouse phone rang. It was the Sheriff's Department. They ask for Trey and when he took the phone they asked him if he would come into town and check in with an Officer Derrick at the Police Station, that charges had been filed. Then Ilene called the bunkhouse. Clarence answered and she asked him what was going on, she'd received a call from the Sheriff as well. Clarence told her he'd explain more later, but that Trey had been in a barroom scrape over Jen and hurt a guy pretty good. Ilene said,

"Oh, well hell then. I thought it was something important. Did she set it up?"

"Seemed like it, from what Trey said."

"Thought so. She seemed like a type, you know what I mean." Ilene's tone sounded like a statement, not a question.

"I know." Clarence said, "Some women are always on the make."

Ilene laughed as she hung up and Clarence felt the ruddiness of her and the way she understood things like this. The old way of women understanding men. He hung up and told Trey the message again. Then he said to him,

"Look, I'll call Weismann. I want to go in with you. Let me drive you and we'll go from there. But, let's see Weismann first."

Trey went back in his room to change clothes for town. Before he stepped out to leave he stuck his toothbrush in his front pocket.

On the drive in Trey was stone quiet. Clarence talked about the dream he'd been having. It was more than once now and since it was about problems with women, it seemed to fit the moment.

"I wanted to tell you why I said no to Ilene coming over and doing cooking or paperwork or whatever." Clarence said

Clarence told the dream to Trey and as he listened, Trey could sense the passion and the longing in the story. He could see the back of a young Ilene in the dimness, in her close-fitting Jeans, trim at the waist, well fitted denim jacket. In fact, Ilene still dressed that way and still had a good figure for her age. Trey could also see the distance between Clarence and Ilene that the dream told of. The gap that could no longer be breeched.

When they drove up to Weismann's office Clarence's story was finished. Clarence parked and they both got out. Trey stuck coins in the parking meter while Clarence dug in his truck for a notebook and a pen. When he had it, he looked up and Trey was standing there looking at him.

"What?" Clarence said.

"Are you going to tell her?"

"Tell who-what?" Clarence answered and then added, "Tell Ilene I love her, tell Casey I don't. Tell who what exactly?"

Trey turned and shaking his head, walked into the building. When he got to the door of Weismann's office he stopped and turned back to Clarence, who was standing right beside him,

"Yeah, I see what you mean." Trey said. Clarence nodded appreciatively and said,

"Thanks. It's sure nice to be understood. Now go in and take your medicine."

"Ok," Trey said, "Right Square on the chin, just like Carl, but at least I got a warning first."

"I know what you mean." Clarence said.

"What do I mean?" Trey asked.

"Well, hitting a man that don't see it coming, you can get the job done but you can't brag about it afterwards. I mean, it's not like a conquest."

Trey literally jerked with the meaning of Clarence's words confirming what he already knew. He muttered a series of cusswords under his own breath. Clarence laughed and put his hand on Trey's shoulder and kind of shook it.

"Well, your turn now." he said as they both were shown in through Weismann's door.

"Maybe you'll figure a way to make it up someday. I got faith in you. Stop kicking your-self." Clarence added.

Weismann sat forward in his desk and listened close to every detail of Trey's story. He ask a few questions. When he had heard enough he could only see one way to handle it.

"Who saw it?" Weismann ask, again. Trey told him he wasn't sure but Jen for certain.

"Trey, this is a problem for not just you but all of us. I want you to go straight at this. You'll go over and give yourself up. You will be arrested. The judge will see you tomorrow morning and will state the charges and then set bail. Whatever that is, I will make it and we'll walk out and come back over here. By then I will have it laid out. The way we will approach this, that is. The goal will be to settle out of court for as little as possible.

They will have to measure your net worth and prove your income. And, a list of everything you own and an approximate value. You can do that for me tomorrow afternoon. The other money, and you know of what I speak, will not be mentioned. It does not exist. We will establish that you do not have much money, if any. Can you give me an idea now? Did you add cash to your bank account from the other?" Trey nodded yes.

"How much?"

"One deposit for $10,000, another for $5,000.00."

"Can you figure a way to explain that cash if it comes up?"

"No." Trey said.

"Anything else? Have you bought anything expensive?" Weismann was sounding pissed off. Trey shook his head "no" again.

"Well get busy thinking about where those deposits came from. They will want to know a lot about you if this goes to court."

Weismann was showing a little annoyance now. This was not a good time to have Trey scrutinized by anyone, especially the law. They all needed to keep their heads down. He chewed a minute on nothing in his mouth and twisted a little in the chair. He stared at Trey hard. Trey looked back and strangely enough felt the urge to hit something or somebody again. He just could not help that thought coming up and he immediately broke eye contact with Weismann and turned to Clarence's friendlier face. Clarence was making a move to speak. He actually raised his hand like a kid in school.

"Bonus." Clarence said. "Bonus from Fenwick for a job well done."

Charles Weismann looked at Clarence sharply and a sliver of a smile came across his face. It was a short, quiet moment that passed quickly. Then he said,

"Perfect," very quietly. "I can make that happen. Or look like it did anyway." Weismann relaxed and leaned back smiling. He looked at Trey and said,

"Now go to jail and keep your mouth shut about everything and anything."

Trey frowned a little at this dismissal. He pulled his jacket back and said,

"I got my toothbrush right here."

"Sounds like you've done this before?" Weismann said.

"Maybe once or twice." Trey answered and then he got up and as he and Clarence were moving to the door Weismann said,

"I'll see you in the morning."

Clarence drove Trey to the police station and stopped out front.

"Far as I go. I've been in one before too." Trey laughed at him, got out and started walking. Clarence stuck his head out the window and said,

"I'll see you tomorrow," and then backed up and drove off.

Trey was checked in by a police officer, given a cell by himself and a kid with a cart came by and ask if Trey wanted a magazine.

"What's your deal?" Trey asked.

"Trustee." The kid said, "You?"

"Just another fool over a woman," Trey said.

The young man laughed and handed Trey a couple of magazines. One was a Western Horseman. It was five years old and looked it. On the cover it had a picture of a Cowboy on a horse with a sunset. The title underneath said, "The American Cowboy, A Dying Breed."

"Jesus," Trey said to himself. "Ain't we though." And then he went to the bunk, laid down and opened it up to read.

***

After they had gone Weismann sat at his desk and knew that he was going to have to represent Trey on this even if it wasn't his area of practice. Protection of their collusion was just too important to do otherwise. He knew Jen Coffer. He knew she was working on part of the Ranch Sale. He thought of a way to throw her a bone in the deal. He decided to call her with a question about the sale and then see if he could meet with her to talk about it. Not to bribe really, that would be too obvious. A woman feeling threatened by a man in this day and time was a heavy weapon in a court room. Charles Weismann needed to head that off. Weismann decided to give Ms. Coffer a call.

He buzzed his secretary and asked her for the files on the Ranch Sale. He would find something there, a short coming, some reason to blame Coffer for an oversight in her paperwork. But, compliment her efforts and offer something down the road that would be enticing and pay well. Then, a few questions about the incident at the Buckhorn. he would suggest, what a good man Trey had always seemed. And how surprised Weismann was, over this fight. Maybe tell her he offered to help because Trey had so little to spare, being just a Cowboy and all. He'd tell her he was helping Trey, fee-waved, for his years of good service out at the ranch. He'd search for a little conscience there. It was obvious Trey loved her, wasn't it?

As far as this Mr. Carl character, Weismann would suggest how embarrassing it might be to have a public trial because he lost a fair fight between two grown men. After all, we are all still men, aren't we? The DA might buy into that one too. He was always strutting like the macho man, around town, jogging, working out at the Gym. He might not want to be seen acting indignant over a plaintiff that lost a fist fight.

Weismann leaned back in his chair and closed his eyes. He was smiling. His confidence in himself in taking the right course of action was solid. And, deep down he loved this shit. He lived in a world and worked at a profession where knowledge was pure power. As a CPA with a larger firm back east he had known where all the bodies were buried. It gave him a lot of stroke and a huge severance package when he left the firm after fifteen years, the last five of which he was the CEO.

He looked over on a shelf at a picture of his father when he was a young attorney back East. Once, when Weismann had come home from school, after taking a beating in a fist fight from another kid, he was in a rage and wanted to take a baseball bat and go looking for the bully. His dad stopped him and set him down. When he had cooled, his father told him,

"Son, if you want to kick some ass go to law school. When you are a lawyer nobody will fuck with you."

12

Goodbye Old Paint

When Spring was in the air and on the muddy ground, Clarence drove out to the winter range of the Dagger horses. He sat in the truck bed and drew them in with his calling and a little horse feed. They came up and circled him. They pushed, shoved, bucked and kicked around him as if they were mocking him, as if they were saying, catch me, ride me if you can. It made him feel old. As they saw him just sitting there on his tool box, they quieted down and some began to come closer.

He thought about the spring round-up coming and the younger of the frisky horses, the cold backs that had to be topped off. That made him smile and think of Jay. That was a time they were really living their lives hard and would not have had it any other way.

At his age now, Clarence could feel every place on his body where a horse had stove him in. Now, there was nothing left to prove. Not to those that knew him, not to those passed on and not the ones he rode with now. As far as anybody else was concerned he did not give a damn. He wasn't going to top these horses off. Let the young hands do that. An old cowboy has to learn to let things go. Clarence had earned his spurs ten times over, anyhow.

But, he could think about it. How they would wrap the swells of a saddle with a slicker to give them more to get their thighs and knees under. How they would change out the big winter stirrups for oxbows and take up the length a notch or two. For the real young and tough horses, you stayed in the round pen and pulled your old bronc saddle out. You needed that association size tree to stay on when the horses head ducked out of sight between his forelegs and refused to come back up until you came off or the horse was just done. He sat for a long time, deep in those memories and stared off at the distant countryside.

When he snapped out of it nearly the whole herd had lost interest and meandered off. Only a dozen or so were still standing near. It took a moment for him to see it, and then he realized they were his string. Every one of them that stayed were in his string. They were the older horses on the ranch that he himself had been riding, some for nearly twenty years. They had stayed together, with each other and with him, like the small and faithful band they were.

Three of them were very near and started to stretch their necks to nuzzle and smell him closely. They were looking for that apple or carrot. Clarence did not disappoint. They were in the deep side pockets of his old canvas coat with the frayed sleeves and collar. The wind gusted up and lifted their manes. Clarence pulled a few cockle burrs from the forelock of one horse and stayed in the moment. He did not think about it being over.

He slid off the truck and pulled the carrots out. He slipped around and among them. They all got a bite. He reached in the truck cab. He pulled out his pocket knife and sliced the apples he brought in quarters. He put the pieces in his pockets, then moved back through his horses and gave each a slice. As he walked he talked to them and spoke each name. He spoke low, like a man-animal purr or code when he exhaled breath and words together. "Heah, easy now, heah now." It was how he reminded them of their manners and they listened. They quit shoving and stood quiet.

As he walked, he moved his hand along their backs. He scratched under jaws, necks, and ears. On some he stayed away from the ears. Those had fought longer than the rest before they yielded to the saddle. A Cowhand gets tired and finally twist or bites an ear. After they are broke you never want to rub it in. Then they'll start to trust you and give you better service.

He instinctively rubbed, then squeezed withers like he was looking for soreness but of course a horse out all winter wouldn't have sore withers. The Ranch bred and rode high wither horses, better to hold the saddle under strain. A good high forked saddle on a high withered horse means you can ease up on the cinch some and let your horse breathe while he works. Its not going to twist out from under you.

Clarence knew well enough who liked the scratching and who didn't. He picked up feet. He knew each of them just by their feet. The size shoe, the split hoof that got the toe clip shoe and more. He knew them all very well. He remembered their scars too, almost as well as his own. He looked at those scars on legs and chest, on heads and necks and he remembered what had happened but not when. He remembered where they had gone down with him in a crash of man and horseflesh. But not when.

Some marks were from a trailer gate, or a mad cow. The worst, the old half down and hidden barbed wire drift fences, out on the vast reaches of lease lands, fallen down and forgotten, not seen in time. When you want to turn or rope a bunch quitter, it's all out. That left its share of chest and foreleg scars.

It was one of those afternoons that a man remembered things that he could still feel. These were the memories an old man recognizes finally, that he will carry with him even to the grave. Everything, all of it was in being there and in the doing of something that was hard enough to make you feel it. The respect of your peers and running with the big dogs of horse and cattle men and holding your own, a place where a man can't hide. It was sometimes life in a whirlwind or a Grizzly on your ass. But, then again it could be as peaceful as a star washed night sky, a whip-poor-will's call and a coyote singing. Like at the end of a long summer day, when the wind stops at sunset and you stop with it, right where you are. You build your fire, stake out your horse, roll out your bed and nothing to do but eat your grub, watch, listen and sleep. The sense of peace that can bring, if you let it, is a welcome release.

***

The Spring round-up, always a big ranch affair, was more than that now. It was a reunion of many old friends and a community event. The local papers got involved and showed up to cover it. Word got out nationally as well and a few large periodicals came to write of it. It was billed as the last of the Great Roundups and the end of that legend of the West, the Double Dagger Ranch of Wyoming. Many of the old hands that were still alive had been contacted. These men, who had ridden for the Ranch in the past, began to get wind of it and most asked to participate. The first few that called and were remembered well, would be put on the payroll. But, the bulk that came would not. They were not needed for the work, so getting paid was not an option. Still, they would come. How could they say no to playing a part in the passing of a great piece of America's Western History.

When the time came Cowboy trucks and horse trailers were parked everywhere. Many brought their own horses just to make damn sure they would not be left afoot. Some of the hands got horseback and directed parking to keep some sort of order. Tents, from Cowboy Tepee's to large wall tents were set up. They called in a contractor to scatter job-johnnies. The area surrounding the ranch headquarters took on the smell of wood smoke and there was a sense of natural cordiality prevailing with everyone.

Many old friends shook hands after years of being out of touch. At night, at several campfires, old hands and young held counsel with each other and the mutual respect shown would carry over in some of the young men's lives for years afterward when they recalled this gathering of older men who could still work hard and still would. A blue grass band from town claimed a spot and played a couple of hours around the fire each night.

There were so many Cowboys that the cattle didn't stand a chance. It was a poor man's way of getting a small piece of a very large action. Every last one of the bunch quitters were busted and brought down hard by hands old and young showing off for each other. A bunch of steers and a few cows that had gone wild on the farthest reaches of the big ranch's range, an area known as the badlands, were tracked down, surrounded, roped and drug from the deepest canyons and thickest brush. The old hiding places that had served as their refuge for years finally gave them up.

Some older men and town horseman on their overweight horses sat on the rims and surrounded the drainages to block the most minuscule of game trails that might provide escape. The young and tough cowboys on young and tough horses rode down into the brush and more than a few old hands took the lead in as well. There were steers that weighed well over a thousand pounds and one that was mouthed later looked to be near 30 years old and himself a veteran of many a chase to catch him. He'd escaped them all till now.

Horse wrecks were frequent. Maybe a chinch broke or the horse just tripped and riders took hard falls. Two horses had to be put down with broken legs. Two Cowboys were hauled out and taken to the hospital. All from different incidents. But, the work never stopped until it was too dark to see. Nobody slept in, in the morning and nobody wanted it to be over at night.

Some of these outlaw steers were butchered and cooked on spits over open fires, some in Dutch ovens, most on grills and smokers. Everybody smelled like horse shit and Bar-b-que. The cowboys and volunteers were on a protein high from having eaten red meat until it was coming out of their ears. You could get a steak, or sliced brisket at every campfire and most did. Beans and biscuits were the side and potatoes too.

Many women cooked and Casey took the lead. She marched all over the place saying howdy and shaking hands. At first, she slept in the back of her little pickup truck and then Clarence set up a cot for her in his room. It was against the rules to let women stay over in the bunk house but what could he do? For some reason, though invited, she would not stay with Ilene.

The biggest issue sprang up when Casey took over Marcos's kitchen. He fumed the first day or two and then he just went to his Mexican cooking roots. It was all beans, cheese and beef tortillas from him as he managed to work around this woman. Casey baked. She baked bread and pie and she baked cake and cookies. It was an absolute blizzard of cookies hitting the camp fires each night.

Since the big feed had taken a red meat direction the only way the women could really compete was by baking. Dutch oven cobblers were special and gravy, bacon and biscuits in the morning disappeared quick too.

Ilene took all the women she could fit and put them up in her house. It was near the end of her days there so she welcomed the company and she made sure they, the women that had come, knew they were welcome to this round-up as well as any man. Many of these women had been horseback with her on the ranch in the old days. When they saw the 1920's collection of women's western wear Ilene had found, they all went nuts. Ilene passed the clothing out. They were tried on, altered and sewed as these old girls stood in line for the sewing machine. Their daughters and grandchildren watched in awe. They'd never seen this side of their mothers and grandmothers. The women laughed, talked and made themselves up like the gals of the old dude ranch heydays. Then, they rode out smelling like mothballs and perfume on bomb proof horses from old Jay's string.

Trey made sure the horses were caught and saddled each morning for these women and kept up for them the next day. He put two dude ranch cowboys from the area on it and that's all they had to do. "Just ride herd on and take care of the women a horseback and the horses at the end of each day and do it until I tell you otherwise." Trey told them.

The old girls were loving every minute of it and some long-out-dated fashions for women's western wear were seeing daylight for the first time in seventy years. Knee high boots, jod spurs, wide brimmed hats with chin string pulled tight, bright colored bandannas and some finely embroidered Cowgirl shirts all gleamed in the sunshine of a Wyoming Spring day. They could be heard a quarter-mile away riding together, laughing and talking. Now and again, when opportunity presented itself, they moved some cattle too.

The photographers went to great links to get the women to pose and the women obliged. Their horses were brushed and bright and more than one old cowboy husband stuck his chest out with pride when the women rode by.

Clarence, with his walking money in his pocket, slipped the photographers cash for the promise to send their copies of all these photos to Ilene. He made sure they had her address and he made sure he had their business cards. If Ilene would remember these last days on the ranch as good ones, then the photos could help make that happen.

With so many to do the work the old tradition of roping and dragging a calf to the fire went fast, too fast for many that wanted the honor of snaking out a loop. Then the last calves to wear the Dagger Brand of Wyoming, the famous Double Hilt Knife ‡ brand, were drug to the fire and the last great roundup was done.

Weismann had advertised it well and the cattle buyers came. Many looked the stock over the old-time way, a horseback and made their bids in various numbered lots. It began slowly at first and then finally in a rush of buying action it ended. The stock was loaded and shipped to the ranch's that had purchased them and the great Dagger Herd was history.

Many of the Cowboys, some with jobs to get back to, left. Some stayed. They helped with the cleanup. All worked now for free. And, then they waited. The horse sale was next and the ones with money started picking the brains of the ranch hands for knowledge of each and every mount.

The decision of what horses were to go to the 2/c had to be determined and a way to hold those out of the sale was not possible. Weismann said they had to run them through and buy them like everyone else. That way the LLC money would not be connected to Clarence and Trey. Still, they listed the horses they would buy back. They had to get Wes and Wiley on board too and they finally decided to do it for Ray and Roland as well.

***

Clarence and Trey had continued taking off in the truck to talk things over. There was just no other way to have any privacy. As they rode out toward the old headquarters barn they discussed the horses in detail. Clarence was having his troubles about Jay's sting. Those and some of his own were over fifteen years old. It was killing Clarence to think these would go now for slaughter. In the past the old horses were allowed to die on the ranch. As long as they could stand and walk and get to water anyway. When they could not do that they were taken to a remote location and humanely put down with a high caliber bullet behind an ear. The selling to a killer for dogfood was not considered except for the occasional outlaw horse. Those buyers, the killers, would show up to pick up what the ranchers, cowboys and horse loving public did not purchase. Then, the old ones would be sold by the pound.

"Trey, I don't think I can stand to see it." Clarence said.

"What choice is there?" Trey answered. "We can't buy them all. We aren't going to make any money the way we are set up now. You know Wiley and Wes are going to pick their favorite horses, maybe ones with age on them. Hell, I'll do the same."

"Shit," Clarence said. "You thinking what age is cutoff?"

"Yes, seven-year old's." Trey said.

"Just duck out at that part Clarence. Don't stay there and watch it. Let the cards fall where they may. We tell the auctioneer to try to get bids for saddle horses first and if there are no buyers, then drop it to bid by the pound."

Clarence nodded his head and knew Trey was right. Sometimes there is nothing you can do about a thing. Clarence had plenty of experience with that in his life. Probably too damn much. What's one more, and then thought, piss on that. It never gets easier.

"Alright then," Trey said. "How can we keep from paying out the nose for the horses we want? There are going to be some serious buyers for them. These horses are famous." Trey knew a horse sale like this comes only once in a lifetime and so do buyers.

"They are going to bid them up real high and if we are seen bidding on them they'll just go higher." Trey said.

"Well, we can't be seen bidding." Clarence answered.

"We need to decide who to buy for us. Couple of these old friends that came in for the round-up are still here for the horse-sale. I know Rocky Duff will do it and ask no questions. He'll do it just like we say. Russ Abbot too. He's still here. They won't ask to be paid for it either, but I think we should pay them something. I never known either of them to have much money. I'm sure they could use it."

Trey pulled up to the big barn and parked. They unlocked the door and walked in. They picked up the cavvy's log book and started to go through it again. They filled a buy sheet out for themselves and did it quickly. Neither wanted to think on it too much. When they were finished they went to the safe and took out some cash for walking money. Trey stopped to think what was left in there. He looked at Clarence.

"That settlement for old Carl's jaw sure whittled us down on cash."

It had, in fact, knocked it down a full fifty thousand dollars. Weismann initially paid it and set it up like a loan from him to Trey. This to keep their cover going. He had not asked for the payment back. Still, Trey took it to him, while he still "had it to take," he'd said when he dropped it off.

Clarence had joked about it not mattering but, it would have saved more horses. He choked that thought back quick. Things happen with women that cost you and you got to get passed it. His whole life money had gone through his fingers like sand anyway. So, what's new?

They took the horse book with them to the truck and drove back to the bunkhouse. It was time to corner Wes and Wiley and tell them more of what was going down, get them to pick their horses. Trey decided he would do the picking for Roland and Ray and not even mention it to them. He wanted some three and four-year old's coming up to give the cavvy some longevity. You never know, maybe the 2/c would have a life.

Back at headquarters, Trey had Wes and Wiley walk outside with him for a conference. He told them they had a job with a new outfit if they wanted it. He told them that he and Clarence were taking it and if they wanted to come on with them they could each pick seven head of horses from their string to take to the new job. Wes asked questions. Trey kept his answers short. It would be a yearling operation on lease lands. These leases would be familiar to them since they were old Dagger range. The living conditions would be primitive cow camps. It would be seasonal only. But, they could stay on in the hunting camp, probably on into November. So, no work maybe five months after that, unless something else was figured out. Then back on in April to get ready for the next season.

"On the pay, I haven't done the budget for it yet, but it will be good as you have now. And, you'll have your best horses with you if we can get them at the sale. We want you to look closely at your seven-year old's and under, nothing any older. Most of yours are around that age anyway. We won't have the colt's coming up to replace older horses anymore. The cavvy book is in the bunkhouse. You might as well go in and get started. No talk about your horse list to anybody." Wes and Wiley nodded quietly. Trey walked off and left them there.

"Cool, that we are doing the hunting camp." Wiley said.

"I guess," Wes answered.

They turned and walked together to the bunkhouse, went in quietly and each with his own thoughts started to go through the book. As they read through the list each wrote down the horses in their string that fit the instructions. Each of them would have to leave half-their horses off the list of keepers. The age slot kept the decisions narrow. The first three or four on the list were obvious. After that it got hard. These were choices made about horses that these young men spent lots of time on. Quietly muttered cussing could be heard from them as they studied, wrote 'em down and pulled brand papers from the folders. Everybody stood clear and let them alone. When they were finished both started drinking hard and nearly got into a fight with each other over something neither could remember the next day.

***

The horse auction would last two days. It would start with one sale on a Friday afternoon and two sales, morning and afternoon on Saturday. The brood mares were shipped to another sale down in Colorado. One for registered quarter horses only. So that was off the chore list.

The buyers could come and view the horses on Wednesday morning. The numbers in the brochures would match the numbers that tagged each horse.

There were no stalls for this many horses so with their hips tagged with the numbers, the remuda was broken up and put out in the smaller pastures. The cowboys brought them into the ranch arena a handful at a time to show them under saddle. A small herd of roping steers were brought in too, so a horse could be shown for its roping and cow savvy in the viewing time before the sale.

The Dude ranch owners and managers showed up from all over the Rocky Mountain States and they asked a lot of questions. They needed Dude horses and they needed them to be gentle. The mounts so marked would be bid high. There were some good kid type horses on the ranch too. Good quarter horses are bred for disposition as well as everything else. Some then, were naturally gentle and always had been.

When Clarence saw an older man with two children prowling the pens he walked up and introduced himself and they talked. Yes, the man was looking for two good horses for his grandson and granddaughter. The children stood beside the man holding his hands. They were seven and eight years old. The man held the brochure to Clarence and ask for a suggestion. Clarence shook him off on the paper and said...

"I don't need that. Come with me." Clarence walked them back and over to a paddock that held his own string. He talked to the man and asked him some questions. Clarence ask where they were from and how much pasture did he have, barns? Things like that. The man gave a good picture of his place in words Clarence understood. Forty Acres of irrigated hay meadow, a hundred and ten acres of native pasture. All under new fence, good barn and tack room. Just a nice little hobby ranch. He even had ten head of cows to keep the horses company.

"Good, cows will keep 'em honest." Clarence said.

Clarence was impressive to watch. His old hat was back on his head, he was chewing tobacco, he had skipped his shave. His skin was sun burnt again, after leaving the kitchen and working outside all these weeks. With bushy eyebrows curling up he squinted at the horses. This was his chance for a good home for them and Clarence wasn't about to let it pass.

"Well I got two for you and they're right there. The smaller Blue roan and that stout little Bay horse on the right. These two are bomb proof. I know them as well as I knew my own mother. We've rode up on Grizzle Bear together and both will do nothing but stand still and wait for instructions from you. They have packed out game from the mountains. They've got handle too. If your grandkids get upside down under either of them I swear to you these two won't take another step until the kids can kick loose and you fix the saddle back. I trust them with my life and have done so many times. Both are sound and sure-footed on Mountain trails and in the pasture at a dead gallop neither has ever fallen with me. They know what whoa means and a few other words I won't mention in front of your grandkids. Now, do you have a horse?"

The kids had climbed up on the rail fence, their eyes big as saucers as they looked at the horses. Clarence walked through the gate and up to the roan. He walked all around it up close and the horse did not move. Then Clarence went to the Bay and did the same. He picked up their feet. He led the bay over by its mane and when the bay started to pull away Clarence said...

"Whoa," and the horse stopped and then came with Clarence as easy as if it had a halter on.

"Do you have a horse?" Clarence asked the man.

"No, I don't."

Clarence let the bay go and walked over to a tall Sorrel. He stroked its neck and looked back and forth from the man to the horse. The Grandpa was about six feet tall and looked fit for his age.

"You've ridden before I'm thinking?" Clarence said.

"Oh sure. Been years, but as a kid I helped with ranch work some and got horseback with neighbors. I wanted my grandkids to have the same good memories of riding that I have."

"Well, ok. This big fella is your boy. He's sound, sure-footed and has handle. And don't speed him up unless you mean it because he is fast. But, he will walk with his head down and on a loose rein and do it all day long if that is what you want. Your kids get in trouble and he'll take you to them as quick as you let him. He won't do well on a tight rein, you don't ride like that do you?"

The grandpa's eyes were gleaming now. He shook his head and smiled. He wrote the numbers down in the brochure and then turned the page to them as Clarence came out the gate. The man looked up and started to say something but Clarence held his hand up and said,

"I know, I know. They got a little age on them. But, that is what you want if you want experience. Look at you and me. Look at them. They got some good years left in them and so do we. The bidders will concentrate on the younger horses and bid them through the roof. These you'll get a better price on. And, their teeth are still good. That's how I know they got good life left in them. With an old Cowhand it's his knees that go first. With a horse it's his teeth. If you want more, let me know now. See that Buckskin over there, well he's..."

Before it was over Clarence thought he had the Grandpa signed up for four of his old horses and maybe even five. Grandma was still alive and the kid's parents might want to ride now and again. The man had the pasture too. That was important to know for Clarence. He'd always hated it when he had to put a horse out on poor grass.

Clarence's feet hurt. He'd walked too much around the Headquarters lately. He just wasn't use to it. He saw Trey at a picnic table talking up his own string to a man. Clarence walked over to him and sat down. Before he was situated Casey sprang on him out of nowhere with a thermos of coffee and a bag of cookies. She sat it in front of Clarence, gave him a kiss on the cheek and marched off. It was so quick that it made Clarence suspicious.

"Has she been lay-in' for me?" he asked Trey.

"Well, looking for you, yes. You better get used to the attention. I don't think she's going anywhere."

Clarence gave Trey such a helpless look that the other man at the table laughed out loud at it.

The sale date arrived and the Ranch again was packed to the limits as buyers milled, talked and viewed the horses. When the Auctioneers gavel hit the table on Friday afternoon the arena went silent. The man was standing on a platform over the round pen, used as the sale ring. Ilene sat on his right side and the auctioneer's wife and secretary sat on his left. Both had pen and paper ready to keep records of each buyer and each horse sold. Four men in identical white, western dress shirts and black hats moved forward into the crowd to act as bid callers. The Auction began…

"I'd like to welcome you all here on behalf of the Fenwick family and the Double Dagger Ranch. I have been selling horses for fifty years all over this great nation of ours and I have never been more honored as to be a part of this sale today. This Ranch had its beginnings over one hundred and thirty years ago when a young settler drove his stake and had his brother drive a herd of mustangs up from Texas and put them out on the range with Thoroughbred studs from Tennessee. Some of the finest quarter horse blood in the country began here and much was added over the years by knowledgeable men. The history of the breeding is in the attachment to the Sale Book. It was written by Mrs. Ilene Parkston, a longtime resident on the ranch and wife of Jay Parkston the longtime manager, now passed on. She will be helping with the sale today, Mrs. Parkston…" The Auctioneer nodded to Ilene and she stood up and smiled at the crowd and they gave her a generous applause."

The mike squeaked as Clarence looked up at her. She was looking out over the crowd, her expression as stoic and poised as any highbrow woman Clarence had ever seen and he felt very proud of her. She sat and the Auctioneer continued...

"The Dagger Ranch Cowherd has been sold and this Remuda has got to go. So, this is your chance to own a living piece of the legend of this great ranch. There are horses here for everyone. The Dagger hands will ride them in, do a turn or two and pull the saddles, so you can see their backs. You have all had a couple of days to look them over. Now this sale will begin. Bring 'em in boys."

He popped the gavel down hard, then he leaned into his microphone and started the bid on what was as fine a cow horse as anybody would ever have a chance to own. The way the bidding went showed that the audience knew it too.

Clarence looked back over the crowd and located the 2/c horse buyers. They each held their separate list of horses to buy and with head down, were checking the numbers. They were separated by several rows, way apart as instructed. It was in their hands now. Clarence saw Trey walk out of the sale area as Wiley rode the second horse in. Maybe he was going because he couldn't watch, or maybe to help and supervise in the back. There were some area Cowboys helping that did not know the horses and so Clarence followed too. Best to keep busy now, busy, busy, busy. Don't think about it, just keep it moving.

***

Benedict Kane sat in his house, muddy, wet and cold. He stared at the money out on the table. It was two hundred thousand dollars. He was feeling a genuine rush of excitement at his successful, early season trip into the mountains. He'd even packed out some Antler Sheds to cover the reason he had gone in. There were only a few people around that would risk the tricky picking of a trail through mud and spotty snow patches and creeks still holding ice on the banks. Creeks were running high with spring runoff and had to be crossed. To be first in the mountains in Spring can be a tough chore. But, the shed market was strong and you could pick up a couple of thousand dollars' worth for the Asian Market if you knew where to look.

But, Kane had gone for the plane. He packed chain and two come-a-longs. He carried two small, economy car jacks. He carried axe and chainsaw. For the business end of a pole he had the metal paw of a common garden tool. He took a snow shovel too. When he got to the plane he went to work to force his way into the pilot's cabin at the front of the plane. Finally, after a day and a half he made some headway. He was able to pull a boulder off of the side of the cabin and then with the chainsaw he cut out a piece of log over two feet in diameter and four feet long. There was a hole in the side of the pilot's cabin where the windshield had been and with the jacks he opened it more. With a pole, rigged with the garden tool claw on the end, Kane started to patiently dig through the clothing and bones of the occupants and materials in the cabin. The small space he raked the human remains in, quickly filled and with indifference he picked the bone and fabric up and threw it behind him onto the rocky scree. He was finally rewarded. In each of the cabin's two seats he found a common, zipper-locked bank bag. The kind you would see small business owners use to carry their register change in. In each of these bags were bundled one hundred-dollar bills. He raked until he was exhausted from the cold, the awkward position and the hanging of his head down in the tomb-like, darkness. Finally, with the last of his flashlight batteries going dim he realized he had found all he was going to. He gathered his tools and the loot. He took three trips to get his gear up to the pack animals. He loaded up, put the loot in his saddle bags and buckled the pocket flaps down. Then he rode out.

He shook with excitement and the cold as he rode. He shivered and thanked himself for his own effort. For the first time in many years he felt proud of himself. For a man like Benedict Kane that kind of pride could only be expressed in one or two ways. One by gloating, the other by bragging. With some liquor in him he'd throw in some bullying too. By the time he tied up at his old stock trailer at the bottom of the mountain he had already spent half the money, just in his mind.

In the heavy drinking days that followed Kane told first one and then another that he had found the plane. He had not meant too but it seemed he could not help it. When he sobered up he knew he had screwed up. It made it necessary to tell the authorities.

The local wilderness rescue team, Sheriff's department and US Forest Service all wanted to go in as soon as possible. When they did what they found was the mess Kane had left. Kane was smart enough to keep his explanation simple.

"That's the way I found it." He said.

***

Marcos brought the news out to the Ranch. He had copies of the local paper with pictures of the plane, the story of its occupants and a piece on Kane stumbling onto it while shed hunting in the mountains. Marcos said,

"Helena is relieved, now that she will finally be able to bury her brother. And, there is much interest in the Hispanic community about the money."

"What money?" Clarence asked, as casually as he could.

"Well, the long-time talk, the rumors about it, I am not sure I would want to be Mister Kane right now."

"What do you mean by that?" Clarence said.

Marcos's enthusiasm faded a little. Clarence waited for an answer. Marcos seemed to weigh his words carefully.

"Our Mexican community has a lot of gossip and news of its own. People seem to know what is going on without talking about it outside their circles. The women gossip to each other. In time the news of this plane being found will pass to somebody out of this area. The Cartels are at work all over. If the rumors of drug money on the plane were true, they have not forgotten about it. If they think Mr. Kane has found the money they will not let that go."

"The article don't say anything about any money." Clarence said. He was sitting at the table holding the paper. Trey listened and kept quiet. He decided to get Clarence to make a beer run with him when Marcos was finished.

Before driving out, Clarence answered a phone call and it was from Weismann. When Clarence hung up he and Trey left and drove straight to town to meet with him. When they arrived, Weismann got right down to business. He was excited about the plane being found and it showed when Clarence told him what Marcos had said about the Cartel.

"Move off the Dagger. Move out to your cow camps. What's the nearest town?"

"Milford." Clarence answered.

"Right, get a PO Box there. Don't take mail at the Conant place. Don't tell people where you are for a while. Just take care of your business and mind your own."

"We should hear from the Forest Service on the Hunting Camp permits any time." He continued. "I am fairly certain they'll sigh them to Ilene. You'll have a way now, to get money to her like you want.

Who's getting their Outfitter License?"

"Either me or Wiley Phillips." Trey said.

"Ok, This Marcos, what's he like, do you trust him?"

"Yes," Clarence answered.

"It would be good to keep in touch with him. Can you use him out on the lease?" Both Clarence and Trey shook their heads.

"We need to keep our labor cost down. We'll all be scattered out anyway and have to cook for ourselves." Trey said.

"You need to stay in touch with him for the rumors and information he might come across." Weismann said.

"I could try to get him on with Casey. She has an interest in the Rancher Bar and they are always looking for cooks. Maybe we can supplement the pay scale to keep him there, make it more attractive to him." Clarence said.

Weismann listened and considered it. He was satisfied Clarence understood the need to keep this Marcos close.

"He has already told you that Kane could be at risk because he found the plane. That is a lot to think on and it's not just a speculation. Everything is fine right now. The plane is clean. Nobody can place you up there, let's hope it stays that way." Weismann said.

"I don't like involving other people." Trey said.

"Don't worry about that now." Weismann spoke sharply and he saw the look Trey gave him. It might not be a good idea to dismiss this Cowboy's views. At least not to his face. Weismann continued in a softened tone,

"We are just letting ourselves keep a contact in the Mexican community. He's just there for you to occasionally have a conversation with. Keep him friendly, so he's comfortable talking to you. You guys have lived and worked together now. Just keep him close."

Trey and Clarence left the meeting, went to the grocery store for a few things, then stopped at the bar for a drink and to say hi to Casey. Clarence ask her if she could get Marcos on and she said she could. The why of it did not enter into the conversation and left it easy enough to drop further discussion. Trey and Clarence left. They picked up a couple of cases of beer and headed back to the Ranch.

"Clarence, this is something that could bite some people on the ass, never see it coming." Trey said.

"We are moving away. We're going to be out of sight in Wilford County. Kane is the target, not us." Clarence countered.

"You believe that, then all-right." Trey answered.

"It's a time frame kind of thing Trey. Like a season, like a hitch in the army. See it through is all you can do once you are in it."

Clarence pulled up to the bunkhouse. Marcos was there and he was packing. He had his little car backed up near the door with the trunk open.

"You got another job yet Marty?" Clarence said, as he walked in.

"No, but I will have soon enough with the summer season starting."

"Call Casey, you got her number?" Clarence asked. He wrote it on a napkin in the kitchen anyway.

"I got dinner ready if you guys want to eat. I am going to stay tonight if that is ok." Marcos said.

"Of course," Clarence said. He turned around to see where Trey had gone. Clarence looked out and saw him backing his truck up to the lowboy trailer.

"You ready to eat?" Clarence hollered to him from the door...but Trey didn't answer. He drove off pulling the trailer. Clarence pulled a tab on a beer and stood thoughtfully watching out the door. He looked at the western sky and saw clouds mixed with the sunset. His mind went blank as the beer hit his tongue and throat. He went for whiskey and poured a shot. He went in and turned on the TV. He wondered if they had the electricity on at the Conant lease yet. Marcos came in and set down. He had a beer too.

"Where did Trey go?" he said.

"He went to get the Chuck wagon, I think."

"A Chuck wagon, can he load that by himself?" Marcos said.

"He didn't ask for help. He's got the winch on his truck and the lowboy."

"Why did he buy a chuck wagon?" Marty said.

"Well, that would be about the sentiment." Clarence answered. Marcos, now comfortably known as Marty around the ranch, stared at his new friend and studied on the word Clarence had used.

"Sentiment." Marty repeated. "Trey bought a chuck wagon from the old days and taking it with him because of sentiment. Ok, I get it." Marty said as he nodded his head.

"I like it," he added. Clarence leaned back and closed his eyes. As he dozed off he said,

"Yeah, I do too."

13

Slow Death by Shame

Wiley and the boys had brought in hay. They strengthened and repaired the Conant ranch stock pens. The pasture to those pens, a one hundred seventy-five-acre hay field, received the horses. Wiley kept two up for the wrangle. They put them in a paddock by the barn. Every morning two of them would ride out at daylight and pen the horse herd. They had fifty-two head of the best cow horses in the country still wearing the Dagger brand. They would throw them a little feed and keep them up part of the day then swap out for two fresh mounts and turn the rest back out. They did it to get the horses in a routine on the new outfit and find the gates.

Once the fences were pulled back up and tightened and the gates re-hung, they turned to the barn and tack room. They cleaned and organized it and then the horseshoeing began. It had been a Dagger Ranch rule that you had to shoe your own string. This would continue on the 2/c.

The house, empty of furniture for many years now, was swept of rat droppings. They dusted, cleaned the bathroom and kitchen and washed off the windows outside. Cowboy bedrolls were thrown out on the floors, lawn chairs from somewhere appeared in the rooms. An old monster of a gas stove was still there but not working, so they cooked in the yard on the rock grill, made sandwiches and made do.

The water trough was full of cold water. It also served as a good beer cooler. The set up was rough for a few days and then service men from town came out. The electricity was turned on, a plumber got the water flowing from the well house and a brand-new hot water heater was installed. The propane tank was filled as well and the kitchen stove now worked. Things were getting comfortable and looking up.

On the still cold spring nights, they built a fire in the big ranch fireplace in the living room and listened to Wes's radio. On one of those evenings Clarence and Trey drove in. They were both half drunk, had eaten in town on the way out and had little to say. They threw their bedrolls down in what may have been the dining room and before Clarence crawled in his sleeping bag he set up his twenty cup, professional model, electric coffee peculator on the floor, ready to go. Within a week Clarence would stop using it and go back to boiling coffee in his old-time, well blackened coffee pot.

Before first light the smell of coffee and bacon filled the house. Clarence, out of just plain meanness, yelled out...

"Drop your cocks and grab your socks gentlemen, the cattle are here."

And it worked. They got up quick and scrambled to get dressed. Clarence, laughing, said,

"Just kidding about the Cattle. It'll be a few days yet. Take your time. Get your coffee, eat, it won't be light for another hour." They cussed him good but nobody went back to bed. That was the first day they all worked on nothing but the old Conant Ranch House. They turned it into a bunkhouse and did it all from barn scrap lumber and old fence posts lying around the place. Plank board bunks, plank board tables, plank board benches and plank board shelves appeared in every room.

The day after, they rolled the Chuck wagon off the trailer and Wiley and Clarence pulled the empty low-boy to town to scavenge some used furniture. The town of Wilford had a Good Will store and a used everything store and that was how the 2/c got its base camp furnished. Before the cattle arrived, the boys had TV going, rigged up to the old outside antenna. They picked up two channels. Old couches and chairs set in a semi-circle before it. The chairs and couch they covered with old sheets and faded horse blankets to dress them up a bit. Scrap carpet of all colors were thrown down in all the rooms and a fresh new shower curtain hung in each of the house's two bathrooms. Old blankets and towels served as curtains on the East and West facing windows, blocking direct sunlight. The North-South window panes were left bare to stare out on this wide, flatter country they were about to cover and you could guess the wind speed each day by looking out at the long uncut yard full of tall Ghost grass waving there. Clarence would look at that glass pane picture and think about getting the brush hook out and whacking those weeds down. But after a time, he got used to it and finally kind of liked it. It was something different to watch tall grass sway in the wind from inside and not hear it rushing in your ears. It was dream-like.

When the load of hay arrived they all pitched in and unloaded it and tarped it beside the barn. Then the cattle came. Semi-Truck load after truck load. Each truck dropping its load of yearlings in the pens. The crew pushed them through the chute, branded them, shot them all the vaccinations, put them in fenced-off lots and fed hay to dry them up from the scours of the trip. The boys rode the pens like they were in the feed lots prowling for sick cattle. When one was found they cut it out to the chute to doctor and then to a separate lot until cured and no longer contagious. As the new cattle settled in the sound of the those newly weaned, bawling for their mothers finally started to die down. The first steers in were moved out to the pastures and just like the old days the boys rode herd on them and milled them and closed them up and let them scatter again and got them comfortable with being handled by men a horseback. That would make all the difference later when they changed pastures or gathered them up for shipping.

They put out salt and mineral blocks near every water hole and tank, at first by pickup truck, then later by pack-horse as the cattle spread out to the furthest reaches of the range they were grazing, a range un-accessible otherwise. The cattle started fleshing out and the work load eased up. Now it was time to let cattle put on weight.

The Cowboys each stayed in the cowboy version of a Tepee out on the range they were assigned to cover. It was quick and easy to move and set up. Another accessory was a tarp fly used to cover a small cook fire and sit under in rainy weather. These camps were cached with food in bearproof containers or hung from meat poles in nearby timber. Now and again you would see a deer or antelope hanging there, cooling in the shade. The old ways had come back to the range. Men on horseback, not fences, kept the cattle where they were supposed to be. When the cattle meandered off the lease boundaries they were tracked and brought back and the boggiest water holes were checked routinely for cattle stuck in the muck.

When they visited each other, the discussions ranged from the best big circle horse to the mountain lion kill to the longest kill shot you could make with an open sight 30-30 lever action saddle gun. These guys lived in their own world of wind and campfires, of horses and dreaming of the girl back home.

They started taking turns going to town. They were too far away from civilization to do it in a day. First you had to have your relief rider show up. Whoever that was would ride your horses while you were gone. It was common to say something like, "don't screw up my horses," when you left out. Unless it was Trey or Clarence relieving you of course. One-night, Wiley came into headquarters and said,

"I'm not relieving Wes anymore."

"How's that," Trey said,

"When I ride one of his horses he acts like I'm slow dancing with his wife or something."

This had come up before and Trey knew how Wes was, but it was still funny. After a while everybody that relieved Wes would act like they were romancing his horses in front of him. They would make kissing and sucking noises and act like the horse was a house pet. Wes got the message and quit complaining.

The town of Wilford did not get the tourist traffic. So, Two Ocean was still the place to go for any night life. Clarence went because of Casey, Wiley and the others for the tourist women it promised. Only Trey stayed away.

Trey kept on the move by pickup truck, keeping the herder's camps in supplies and relieving them some himself. With things going smooth he let Wiley ride on the herd closest to headquarters to work on his Outfitters License and applications. They had no clients for it but Ilene had gotten the permits and she and Weismann had given the Outfitters Association Wiley's recommendation letters. The process was moving forward.

Clarence helped Wiley start putting a basic hunting camp together. The Dagger Ranch had always had pack saddles and panniers. It had wall tents too and Clarence had bid on the ones he thought were still good enough to get them through a season or two, when the equipment sale went off. Some of the pack saddles needed repair work. Clarence had this down pat and Wiley, like every Cowboy, was fairly good with leather work.

The plan was, after they shipped the cattle, they would all pack into the mountains for a good Elk and Deer hunt. While there, Wiley could learn his country better and if the rest of the crew would get a good taste of that kind-of work they might like it enough to keep doing it each fall. This would stretch out their employment another two months and Wiley would have his crew.

**

Benedict Kane was set to meet his three clients at the trailhead at seven a.m. He had driven in the night before and finding the Dagger corrals locked up tight, he cussed it but left it alone. He un-loaded his mules and horses and fed them tied to the side of his trailer. He threw down his bed-roll after mid-night and at five a.m. he got up and started saddling and packing up for the ride in. He was ready and waiting for the clients and their gear when they drove up. He was a little surprised that two of them were Mexicans. One, the one he had talked to on the phone was white. He told Kane that he wanted to see the plane that had crashed and do some scenic rides in the area for photography.

Kane did not see any cameras with them but they each had a side-arm buckled on. The bags seemed extra heavy when Kane strapped them to the sides of the pack mules. It occurred to him that he might have made a mistake to take these guys up there without finding out more about them first. But, he was always looking for new clients, he had trashed so many over the years. And, they were paying cash. So, he booked the trip without thinking past tax-free money.

Kane had already taken law enforcement in and family of the Pilot had gone in as well. Another Outfitter took the news media in. The clients he had now sounded normal enough on the phone, friendly, excited like any tourist. It was the peak of the tourist season. There were several cars in the parking area left by Backpackers and Hikers. When Kane had the string of pack animals ready he noticed the Mexicans looking at his new horse trailer and new truck. They were talking to each other in Spanish. They spoke over their shoulders to the white man, Tony, and he answered in Spanish. Tony saw Kane looking at them. The smiling had stopped. Tony said,

"Nice rig you got there. Looks brand new."

Kane went to his truck and took out his short-barreled 12 gauge pump and put it in his saddle scabbard.

What's that for?" Tony asked.

"Bear." Kane answered. "Lots of them around this time of year."

***

The clients slept late the first morning in camp. Kane was up early, even though he had not slept well at all. He made coffee, wrangled the stock and drug up some more firewood. The men started coming out of their tents after nine o'clock. Kane started to fix breakfast but one of the Mexican clients took it over from him.

"We had a long drive up here from New Mexico," Tony said. "We haven't had much sleep lately."

"That's fine," Kane answered. "It'll still be there."

When they got to the edge of the drainage that held the plane, the clients dismounted and without speaking went down to the crash site. They were systematic, sticking their heads in any place that offered an opportunity. The smaller one crawled in the hole behind the left wing with a flashlight. Kane stood off and watched.

The two men moved around outside of the plane. They moved across the rock slide peering into the openings and generally poking around. Finally, they climbed to the ridge on the far side and seemed to take in the landscape. Tony stayed at the plane a little while and then climbed up to where Kane sat and said,

"So, what did you find here Mr. Kane?"

"Just what you see. The Sheriff's office dug out the remains. They took the luggage and ID's for next of kin."

"You weren't curious when you found this plane? You did not look it over or crawl into it?" Tony said.

"No, I don't crawl in holes. I saw the plane and I reported it when I got out of the Mountains. I'm too big to get into small places like that." Kane smiled at Tony as friendly as he could fake it. He looked up and saw the two Mexicans coming slowly down from their climb. Tony stood there beside him while the Mexicans walked across the scree and up to where they stood. They spoke in Spanish to Tony and several times looked down at Kane, still sitting, as they spoke.

"If you guys are going to talk about me I am going to tell you to speak English." Kane said and stood up.

"Sure," Tony answered. "Let's just all go back to camp and take a break."

This was not Kane's plan. A scenic ride was what he expected to do. But he went back to the horses, mounted and waited for the clients to do the same. Kane was thinking hard as they moved through the timber to the meadow and their camp. Now he knew what these men were here for. It was not his nature to be afraid, but he had not been very smart many times in his life. With that thought, he led the three men to the camp with one simple idea. He was going to ride off and leave them at his first opportunity.

When they rode into camp Kane dismounted and tied his horse up quickly. One of the Mexicans was quick too. The small wiry one, with a hatchet like face, had been riding up close behind Kane. When they arrived at camp the man dropped his reins, kicked his feet out of both stirrups and jumped straight to the ground. Kane was just starting to tie his mount from the near side of his horse when the man moved quickly to the off side, jerked the shotgun out of the scabbard and walked away with it. Kane was stunned.

"Keep your hands off that," Kane said loudly and moved to follow the man. Then Tony stepped right in front of him and blocked his path. Kane pushed Tony out of the way and then felt the pistol of the other Mexican, the stout one that looked more like an Apache Indian than a Mexican, sticking hard into his ribs. Kane stopped dead in his tracks. Tony recovered his balance and speaking calmly said,

"Come over to the fire and we'll have some lunch and talk some more."

Kane, with face flushed with rage and embarrassment, did as he was told. His jaws were clenched tight as he sat down on the log by the fire pit. Tony sat across from him. The man with the pistol stood by and the one with his shotgun sat down and leaned against a tree behind him. Tony removed his ball cap hat and scratched his head. He looked down at the ground and picked up a stick. He broke it over his knee to the length he wanted and started digging back and forth in the thin soil. Kane watched and waited. Then, Tony pointed the stick right at him and said,

"You have to own up to this now man. I am waiting." Tony's leg started doing a nervous twitch. Then he jumped up so suddenly that Kane's reaction was to jump up too. There was a nervous moment and then he was struck from behind and he blacked out.

When he came too he was on the ground. He could see he was back in the trees that surrounded the camp. There was a sharp pain in the back of his head and his eyesight was blurred. He tried to bring his arms up but he could not move them. Then Tony bent over him and said,

"We're hiding you back here in the trees in case someone comes by. We'll gag you too, so you won't make any noise. I want you to notice first thing, that we are showing you some compassion here. You cannot count on that to continue. Your hands are tied in the front for a reason. That is so you can watch, with your head propped up on the hard rock pillow. You will see it, while I pull your fingernails out. Will I have to do that?"

Kane shook his head 'no' and stared, incredulous at this turn of events. Kane had been playing for time that he did not have coming. He shook his head, 'no' again with exaggerated measure.

"Good. Now then, a man named Hector Gomez was on that plane. Hector, he was employed by some friends of mine. You found the plane. The two men were the only passengers on the plane. So, they did not run off with anything. The plane did not burn up. That means the money was still there. What did you do with it besides buy a new truck and horse trailer?"

"You can't come up here, do this shit to me and get by with it," Kane said. "There's laws in this country. This is fucking Wyoming, it ain't Mexico."

"Not laws for us. Gringo laws are for gringos, not us. We can kill you right now, ride out, get in the truck and go back to Mexico. The whole nation of Mexico is our safe-house. We do what we want and right now we want the money from this plane."

The two Mexicans came up and bent close. One had something in his hands. It was Kane's long handled plyers from the shoeing bag. He had wire cutters too. Tony took Kane' left, little finger in his hand and held up the plyers.

"Damnit, ok" Kane said. "The Truck and trailer I paid cash for. That was about $75,000.00 of it. I got a little over $100,000.00 stashed at home in cash. You can have it all. I can sign the truck and trailer titles over to you too. It's all paid for."

Tony spoke to the other two in Spanish. Kane watched. He expected a good response but he did not get it. All three were shaking their heads at him. One of them did a mocking frown. Tony took the plyers, bent down and as he gripped Kane's little finger in his left hand, gripping it tight, he said...

"Man, you are just not getting it are you..." then, quick as a snake strikes he snapped the end of the finger off and tossed it aside."

Kane began cussing hard with the rush of pain and tried to rise up. One of the Mexicans kicked him solidly in the ribs and the wind went out of him. He stopped struggling. He laid back, gasping for breath and tried to control the fear he felt rising up inside him.

"Mr. Kane, I think he broke one or two of your ribs." Then Tony spoke in Spanish and the Mexican squatted down, grabbed Kane's kerchief from around his neck, untied it and tied it tightly around the bleeding stump of the finger. Then the man held Kane tied hands up in the air as if he were trying to slow the bleeding.

"Mr. Kane, you keep telling me you just have one or two hundred thousand from this plane and you are going to be missing all your fingers and your toes too. One by fucking one." Tony said.

Kane was surprised to hear argument over a dollar number and the pain was not helping him think. His adrenalin had kicked in and he found he was able to take a shallow breath. His head cleared a little.

When he found the money in the plane he was happy enough about it to think of little else. Anyone who found the plane first may have found money too and run just like he had. He looked up at Tony and said,

"Somebody was at the plane before I was. There were other hunters in the area. There always are in hunting season."

"I'm listening, go on," Tony said.

"When I rode in, the Dagger Ranch corrals were not being used. So, I used them. When I came out they were there, their trucks and trailers anyway. I came back a second time and they were parked inside the gate and there was a new lock and chain on it."

"So why them, you think?" Tony said.

"Very few hunts go this far in from that trailhead. They are the only ones that have a permitted camp up here. The next nearest Outfitter uses a trailhead in the next drainage over."

"So where is this Ranch camp then.?" Tony asked.

"Let me up and I'll take you to it." Tony translated to his two companions. They talked it over.

"I don't think ribs are broke. I've broken 'em before and this don't feel that bad." Kane said. "I can ride."

"How long to the other camp?" Tony said sharply.

"It'll be near dark when we get there. It's about two hours from here." Kane said and immediately regretted telling them the distance. He heard them walk off discussing it. In a few minutes they came back with Kane's bedroll, spread it out and put him in it. They took his bloody bandana off his hand and tied the wound off with a bread tie. They gagged him. Tony said,

"We won't ride in the dark. Too risky, we might lose you." Then he walked off.

Tony went to the fire pit and built the fire up again. Chalito moved off and came back with the food pannier. While he and Vaca put a dinner together Tony stayed quiet and watched and thought about his partners in crime. The heavy-set Chalito was a bad hombre and already growing impatient. The other one, Vaca, was always the same. Tony never knew what he was thinking. But Vaca took his lead from Chalito and it was Chalito that told Vaca to get the shotgun. This was Chalito's way of letting Tony know, speed things up or he would.

Chalito just wanted to get the money and get back to Mexico and his very good lifestyle there. Tony was an interpreter and a front man for the Cartel in the U.S. That made him vulnerable since he could not simply disappear over the border as easily as they. Eventually, he had to get back in. He lived in this country.

The hardest part of this kind of job was patience. It can take time for things to develop. Now, Chalito had stepped up the game and without some sort of angle on Kane, something to keep him silent, then when it was over they would have to kill the man. But, you have to get the money back first. Tony hoped a confrontation with Chalito could be avoided.

Tony waited until Vaca and Chalito were well into their cooking project and then got up and walked off into the late afternoon light. He walked to the horses that were still tied and saddled, and then he circled around to the spot Kane had been left, all bagged up.

Kane heard him walk up and opened his eyes. They looked at each other closely. Tony could see that this backcountry outfitter was a tough, old time throwback of a white man, with plenty of strength and meanness in him. Tony knelt down beside Kane and un-tied the gag. Then he quickly put his finger to his own lips and said,

"Shhh, listen to me. I want to tell you, your situation. My compadres think you have all of the money. Our number is over three million dollars. I don't know if your story is true or not. It is plausible to me that someone found the plane before you. But why would they leave any money at all? My friends know only the newspaper account about you being the one that found the plane. Just you. Here is what I think we should do. I will offer that you can keep some of what you found. It will be your finder's fee. I am pretty sure I can get my guys to agree to that. You tell us where the money is and I mean all of it. You give that money to us. Maybe you just keep your new truck and trailer. But you will have to tell me where all the money is and in some detail. You have to get the money to us, in our hands. Ok?"

Kane was shaking his head and feeling the desperation. His breathing was shallow and irregular. He gathered himself as much as he was able, took a couple of deep breaths, looked up and with a painful groan in his voice said,

"Listen, I only have and only know of the money I found here. It was two hundred thousand dollars. I saw sign that others were in the cargo area, behind the passenger seats. Somebody was there before me. Who they were I can only guess at. It's probably some cowhands that work for a local ranch. We should go over to their hunting camp and take a good look around. It would make sense for them to hide a big chunk of that kind of money up here. If I had known how much money was on that plane I would already have taken that camp apart."

Kane was thinking this could buy him time. It might present a chance to get away. Tony did the 'Shh,' again and put Kane's gag back on. He stood up and walked back to the fire.

Chalito was standing up by the campfire watching him, as if expecting some clarification. Tony told Chalito what he had said to Kane and the man's reply. Vaca listened and said nothing. He shrugged his shoulders as if to say it was all-right with him, whatever had been said. Tony went to the waiting food and filled a plate.

The rest of the evening passed. They were all tired from hard traveling and the stress of this collection job. Just at sunset, Vaca went over to the horses and took them down to the spring to water. Tony took his canteen and a bean tortilla and started to go over to Kane. Chalito saw it and stood up shaking his head no. So, there would be no food or water for their prisoner. Tony sat the food on a rock, then took his canteen and stretched out on his bedroll by the fire.

Tony 's last thought before sleep was that Kane did not have all of the money. He only had what he said he had. It was down to simple logic to Tony. Why else would the man still be doing this shit in the woods thing? Most men would be off to Vegas or something, living large and long gone by now. You don't find money like that and just buy a new truck and ride around in the fucking woods on a damn horse. Not with three million dollars in your pocket.

14

Stolen Cattle & the 2/c

When Trey and Wiley drove into the trailhead, the green USFS truck was parked in front of the Ranch's gate. They stopped behind it. Trey saw the Ranger standing off to the side, beside a shiny-new Ford dually hooked up to an equally new horse trailer. Both backed up, neatly into the trees. There were some campers, hiker types, talking to the Ranger. Trey read the name badge on the Ranger's shirt as he walked up to him.

"Hello Edwards," Trey said. The Ranger looked up from his notebook and without saying hello, he said.

"You know who's rig this is?

"No, but I need to get in to our corrals."

"I thought Dagger Ranch sold out." Edwards said.

"It did. This is Mrs. Ilene Parkston's now. We will be working for her"

"Right, guess I'd heard that." Edwards said.

"Who's going to be the Outfitter?"

"This young man right here. Meet Wiley Phillips. He'll be getting his license in the next few weeks."

Edwards grunted and barely looked up. Wiley and Trey looked at each other and Wiley's expression showed that he detected the attitude.

"Can you move your pickup for me…?" Trey said.

Edwards turned and walked straight to his truck and moved it without saying a word. Wiley looked at Trey and said,

"Kind of a rude SOB,"

"Well, locals complain to them a lot about Outfitters. They get tired of it. Some of these Outfitters are bigger crybabies than team-ropers." Wiley laughed out loud at the comparison. If you had ever-Rodeo'd, and they all had, you'd heard that one before.

"Why'd you think I didn't get the Outfitter's license?" Trey said as they both walked back to their truck. Trey told Wiley to drive and went with his key to the gate. The chain and padlock were still in place but the pad lock shank was cut through.

"Hell, I got enough enemies now." He said, then held up the cut padlock. He opened the gate and Wiley drove through and parked.

"Clarence says anything like this, it's Benedict the butt hole?" Trey said, pointing to the cut lock.

"So I've heard," Wiley said.

They walked to the back of the trailer and unloaded the horses. They were busy with their work when Edwards came over and in a friendlier tone said,

"Are you leaving any livestock in your pens tonight?"

"Nope, all going in with us." Trey answered. "Why?"

"Well, I don't know who this fancy rig belongs to but the hikers told me that the horses have been tied to the trailer un-attended for two days. There's three horses tied up and a couple of mules wondering around. The rig is locked up. I've called the office and they are trying to find out who owns it."

"Put 'em in our corrals. The water is good. You can hay them from our stack over there. Stay away from the bottom bales, they're wet and moldy."

Edwards hesitated, as if there were more and Trey took it as a cry for help. He hollered over to Wiley,

"Hey, I'm going over to get those horses and put them in our corrals."

Trey did not wait for an answer. He walked with Edwards to the trailer. He checked the door on the side and it was locked so Trey opened the end gate and swung it wide. He untied and led a horse around, stripped the saddle and threw it in. He handed the lead rope to Edwards and took the horse he had and stripped that one quick too. Edwards led the two horses over to the Ranch pens and put them in as Trey came with the third one. They stuffed the manger with hay and it was done. The three horses were sucking the water down so fast that Trey worried about them. He looked at the brands and said,

"Those are Benedict Kane's stock. I've seen the brand." Then Trey took the halters they'd taken off the horses and handed them to Edwards.

"You better pull them off the water and tie them for a little while. Then let them loose again before you leave." Trey said.

"Why?" Edwards said.

"They might founder if you don't."

Wiley moved around his horse to where Trey stood. He looked

over at the new truck and horse trailer.

"There must be money in it if you can drive a rig like that.?" Wiley said.

"It's hard to think Kane would leave his stock tied up for two days." Trey said.

They finished up and rode out. Wiley pulled the pack string and Trey rode behind him to watch the loads. A short way out of the trailhead there were two mules in a small meadow grazing away. Trey quick trotted his horse over to them, looked at their hips, then drove them back to the trail and sent them trotting down the hill toward the parking area. They had Kane's brand too. Trey took them all the way down and penned them. Edwards held the gate. Then Trey loped back up the trail and caught up with Wiley, still moving steadily up the canyon.

They puzzled on it for half the trip and through the conversation, concluded that Kane wasn't the first man to lose his stock in the mountains and have them go home without him. Some camper probably tied them up for him.

"We might meet him hiking down to get 'em back." Wiley said.

"I'd kind of enjoy that." Trey said.

They rode into the old camp just after dark. They unloaded and unsaddled quickly, held a wrangle horse up for the morning, belled and hobbled the string and sent them off into the meadows to graze. The sky was clear and the stars were bright. They dropped the bedrolls down by the fire pit and settled in.

***

Clarence, out on the lease lands, drove his truck and trailer as far as he could go. This end of their range had a series of washouts that prevented driving any further. He got out and looked around. It was mid-afternoon and a fair day. The wind was barely stirring. Distant mountains were in view and a few clouds hung above them.

He was doing a re-supply drop on Wes's camp. From where he parked his horse ride would be under two hours and only one pack horse was needed for Wes's grocery requirements. He brought his own bedroll too. He didn't feel like riding all the way home in the dark and a night out on the prairie might help clear his mind of town stuff.

He had driven to the town of Two Ocean and arrived early the day before. He had cleaned up first. He had arrived reasonably sober. They went out to a party for a girlfriend of hers. The folks throwing the party had reserved a section of the restaurant that adjoined the bar and dance floor. They ate, they drank and they danced. Nothing wrong except maybe that Ilene was there. She was a friend of Casey's friend too. Clarence could not help but take Ilene out on the dance floor and Casey had said he should do it. Later, it seemed she had not been sincere. The second time Clarence danced with Ilene, Casey, normally a good date at a party, clammed up. She did not say another word to Clarence the rest of the night. She then became very friendly with Ilene and ended up moving her chair and sitting next to and talking with her. It was like Clarence was no longer there.

So, he drank and tried to talk to the husbands, also alone at the table, while their wives line-danced and mingled. But he just could not move them to drink much with him and loosen up. They acted like they were on some sort of escort duty. Clarence could usually turn up his charm and get things moving but not that night.

He and Casey drove home in silence and went to bed. Casey was so curled up in her corner that he'd have had to stretch his arm full length to touch her.

The fight came in the morning. Clarence woke up first and while Casey was still snoring deeply he carried all his clothes into the living room and got dressed. Fine, so far. Then he wanted coffee so into the kitchen and quiet as could be he put it on. His mistake was putting his boots on first and walking in on that tile floor. It was noisy and his footsteps woke her. He heard her raspy, hung-over voice say,

"I'm still sleeping you know."

Clarence did not answer. He had to pee bad. The boots he was wearing were tight. They would be hard to pull off and on again. So, he tip-toed to the toilet. His stomach gurgled and bubbled and he farted as he walked. He closed the door softly. When he came out he forgot to tip-toe and immediately regretted it.

"Can't you let me sleep?" She said, sounding very agitated now.

Clarence got his coffee, poured it in a go-cup and looked around for his hat. Before he could find it, she was in the kitchen in her robe looking very unhappy. She got her coffee and went to her chair, sat down and began sipping it. While she sipped she glared straight at him.

"Nice seeing Ilene last night." She said. "I wonder how she likes being woke up when she's been out late."

"I wouldn't know" Clarence said.

"Wouldn't you?"

"Wonder all you want. I got to go." Clarence saw his hat. It was on the floor by the chair Casey was sitting in. Damnit, he was going to have to get close to her. He walked over and carefully, staying at arm's length, bent stiffly, picked it up and farted again. He laughed when he did it. He could not help laughing any more than he could have held the fart back. He did not look at Casey. He put his hat on and started for the door.

"You are a nasty old bastard you know." Casey said. "I wish sometimes you could be polite and quiet in the morning. You could at least do that."

"No, I can't." Clarence stopped and turned around. "I can't tippy-toe around people. I have never been able to tippy-toe around people. When I tippy-toe I am getting ready to kill something. Like when I'm hunting or in a war zone. You really don't want to see me tippy-toe around you."

"Is that a threat?" she said.

Clarence looked at her and then he farted again, but this time forced and on purpose. He raised one leg off the floor just for effect. She could not keep a straight face. She stared laughing at him and it gave him the smile he loved to see. He went back to the couch and sat down. He held his arms out and she came over and sat on his lap and they kissed and he hugged her.

"You hug good Clarence."

"Takes two. I always appreciated a sense of humor. It's rare in an older woman you know."

"Oh yeah? we laugh plenty when men aren't around." She said.

She released the hug and gave Clarence a frown. But, she decided to let the older woman thing go. She squeezed him again, then stood up. She walked back toward her bedroom, stopped for a moment and said,

"Don't forget to lock the door on your way out. And, I think we should see other people." Clarence went to the front door and closed it quickly behind him and left. That was the kind of conversation that he did not want to have. She would have kept him in there all morning talking about their relationship.

Now, he was out on the range getting ready to ride and instead of the job on his mind he was wondering what other people she was talking about. And, at their age. Like there was a banquet of babes waiting to date him and men lined up at her door.

Somewhere over an hour into his trip he realized she was not talking about other women, or herself and other men. She wanted to see if he would take the bait and start dating Ilene, a woman with whom a relationship with him had long since, missed its chance.

When Clarence rode into Wes's camp the kid was not there. Clarence un-loaded and-un-saddled his packhorse, led him out on the side of the hill and staked him out on some grass. He was unsaddling his mount when he realized he had ridden through some cattle without even looking at them. They could have been starving to death for all he knew, dying of some plague or something. It really upset him. He tightened the cinch back, mounted and rode off to do his duty, to ride to cattle and look them over and judge their overall condition. And, he needed to look the grass over good too. It might be time to move this bunch. Hadn't been any rain lately.

When Clarence rode back to camp it was past dark and Wes was home. His dog came up to Clarence to say hello. Wes stepped out of his tent,

"I am sure glad to see you. We got trouble, we got rustlers." He said, and there was urgency in his voice.

"I hate to hear that." Clarence did not get his head around that thought very quickly.

"I found a hide drug up by a coyote. It had the 2/c brand on it. Somebody skinned one of our steers." Wes said.

"How far away?" Clarence said. Wes pointed west-north-west.

"It was that way, probably seven or eight miles."

"Let me see the hide."

"I didn't bring it. I'm riding Skeet here and he wouldn't let me mount up with the stinking thing. I couldn't take a chance of walking home."

"Hell, I told you a long time ago to put a night latch on your saddle. We'll go in the morning. Take care of the horses and I'll fix some supper." Clarence said.

"You mean a sissy strap don't you." Wes answered.

Clarence ignored that. They'd had this conversation before. A night latch on a saddle is just a precaution on a sketchy horse when you are far from home. Real nice when you are riding at night too. Lots of these young buckaroos did not get it. Not yet. You needed a little age and experience to catch on to that one.

As they ate, Wes talked and Clarence started to put the kid's story together. They'd had rustling before but not in a long time. Skinning it out meant it was a meat only kill and did not necessarily mean there would be more. You rack those up to the cost of doing business kind of stuff and hope it went to a good cause, like a hungry family somewhere. But, you needed to check it out and stop it. They turned in for some sleep. It would be a long day coming.

"Good night Wes." Clarence heard Wes stirring about in his tent. Clarence lay on his bedroll, out by the fire for some star-gazing.

"What'd you think of the cattle?" Wes said.

"Fat and sassy. Another week we'll move them."

"Ok," Wes said.

The morning came on quiet, no wind, just the high glow of a summer's day. They ate, wrangled, saddled up and rode. The area where Wes had found the hide did not have much sign around it. Wes had put it up in a sapling. Clarence cut the brand part of the hide out and put it in a plastic bag he'd brought. Then he put it in his saddle bag. They saw no tracks but Wes's. They began to circle out around the area and the circles got wider and still nothing. Then, Clarence hit some cattle tracks, just a few head and then some four-wheeler tracks moving off more to the South. Clarence waved Wes over to him.

"The nearest highway is southwest. Let's just take a straight line toward it and make some circles out along the way to see if we keep crossing these tracks."

"Shit Clarence there is twenty miles between here and the highway." Wes said.

"I know, but maybe we don't need to go that far. They had to come in on a road. You got a fresh horse anyhow."

"Ok, let's go get 'em. " Wes said, realizing the time was now. They rode all the way through lunch and could see the random sort of path the four-wheeler had taken to find the cattle. They were eating sandwiches while riding when Wes's dog sniffed up something and it was hides buried and partially dug up by varmints. It was here they saw plenty of sign and 4-wheeler tracks in soft ground. Wes was moving off to look for more tracks when buzzards flew up from a ravine. They found what was left and counted six head, butchered. Wes threw a cussing fit.

"Wes, there is an old home place over the next ridge and there is a road to it from the highway. We've seen this before. I am guessing there are some folks selling fresh beef to town for half-price or something. That's an old racket. Lets' ride over the ridge and see what we can find out."

They both kicked their mounts into a short lope and rode straight to the ridge following tire tracks all the way. When they got to the base they found a dirt track that traversed it and went to the top. They rode up until they could see over it, then dismounted to look out to the flats below. They saw the old ranch place below them. It looked deserted as it should have been. There was no longer private property left this deep into BLM land. A dirt track road coming into the place was easy to spot through the sage brush. It headed south toward the highway. Clarence cupped his hand to his ear,

"You hear it Wes?"

"Sounds like a motor running. Maybe a truck is down there somewhere." Wes said.

"No, that is a generator and a good size one. Hear that chug-a-chug sound. Diesel on low idle."

"Let's ride down," Wes said, and started to move but Clarence stopped him,

"Why not? I've got my 30-30 and you got a pistol. Lets' see what's up."

"Give me a minute. Need to clean my pipes." Clarence said. He handed the reins to Wes and walked off a little way and pissed. He came back, took his canteen down and got a long drink of water. He put a fresh dip of snuff under his lip and re-mounted. Then, he pulled his hat so far down it bent his ears. Wes watched him impatiently and was smiling in a grim sort of way. Clarence knew the kid was smelling blood. He had a predator like gleam in his eye. Clarence made a mental note to keep a little salt on his tail.

"Take your time Clarence," Wes said in that mocking way he had.

"I like to be comfortable before getting into a shootout. And, if you can, always drink water before it starts because you'll get thirsty real fast and you'll stay that way the whole time. And, if you run out you'll…'lick the boots of them that's got it.' "

"Wait a minute." Wes took his canteen off his saddle and drank deep and then put it back.

"I've heard that before." He said and burped.

"Yes, it's Kipling. I lent you one of his books. So, you actually read it?" Wes nodded his head and said, "yep."

"Excellent, so ok then. We swing out to that clump of trees down on the right and watch for a minute. That looks like a high enough place for you to watch the road past the house too. If all still looks good I will ride in alone. That way you can help if I need it. No sense both of us get cornered at the same time by somebody, ok?"

"Yeah, I can see that." Wes said.

They rode down and Wes tied up in the trees. He took his rifle out of its scabbard and put a round in the chamber. Clarence waited for him to get settled...

"I'll try to stay where you can see me. That old board fence by the barn, that's where I'll tie my horse." Clarence trotted off and in a few minutes he was to the fence.

He could hear the generator loud and clear now. The barn had no windows but it had plenty of loose boards. Clarence moved around on foot and could see a pickup or two had been in and out around the front of the barn. He peered around and saw the door, it was chain and padlocked.

Clarence watched the house for a few minutes. If anyone was there he couldn't tell it, not without going up and knocking on the door anyway. That he was not going to do. He went back around the barn and boldly pulled up a loose board and stuck his head in. There were ice chests stacked up in there and at least two good size freezers running off the generator. There were rolls of meat wrapping paper and a very large butcher's block in the center of the barn floor. There were plenty of flies too and the smell of raw meat hung heavy. Clarence moved to his horse and rode back up to Wes's hiding spot.

"Mount up Wes, lets..."

"Here they come Clarence." Clarence looked and saw it too. Dust was boiling up from the road a mile or less away.

"Let's ride," Clarence said and Wes swung up so agile and quick it made Clarence feel his age.

"Wish I could still do that," Clarence said as he leaned forward in the saddle, grabbed some mane for the hill climb and touched spur.

They rode over the ridge in a full gallop, laughing like two school boys on a prank and were out of sight before the pickup ever got close enough to see them. They fox trotted their horses in the old big circle style and reached Wes's camp before nightfall. Clarence decided to stay another night. He and Wes made their plans as they gathered firewood, cooked supper, staked Clarence's horse out and wrangled a fresh one for Wes for the next day. They took shots of whiskey and before bedtime Clarence had his plan made.

"Wes, I don't want you to go anywhere near that rat's nest by yourself. I want you to go on like usual but start pushing your cattle to the northeast toward those little bumps of hill. You've seen 'em over that way?"

"Sure," Wes said.

"That's the end of your range, just the other side of them. The drainage is Camel Hump creek and its good grass. Just move them away from here as much as you can. I will have to pull in Ray and Roland and send them over to you. Wiley and Trey are in the Mountains but they'll be out any time now. They might be already. Then we'll move your camp. This grass here is about done anyway. We can't let the cattle start falling off."

"We're gonna' bust these Rustler's, aren't we?" Wes said.

"Hell yes. I will head in to the sheriff's office. We got to find that dirt track of a road in they are using, where it meets the highway. Should be easy to hold them in there. I can't see they'd try to get away across country and have to leave the tools of their trade behind. They have money invested in this thing. If they can't get any more cattle they'll move on. Might anyway if they notice our horse tracks around that place."

"That'd be too bad." Wes said.

"Let's hope they don't. We put the cattle out of their reach meanwhile. It'll work."

Wes stood and stared off at the sunset. Clarence stared too. A beautiful ribbon of orange light spread across the horizon. They stretched out on the ground by the fire and talked a little about random things. Then they caught themselves dozing off and they both turned in. Another long summer day was behind them.

Clarence rode at daylight like he said he would and Wes went to find some cattle to push toward the Camel Humps.

15

CYA

In the morning Trey and Wiley could clearly see the mess around the hunting camp. The log poles for wall tents, once neatly stacked in the trees had been pulled out and scattered. The tree cache and the few things stored up there had been pulled apart. Camp tools were scattered about on the ground beneath it. There were holes dug as well and the camp shovel from the cache was down, leaning against a rock. A large, dead tree that had fallen had been rolled. Much of this could be explained by a bear's interest but there was no bear sign, no scat, and no tracks. Claw marks should have been on the rolled tree trunk but none were there.

They did see the fresh horse droppings and pawed up ground around several trees. The bark was worn off of live trees where a horse rope had been tied long enough to scar the tree trunk. They could speculate on what happened but they had plenty to do to clean things up. If the Forest Service rode in and saw the camp that way, Wiley would have some explaining to do. It could block his approval for the license with the Outfitter's Board. They started on the Cache first and chalked it all up to vandalism, suspect Benedict Kane.

Wiley stood on a limb in the big Spruce and caught the piece of rope Trey threw up and got ready to lash the log pole in place. The old cache was getting an all new frame and decking. All the new poles, they cut from standing dead timber near the camp and drug them over horseback.

"Make a great tree house." Wiley said. Trey stood below trying to get a piece of bark out of his eye. He wasn't having much luck so Wiley came down and with the corner of a bandana helped him get it.

"We need to replace the pole above the deck too. To hang the block and tackle on." Trey said.

"I'll get it. Keep washing your eye out." Wiley swung up on his horse and rode toward another grove of dead trees. It was off a way, at the end of the largest meadow. Riding loose in his saddle, with his eyes gazing all the way across the open space, his horse suddenly jumped sideways as if it had stepped on a Rattlesnake. It was all Wiley could do to stay in the saddle. When he looked at what had spooked his horse he could see a dead mule lying in the brush. It had bloated up and the thing was crumpled like it had died suddenly on its feet and collapsed. Wiley rode past it and almost immediately came up on another mule and then he saw a dead horse. Wiley turned around and rode back to camp where Trey stood, holding a cup of coffee.

"You ain't gonna' believe this." He said to Trey. "I think somebody went nuts and killed their stock."

Trey went quickly to his horse and rode back with Wiley to have a look. Trey tried looking at each animal from the saddle but his horse kept shying away. Still, he saw the brand he had seen at the trailhead. It belonged to Benedict Kane. They rode over to the timber and tied the horses up. Both men walked back and approached the carcasses from the up-wind side. Trey looked closer now and he could see that each animal had a bullet hole behind its left ear.

"They were shot?" Wiley asked.

"Looks that way to me." Trey said. He didn't want to understand what had happened to cause this but his first thought was he did know. What he had feared, since news of Kane finding the plane came out, had come calling.

They went back to their horses and Trey noticed a strong sapling nearby. He'd almost tied his horse to it. There was a couple of pieces of cut rope at the foot of the tree and there were dark stains on the rope. There were stains at the base of the tree as well, and boot prints on the ground around it.

They rode back, gave the dead stock a wide distance and tied back up in camp. Trey pulled a canteen out and took a long pull.

"Well this trip is over. We got to go in and report this." Trey said.

"What are you thinking happened?"

"Damn if I know. If I had to guess I'd say somebody was tied to that tree facing whoever was shooting the stock."

"Why would anybody do that?" Wiley said.

"Damnit," Trey said. And he knew just as clearly as if he had seen it. Kane had some un-welcome visitors. Trey stood there with Wiley and he felt a pang of regret for not telling him about all this. He had known that if things heated up he would have to do it. This was damn sure heating up. For now, they had to get out of there. If a body was going to be discovered let the sheriff's department find it. They began to scramble and get ready to leave.

The canyon ride down was dark and cold as the sun set, and the night shadows closed in. Trey shivered just thinking about being tied to that tree and knowing it could be him. He felt exposed riding down into the canyon. Wiley was out front with no idea of what could lie ahead, on the trail or at the base camp corrals. Trey started to ride out and get ahead of him to meet any danger first, but Wiley disappeared into a thick stand of timber as the night fell around them. It grew so dark that Trey never caught sight of him again, not until they rode into the trailhead and a campfire glowed across the road and silhouetted Wiley as he rode past it.

Trey drew his coat collar up from the chill. He reached and felt his pistol for comfort and cleared it from his coat. The sickening thought of Wiley and him riding right into a gang of outlaws seemed real and his shivers came from more than just the night air.

They stripped the saddles, put the stock up and fed. They dropped the trailer in place, left it and drove straight into Two Ocean. They made the report to the night dispatch at the county Sheriff's office. She thought it was important enough to call the sheriff at home and apparently, he did too. He said for them to come to his house right away. It was almost mid-night when they got there. Trey told the sheriff that the dead stock carried the Kane brand.

The sheriff said he had already been out to Kane's home. He went out after the Forest Service had called him to find out who owned the stock and the truck and trailer. No one was home but they discovered the house had been broken into. They had seen enough to treat it like a robbery.

The sheriff asked Trey to take him into the wilderness camp as early in the morning as possible. Trey turned to Wiley and said,

"Will you do it? I have to get back to the ranch."

"The county will pay you." The sheriff said.

"Sure, no-sense in both of us going back in." Wiley answered.

Trey dropped Wiley off at a motel on the way out. Trey went in and paid for it. The sheriff was Wiley's ride for the morning and Trey, or somebody from the 2/c would pick him up at the trailhead when he came back out. Trey helped Wiley carry his bedroll and saddle into the room.

"You be careful. And stay armed."

"The Sheriff will be there." Wiley said."

"Don't forget the Bears will be on the kill," Trey answered.

Trey arrived at the 2/c in the wee hours of the morning. He found Roland, Ray and Clarence just struggling out of bed and trying to get a start on the day. Trey startled Ray in the kitchen and asked him, accusingly,

"What the hell are you doing here?"

"I brought them in. They are going out to Wes's range." Clarence hollered from his corner of the bunkhouse.

"They will help him move all his cattle over to the Camel Hump drainage and then help him move his camp. So, where is Wiley? I kind of need him."

Trey shook his head and was so tired he could hardly think. It was early to move the cattle, or was it?

"I have to get some sleep. What time is it?" Trey said. His voice revealed a gnarly mood and Clarence could tell it.

"Four am." Clarence said. "Go now, go sleep. We'll talk later. You already barked Ray's head off."

Trey went to his bunk, pulled his boots off and lay down on top of his bedding. As the sun came up Clarence walked out to send Ray and Roland on their way.

With the trailer loaded with two of Clarence's horses, Ray and Roland got in the truck. Clarence leaned down to speak to them.

"Like I told you, just Camp yourselves at roads end. Don't bother to move your stuff to Wes's camp. Just go there to tell him what we are doing. He's expecting you. Start bringing his gear and camp out to where you left the truck. It's closer to the Camel Hump on this here road and you can haul your gear in the truck much of the way." Clarence pointed to it on the map, again.

"You are all three to carry your rifles and you are all three to stay together as much as possible. I doubt these rustlers are dangerous, but if you happen to run into them I have to tell you to leave them alone."

"My ass, leave 'em alone." Raymond said,

"That's what I thought you'd say, but the point is to move the cattle, not get in a fight. If you get shot there is nobody to move the cattle, ok?" Clarence said matter-of-factly.

Clarence saw Raymond glance at Roland and though it was only a split-second look, it was telling. Clarence thought he and Trey were going to have to get out there and do something quick. Cowboy herders build up a lot of potent energy in their lonely life. It was a thing that could explode. Clarence had seen it happen.

The boys drove off. They had bread, sandwich meat, cans of beans and beer in their ice chest. They took horse feed and had their rifles. They looked pretty punchy pulling the trailer out with the bed-rolls and saddles stacked in the back of the truck. 'Living the life,' Clarence thought. He had been slow to warm to them but he was getting to be kind of proud of this cow crew.

Clarence went back into the house and to his padlocked closet. He opened it and drug out the foot locker. He got out a couple of his rifles and pistols and set them out on his bunk. The longer barreled rifles, in gun cases, came out from the closet corner as well. Then Clarence picked his weapons of choice and started to wipe them down.

At a few minutes before noon Clarence re-heated the coffee, poured a cup and went to a chair beside Trey's bunk and sat down. He sipped the coffee and stared at his friend and waited. It was only a moment that passed before Trey opened one eye and said,

"We got to talk."

"Yes, we do." Clarence answered. Then he got up and went into the kitchen and waited for Trey to stagger in. When he came in Clarence poured him coffee and then waited some more. Trey was sitting there, not saying a word. Finally, Clarence got up and went to the cabinet and took out the bottle of whiskey, poured a shot and set the glass down in front of Trey.

"Will that help?" Clarence said.

"I thought you'd never ask," Trey said. "Man have I got a story for you." He tossed the whiskey down and chased it with the coffee.

"Not as good as mine." Clarence said. "We got a real problem."

"Not like this one," Trey said.

Clarence stared at him blankly and wondered if Trey already knew about the rustlers somehow. Then, Trey started talking and Clarence could do nothing but listen carefully to every word of it. When he was finished Trey drank his coffee and waited for a response.

"So, you think that was Kane tied to the tree.?" Clarence said,

"The new truck and trailer means he found some money, is what I think. Some bad people have showed up. I think it was money I failed to find. Kane must have opened the wreck up some more and gotten into the pilot's cabin. I don't know how he did that but,"

"But, he is a stubborn and industrious man." Clarence finished Trey's sentence. "I'd say that fits him."

"Damn Clarence, I should have made sure that plane was cleaned out."

"Don't go thinking that. Kane would still have reported the plane found and these guys were always out there. We knew that going in. We need to talk to Weismann."

They got in Trey's truck and drove up the little mountain beside the ranch's horse pasture to get a strong signal for the truck phone. Trey called Weismann's office and the secretary answered.

She told Trey that Mr. Weismann was on vacation and would be for another month. But, she could give him a message. Trey told her to hold. He looked at Clarence…

"What do we say?" Trey said,

"Nothing, we ain't got a month. Tell her never mind, we'll call her back if we need to." Trey did that and hung up.

"We have to handle this ourselves." Clarence said.

"Tell me about it. So now, what's your story?"

"I'll tell you on the way." Clarence said. "We need to drive to the trailhead and get our stock. You got men shooting people's horses. We need to get Wiley back too. You need to find out what the Sheriff found up at the hunting camp. There are bad people looking for us. They just don't know who the 'us' is yet. It's time to circle the wagons."

"And, it's time to arm ourselves." Trey added.

They drove back to the bunkhouse. Clarence selected his lighter, semi-auto rifles. One for Trey and one for himself. Trey had his own pistol strapped on and he picked up his shotgun too. Clarence kept an old army sack full of loaded clips for his weapons. He grabbed it.

As they drove out Clarence told Trey the story about the rustler camp on Wes's range. He told Trey the boys were moving the cattle. When he finished, Trey drove quiet for several minutes.

"Well, what do you think? Clarence said…

"When it rains it pours." Trey answered.

"Don't it though."

"Well, let's just do one thing at a time as long as we can. I'm thinking don't report the rustling, not yet. Damn good idea with the boys together and moving the cattle by the way." Trey said.

Clarence watched the tree tops go by down below them, along the river canyon that ran beside the road. He had a flashback to a helicopter ride in 'Nam. He was watching tree tops go by then too. It was a beautiful country and he could see that, but only in brief moments. Mostly, he saw it as a treacherous place to be. It was a time that he thought he would never see Wyoming again. He would say goodbye to his home each time his boots hit that bloody ground. It's how he would cue in his awareness and do a reality check. It was how he stayed focused on staying alive out there. Now, he was thinking like that again. Deep inside he was always saying goodbye. He'd done it his entire life.

"Come then and welcome life's last day." Clarence said. Trey looked over at him,

"What the hell does that mean?" Trey said.

"Ahh, ah, Faust speaking, I think."

"Oh, well I should have known." Trey answered sarcastically.

***

Casey had just walked into work through the side door of the restaurant when Marcos got her attention and waved her to come back into the kitchen. She went back and Helena Gomez was there.

"I need to talk to you Ms. Casey, it's important." Helena said. Marcos stood beside her with a concerned look on his face. They walked back into the tiny office and Marcos closed the door as he stepped inside with them. Helena started talking.

"There was a man that came to see me this morning. I was in the parking lot getting ready to drive to work when he approached me. It scared me, but I remember him from my brother. He kept his distance and told me something. He said he wanted to talk to the Double Dagger Ranch hands about some business but he did not know how to find them. He said he had called the ranch phone number and that phone is disconnected. I told him Marcos knows these guys. This is where it gets weird Ms. Casey. He said he knew my brother and that he was sorry to know he perished in the plane crash. My brother had some associates I was always afraid of and I came here to tell Marcos because I think I should not have sent that man here."

Casey looked over at Marcos and said.

"Has he talked to you?"

"No."

Casey looked back at Helena and realized the woman was very nervous, even trembling a little.

"I don't understand Helena. Why are you so upset?"

"I think I know who this man is. He is a gringo that speaks fluent Spanish. He works for bad people down south. If he is who I think of then I might have put Marcos in a bad place."

"Who is this again?" Casey said,

"Cartel, this man is Cartel..." Helena answered.

"Should we call the police?" Casey said, Both Marcos and Helena shook their heads, no.

"Why not?" Casey said.

"Miss Casey, these men cannot be handled like that. They just disappear for a while. But, they always come back. When they come back they get even." Helena said.

"Have you ever been out to see Clarence and the crew?" Casey asked Marcos.

"No, but I have Trey's phone number. I don't know where they are."

"Give the number to Helena in case they bother her again she can give it to them." Casey said.

"We'll get the man's phone number and tell him we'll have somebody call him. That should work, right?" Casey said.

Helena shrugged her shoulders. Marcos wrote down Trey's phone number and gave it to Helena just in case they contacted her again.

Later, in the afternoon, when business was slow, a man came to the back door. Casey could sense the man's tension as soon as she saw him. He told her he wanted to talk to the Dagger Ranch people. Casey took her receipt book from her apron, tore off a blank receipt and turned it over on the pad. She handed that to the man with her pen.

"Write a number down where you can be reached and someone will get back to you." Then Marcos gave the man Trey's number as well. When the man left, Casey and Marcos looked at the receipt. The man had written a phone number and beneath it he had written,

"Get them to call me right away."

***

When Trey and Clarence drove into the parking area of the trailhead there was a Sheriff's Department squad car parked just off the road at the entry. The Deputy was just sitting there. Trey, pulled up by the car's driver side and stopped as the deputy held up his hand suggesting the same.

"You stopping people?" Trey said.

"No, not really. More like noticing people. You're Double Dagger Ranch, I know you. Hello Mr. Colton." The deputy nodded at Clarence who waved back.

There was a crackle on the radio and someone said, "Commo-check." The deputy lifted his mike and said, "Copy that, loud and clear," and put the mike back down.

"Can you talk to them up there?" Trey said.

"Well, nearly. There's a deputy on top of the mountain that relays the calls from the guys in camp on the other side. I'm the go-for if they need anything."

"One of my hands is up there and I need him. Any idea when he'll be out?"

"I can call up. It'll take a few minutes to relay and get back to me."

"Ok, we'll be over at our corrals feeding the stock."

The Forest Service truck was there with another truck and horse trailer as well and the Game Warden's rig was nearby.

"Looks like plenty of people gone in." Trey said.

"All hands-on deck." Clarence said.

They both got out, pulled on their work gloves and moved to the hay pile. They stuffed the hay racks around the pen and as they worked the Deputy walked over and told them Wiley was on his way out now. He said that he'd started riding out about an hour ago.

Trey went to his truck and borrowing a blank sheet of paper from Clarence's notebook and scribbled a note to Wiley to wait there. They would be back for him around dark. He put the note in the can tied to the gate and used for a mailbox. Trey did not expect him out any sooner. He wanted to go into town and sniff the wind a little. Clarence put three beers in the water trough to stay cold. Wiley would find them. It was a long-honored custom among them and they did it for each other whenever they could.

***

Casey and Marcos sat at the restaurant table with Trey and Clarence and told them about their visitor.

"Helena told us the man was a business associate of her brothers and had been a long time." Casey said. Casey gave Trey the phone number the man had given her.

Clarence had heard enough. He excused himself, got up and walked out of the restaurant. Casey's eyes followed him out and when she looked back at Trey he just shrugged his shoulders.

When Clarence came back he had the topo map for the leased land they were grazing. He sat down, opened it and they all moved the table settings to make room for it. With the map spread, he studied it closely. He had his spectacles on and his nose practically touched the map. They waited.

Marcos said he needed to cook the hamburgers they ordered. He went back to the kitchen. Casey sat and looked at Clarence and said,

"So?"

"So, whiskey and beer for me and Trey. Send a shot back to Marcos too."

"We don't let our employees drink on duty," she said.

"Make an exception," Clarence said curtly. Casey looked at him a moment and she started to say something. Clarence turned his face up and gave her a look from the corner of his eye that had been completely unknown to her the entire time she had known him. It was a little wild, like the blank stare of an animal looking at you. She decided not to say another word. She got up and went to the bar. Clarence turned the map to Trey and pointed to a particular spot on it.

"So, what?" Trey said.

"It's the rustler's camp. When you call give the Cartel directions to it here, where the dirt track road meets the highway. They must talk to us again to get the exact directions to our location. That will be this old homestead. But, we hold out on that info' until we are ready."

Casey came back with the drinks and set them down. Clarence sent her back to her office for sheets of blank paper. Marcos came out with the bag of burgers. Clarence looked at Casey and said,

"Will you go call Ilene and see if she is all right?"

Casey said, "Sure" and went to the phone at the bar and called the Dagger Ranch Headquarters number and got the disconnected recording. When she came back with that news Clarence said to Trey,

"We need to drive by there and check on her."

In the Restaurant parking lot Trey checked his messages. He had one. The Cartel had gotten his phone number, it was game on...

***

The Dagger Ranch entrance gate was wide open. Trey drove up to Jay and Ilene's house and the lights were on. There was a strange pickup and cargo trailer backed up to her porch. The dogs came out barking and Ilene came out to see at what."

"You are really moving away?" Clarence said it in disbelief. "Why'd you not call me?"

Inside the house boxes were everywhere. One of Ilene's daughters and son-in-law were there. Clarence stood with his hat in his hand, in guilty dejection. He shook hands with them.

"I should be helping with this," Clarence said. The look on his face was sheer pain and all saw it as it hit him. This would complete the separation from his old life. The recognition of all he knew of home and family, the last of it was packing up and leaving. All the years and memories were being packed away to a storage building somewhere and maybe forever. Trey thought for a second that Clarence was going to turn and run out of the house. But, Ilene had him by the arm and took him into the kitchen. She sat him down and started making coffee. Trey reached for the kitchen door and started to close it when Ilene looked at him. She nodded at the door and he knew he was doing the right thing. He eased it shut and turned to her daughter and son-in-law and said,

"I think they are going to need a minute." Ilene's daughter grasped it instantly and took her husband to a back room where they could continue packing boxes.

"I need to run over to the ranch bunkhouse for a minute. Tell Clarence I'll be right back." Trey said to them.

He drove down to the bunkhouse. There was a light on and a familiar pickup truck parked in front. He stopped, got out and knocked. A man came to the door and Trey was glad to see it was somebody he knew, Ralph Meeks, one of the farm hands. He greeted Trey warmly and invited him in, but Trey said no.

"Meeks, do you know if there is some harness left out at the big barn. I bought a set at the auction and when I got home I didn't have the britchens." Trey lied,

"Trey, I don't know. I haven't been down there."

"Is it locked?"

"Yes, I have the key." Meeks walked off to a shelf and rummaged around for a minute, then said,

"Here it is, want me to go with you."

"No, this won't take long. Looks like you're already settled in for the night anyway."

"Need a flashlight?" Meeks said.

"Nope, thanks, got one of those too. Be right back." Trey knew every bump and turn and he drove it fast. It had come to him unexpectedly, that there was something he might be able to use. It was a half-baked idea for now but sometimes you have to follow your instincts.

Trey drove straight up to the big barn doors. Leaving his truck running and the headlights on, he unlocked and pulled one side open to let the truck lights shine in. He took his flashlight from the truck and went to the loft ladder and climbed it. He scared up pigeons in the ceiling rafters and jumped through his skin at the sound. Other than the birds the place was so empty there was a weight to it. He stepped out on the solid loft floor and went to the corner where the ceiling joist beams intersected the wall. He reached over the top of the huge beam and retrieved the back pack with the bundles. He went back to the ladder and climbed down, closed the barn door, locked it and left.

Trey dropped the key on his way out. When he pulled up at Ilene's, her daughter and son-in-law were placing things in the trailer by porch light and Clarence was standing out with Ilene still talking. He had a big box under his arm and started down the steps to the truck. Trey left it running and got out to say goodnight. Ilene came down and gave him a warm hug. He wished her luck and as he walked back to the truck and got in she said,

"You both come see me anytime. Keep me up-dated on the Hunting Outfit."

"I will Ilene. I will talk to you soon. This LLC we are working for will buy it, so money is coming." Trey answered.

She watched them as they backed out. She stood with her legs spread slightly and her hands on her hips like she always did. Clarence could see her figure silhouetted against the porch light. Then, as she turned away he saw the glint of the tears coming down her cheek and he saw her wipe them with her wrist bent. He blinked his old eyes and they came in focused. A burning pain caught in his throat.

Trey drove to the highway and turned toward the road to the trailhead. They would gather up Wiley and the stock.

"Your idea on giving these guys a false location for us, what is it you are thinking?" Trey said as he drove.

"We had to give Marty and Casey a break." Clarence said wearily.

"It'll give the Cartel something to stay focused on, which is us instead of them."

"And, it's the rustler's location?" Trey said.

"It's close. There is a deserted homestead down that road. The rustlers are there and it's a place we can get to from off road, you know, horseback from the Conant lease. Maybe set something up, incognito. We can get a look at them without giving ourselves away? Hell, I don't know. Just looking for some leverage. We could never be trapped there, only they could. Where did you go?"

"I went over to the bunkhouse. Meeks is living there. He's the caretaker."

"Oh. Well good for him." Clarence said. "Guess they are cutting hay about now?"

"I didn't ask. Sure be a waste not too. What's in the box?"

"Pictures, Ilene thought there were some I should have." Clarence answered.

"Now, what do I tell Wiley? We got about thirty more minutes to the trail head and a couple of hours drive back to the 2/c. He's going to be sitting in here with us. I say I tell him, we tell him." Trey said.

Clarence went silent. Trey waited for it, for more from him. But when they drove into the trailhead and saw Wiley in the headlights that word had not come. Just as Trey pulled to a stop... Clarence said,

"Yes, you got to tell him everything. I say you can trust him."

Clarence got out. Trey rolled his windows down to hear and watched his side mirrors. A flashlight shown on the fifth wheel, Clarence dropped the tailgate and Trey backed up to the trailer. He saw the fist closed signal to stop in the red of the backup lights. Wiley hopped in the truck bed and Clarence lowered the trailer. Wiley saw it dead on, latched down the hitch and jumped out. Clarence plugged in the taillights and when they signaled clear Trey pulled up so they had plenty of room to load the horses. Then he set the brake and he got out too.

It was all done in the dark, with a flashlight and Wiley's headlamp and three men who had worked together at things like this so long it had become effortless. In those minutes of silent and mutually shared labor, Trey felt his confidence building. It was getting stronger all the time.

Clarence's idea on getting the Cartel guys off like that, on a road to nowhere, was a good one. Trey may have been wrong to leave Wiley out of the loop this long but that was about to change and change tonight. It is a good moment when a man realizes he is with friends he can trust. Men who can prove that trust and will.

Trey grabbed a cold six-pack from his ice chest and sat it in the backseat of his truck. He stepped to Clarence and said,

"Let Wiley ride up front."

"Sure," Clarence said. "I'll serve the beer and Burgers. Let's get going."

Clarence popped three beers and handed two forward. Wiley grabbed his first burger and tore into it like a starved animal. Clarence had gotten him two of them. He took Trey's and passed it forward, then started on his own.

They pulled past the Deputy and waved, then out to the highway and Trey got the truck up to speed. Wiley slashed through his hamburger and Trey finished his as well. With a break in the eating Trey said,

"So, what happened up there?"

Wiley started talking and was still talking almost an hour later. He said the Sheriff and the USFS were treating the place like a crime scene. The bloody rope had been sent out for analysis and they had called in a helicopter to carry the samples out. They had also extracted the bullet rounds from the horse and mule heads and sent those out. The Game and Fish ended up sedating three different bears to get the evidence from the dead animals. There was preliminary searching for Kane. His x-wife and children had not heard from him for a while but they said that was not unusual. Deputies were in Two Ocean trying to locate him. The rest Trey already knew.

"They are about to bring people in to start a search party. I think that's next if Kane don't show up." Wiley said.

In a wide picnic spot at the top of a hill Trey slowed and pulled in. They all got out and took a leak. Clarence grabbed another six-pack from the back of the truck cooler. Trey put his flashers on, set the brake, got out and walked around the stock trailer. He kicked tires, checked tail lights and looked through the bars at the horses. Everything was good. He called Wiley over to the picnic table. Clarence walked over too. Wiley stood facing Trey who sat on top of the picnic table, his arms on his knees and his feet on the bench. He started talking.

"Wiley, when we were up at the camp last fall hunting, I found the plane. You'd ridden out with your Elk. The rumor all these years was true. I found the money the plane was always said to hold. I didn't tell you because I didn't want to involve you in something illegal. I wanted to think it through and I can see now that from the start I was thinking I would keep it. I just did not know how you would take that. I've always known you to be an honest man. I told Clarence about it because he's got that old outlaw spirit and he is well experienced in life. We decided best was to keep our mouths shut and find a way to include you, Ilene too, maybe the boys once we were past this hard part.

The thing is we could not throw the cash around. I can tell you the business set-up another time, but I will tell you the 2/c is ours and you're getting a cut. It's the hunting outfit. You'll own part of it, maybe all of it If we start making money off the 2/c. Right now, the 2/c has to buy it from Ilene. You'll have all the equipment you need, pack mules too. Everything you need to make it work. You can keep profits when the camp is running, when we are in the black on the business end. Meanwhile, you got a job, no overhead for you and I can get some additional money, bonus money if you will, to you after we sell the cattle from our first season."

Wiley had not taken a drink of his beer or changed position while Trey talked. He just stood there silent in the dark. Clarence slapped him on the back and said,

"Trey counted you in all along. I can vouch for that."

"I don't know what to say…" Wiley answered.

"It's coming around now." Trey continued, "The Drug cartel are here looking for that money. They contacted Miss Casey and Marcos. Since Kane was the one reported the plane found they went after him. I think he found some of the money I'd missed. I know he was in the mountains when you and I were. He must have pointed a finger at us. He was using our camp to scab out of after you and I had packed out. I rode up on them in the dark going back in but I didn't ride into camp. I turned around and rode for a camp closer to the plane. Maybe he saw me. The Cartel are trying to find me and you. I left them my phone number and an idea of where we are. Still, not directly to the 2/c, but in our direction."

"Why?" Wiley asked.

"To get them off Marty and Casey's ass." Clarence answered.

"Had to do it." Trey added.

"Wiley, you don't have to get involved. You had a right to know in case there is going to be a confrontation. The shooting of Kane's stock and him disappeared tells me they mean business their way. Hope you see it as better late than never that I told you."

"You old fuckers," Wiley said, as his tired, half-drunk mind began to grasp what he was hearing.

"If you want I will give you a chunk of cash and you can take off.

No hard feelings if you do." Trey said.

"That goes for me too." Clarence said.

Wiley looked at them with that half-baked grin of his. Then, he looked down at his spread-eagled feet and spit between his boots. He finally took a long pull on his beer, belched and said...

"Sounds like you guys are in it up to your necks. I wouldn't back away from you now anyways, hell our season ain't even over yet."

"All-right then!" Trey said with conviction. Trey stood up and shook hands with Wiley and said,

"Let's get home."

They drove. In the short time left of the drive Clarence, with arms resting on the back of the front seat and his head close between Trey and Wiley in the front, told the story about the rustlers and what Wes and the boys were up to. They drove into the 2/c, took care of the horses, then walked into the bunkhouse and went to bed.

In Wyoming, in summer, a cowboy can work fourteen hours in daylight and go through two remounts to do it. It doesn't take much after that to push it to a sixteen-hour work day. That hour, before sunrise to get somewhere, that hour after sunset to get back. Then, unsaddle, feed your horse and you are there. The take on this has been spoken of for many years in ranching and Cowboy country. You sleep in the winter. In the short summer's long days, you needed to have push and you needed to have a lot of heart.

16

Cartel

Tony was starting to hate working with Chalito. The man moved too aggressively for Tony's style. When Chalito took over the questioning of the man Kane, he really turned up the pain level. Tying Kane up and then making him watch while Chalito shot his mules, then his best horse, that was Tony's suggestion. It was the physical torture that took it over the top and it was all Chalito and Vaca doing it. Tony sat that part out. He wanted Kane to take them to his home and that hiding place, himself. Then, if it was not all there, they could continue questioning him. But, somewhere in the process of torturing him physically, the man died on them.

Tony tried to give Chalito some shit about that. While he complained to the man for killing Kane, all Chalito did was stand there and smile at him and shake his head. Finally, Chalito interrupted Tony and said,

"That's not why he died. He could take the pain. I've been doing this shit a long time."

"Well, what the fuck killed him then?" Tony said angrily.

"He died of shame man."

***

Tony chose to start with Helena Gomez. She was a local and if she remembered anything about him working with her brother she would help, just for that reason. Family members of Cartel are aware of their obligation to cooperate whenever it becomes necessary.

Tony was also certain he was the only one that should see her. He did not trust Chalito with it. The man would have kidnapped her, questioned her and then killed her. He was the perfect black-hearted criminal, no quarter and no remorse. So, Tony kept her identity to himself and now he had a phone number.

Tony sat in his room and made the phone call. Chalito and Vaca were watching TV in the next room. They were drinking beer and eating pizza. Tony dialed and got a voice recording.

"Mr. Trey this is a friend of Mr. Kane. It seems you may have something of ours. Mr. Kane said I should call you. We need to meet very soon." Then he left his phone number and hung up.

***

Trey and Clarence went straight to the hilltop calling spot the morning after picking up Wiley. Wiley had started the day with the hot shower he had been too tired to take the night before. They left him too it and went to the truck. Clarence brought the map. He again showed Trey the location of the old homestead the rustlers were using.

"We need to bide for a little time but here's my idea…" Clarence said.

"We get these drug people to meet us there." Clarence pointed with his pencil and circled the intersection of the Homestead road and the highway.

"It's a ten mile drive in from the highway and only the one road back out." Trey stared at the spot on the map and waited for more.

"I mean to tie them in with the rustlers," Clarence said, "We can cover the back and sides ourselves. Let the Sheriff have the road out."

"With Wiley in that's three of us, but the rest of the crew, do we have to involve them?" Trey said.

"They will be up for this like a jackass eating' briars. They'll love it. Wes is so damn mad about losing 2/c cattle on his watch he can hardly see straight. We go in horseback. Be a big advantage out there in that rough country. If anything goes wrong they won't be able to chase us but we can damn well chase them."

"We're taking a risk with our crew." Trey said.

"Well shit, we didn't tell them to steal 2/c cattle or to make Benedict Kane disappear. I'm saying Wes, Ray and Roland are with us on this. These rustlers and Cartel just get what's coming to 'em. Think they can come up here to our country and push us around? That's bullshit and you know it. Just because the government lets them run all over the country doing what they want don't mean we have to."

"Our Sheriff in Two Ocean has his hands full now." Trey said.

"Leave him out of it. We call the Sheriff here in Wilford county. It's their jurisdiction." Clarence said.

"Right," Trey had forgotten that. "But, all they would know was they were coming after rustlers. Cartel is another thing."

"Can't be helped. All we know is they are rustlers. We need to remember that. They all get arrested and we'll be out of here and long gone before any of 'em get out of jail. We need to ship the cattle in about sixty days anyway. Let's hold onto what we got and stick it to the bastards." Clarence stopped for a minute, caught his breath, then said,

"How long you think they'd get for rustling?"

"Not enough. They might just get deported. Then they can come right back at us." As he spoke Trey remembered he had something to up the ante.

Trey dropped his tail gate and crawled in the back of his pickup. Clarence stepped to the bed rail. Trey opened his tool box and pulled out the day pack. He removed a package and handed it to Clarence.

"I think it's cocaine." Trey said.

"Yeah, I do too." Clarence hefted it and set it down.

"You get caught with that Trey, you're going to have a lot of ex-plaining to do."

"I'm not going to get caught with it, they are. I'm thinking we salt the rustler's place with it."

Clarence's face lit up. He remembered Trey having to go back into the mountains for it. But Clarence had never asked what he had done with it. He didn't want to know.

"I thought you destroyed this? Clarence said.

"I wasn't sure how to. Burn it, dump it in the river, maybe it'd cause a fish kill for all I know. I hid it till I could get back to it. It was up in the big barn loft all this time. But, when this contact from the Cartel happened I thought I'd better get it. I thought maybe we could use it to get past them some way, a bargain chip maybe."

"This plan is getting better." Clarence said. "We got to decide now, when and how to bring in the law."

"I got to call the Cartel guy first. What do you think I should say?"

"Tell him we will call him tonight. Say something that sounds like you are going to cooperate but need a little time to put it together. Just keep it simple." Trey made the call.

"Hello, what is your name again?" Trey said.

"I am Tony. And yours?"

"You can call me Trey."

"Trey, you know of what I am talking about. You have something of ours." Tony said.

"I am going to have to call you back later tonight."

"Just tell me you know exactly what I want and that you will give it to me very soon." Tony said.

Damnit, Trey thought. He did not want to say it, to have it out there like this, on the phone. It sounded too much like a confession. He searched for a response,

"Where is Mr. Kane?" Trey asked on sheer impulse. "Let me talk to him." There was silence on the other end and Trey knew in that silent moment he had said the right thing.

"You will call me tonight, about what time?" Tony finally answered.

"Between ten and eleven P.M." Trey said.

"Ok, I'll be waiting." And the man hung up.

***

Tony sat on the bed in his motel room and could not help thinking he had just talked to another dead man. It did not matter if this Trey had anything or not. Chalito would kill him anyway. And Tony didn't think he should prevent it. They were approaching that time in the crime when it needed to be finished. It was time to get out of this country and go. The longer they were exposed in their collection process the more the risk of getting caught.

This Trey was probably the last lead they were likely to get. But maybe, just maybe the guy would come through. He would give them the money and then all they had to do was kill him and anybody with him and get the hell out of there. No agonizing hours of watching a man moaning and twisting in pain. Watching this drawn out torture shit was too much to have to endure. It struck a deep nerve in Tony. That look, on Chalito's face when they argued, was telling. The look implied, someday it might be you. And, that would be fine with Chalito. Tony was certain of it. Tony went to the mirror and smiled into it at himself and put his right fist over his heart, pumped it and said,

"Not if I get you first Mother Fucker." Then he ducked out of the Motel to grab something to eat. He went to the next room and knocked. Vaca opened the door and Tony stepped in.

"I'm going out for some chow. You want anything?" They both said no. Pizza boxes and beer bottles were everywhere and an American Movie was on TV in Spanish. These guys were dug in and content. When Chalito ask how things were going Tony gave him thumbs up and said they would be moving to collect soon, perhaps the next day. Chalito grinned and he and Vaca toasted it together. Tony pointed to the half empty tequila bottle and said,

"Take it easy," in Spanish. Chalito nodded in a friendly manner and Tony gave him his best professional look and nodded back. It was just a little conspiratorial moment that Tony thought would keep up the good mood they were showing. The commission for this collection would be large for all of them. It had a better chance of success if they cooperated with each other. Even a depraved, Mexican Cartel killer knew that.

***

The three of them saddled up at the 2/c headquarters and loaded the horses in the trailer. They each carried a pistol and a rifle, water and a lunch. Trey had his binoculars and Clarence carried his old spotting scope. They drove out the back gate of the Conant Ranch, headed cross country on rough road and got as close as they could get to the homestead and keep everything mechanical in one piece. Then they un-loaded the horses and rode toward the long ridge of ground Clarence and Wes had used before.

"Now what." Wiley said.

"Pick some advantage points we can use to watch the place and block off escape routes." Clarence said.

There was a drainage, parallel to and about five hundred yards from the house and barn. It had a full view of the place and it would provide a natural escape for the rustlers that the sheriff would not be able to cover from the road.

"Wes and Ray here," Clarence said. "You and me over the ridge and behind the barn."

Clarence showed them on his map where he had marked a three or four-hundred-foot rise off the sage flats. It was further down along the road. It looked to hold a great view in both directions.

"Somebody has to be there..." Trey agreed.

"With a two-way radio." Wiley added.

For now, to really know, they had to ride to it and they did. Finally, all three lay on their bellies behind the rocks, on the top of that hill. It was a perfect place to control things, to watch and radio to others. They rested there, took lunch and talked about it.

"Damn, I'm glad we did this," Wiley said. "It's like a forward observer post in the Army."

"Glad you like it. It's your spot." Clarence said. Clarence took the binoculars and looked away toward the East.

"Where's our truck and trailer you think?" He said.

Trey sat up and pointed east, northeast, "There," he said. Clarence studied the spot through his glass and sure enough he could see the faint glint of metal. He pointed to it and said,

"There, eleven o'clock, get yourselves oriented. I've seen enough, let's go,"

They rode silent until they were well away and then to make some time up, they kicked into a good smooth trot and began to cover ground. They reached the truck and trailer. The Camel Humps were barely in sight from where they stood. Clarence looked at Wiley and while pointing out the direction said,

"We need you to go get Wes and the boys. Tell them we are picking them up in the morning. They need to ride a fresh horse." Clarence had the map out again and showed Wiley the nearest point he could drive to and meet in the morning.

"I'll meet you here." Clarence said, "Or Trey will. They are supposed to be sticking together. He's camped here." Clarence said, and pointed again at a place on the map.

"How far you think?" Wiley asked.

"Easy twelve miles. You should be there in two, three hours. I'll meet you with the stock trailer at daybreak tomorrow. I'll be trying to get you all back to headquarters by noon. I'm thinking this will be set to happen tomorrow night, or the next."

"What do I tell Wes and them?" Wiley said.

"That we are going after the rustlers and with the Sheriff's Department with us. That's all they need to know." Trey answered. Wiley looked at him, a questioning look and Clarence picked it up...

"Wiley, this money, the 2/c, us, we all got to keep our cards close in this game. Later maybe, we can tell them the whole story."

"I got you boss." Wiley said, and in a swinging trot, on his leggy bay, rode toward the Camel Hump drainage.

"He's going to make good time." Clarence said as he watched him go.

***

When Trey and Clarence got back to the bunkhouse they

unloaded the horses and dropped the trailer. Clarence drove alone up the hill to make the call to the Wilford county Sheriff's office.

"The Sheriff is not in now. Can I take a message?" a woman answered.

"Yes, I'm Clarence Colton. I'm one of the ranchers running cattle out on the Conant homestead. I need to see him."

"What is it about?"

"Cattle theft." Clarence answered.

"Oh, well hold on, let me radio him." Clarence waited. He could hear her talking but nothing else. She came back on.

"Can it wait till morning?" She said."

"That's fine, see you in the morning, first thing." Clarence said.

"He gets in at eight," she answered and hung up.

Clarence drove back down the hill and went in the bunkhouse. He looked out the kitchen window at the ghost grass swaying in the wind and hoped for an intuition. But he didn't get one. Trey still had to make his call. That would be later that night. Clarence spread a newspaper down on the table and started cleaning a gun.

***

At ten p.m. Tony took the expected call alone in his room.

"Do you have it?" Tony said.

"No, not now. You got a map?" Trey answered.

Tony told him to hold, got his map and went back to the phone. Trey guided him to the intersection location. He was counting on the man having a Wyoming highway map, only. That would not show any road into the BLM land.

"Is that it?" Tony said.

"No, we are going to have to talk about that. I'll have to give you further directions. I just want you to know I am working on getting this done. Don't bother to come before five thirty pm, day after tomorrow," Trey said.

"Why so late in the day?" Tony asked.

"It will be the best time for me to meet my end." Trey said. Then he listened to the silence that followed and waited.

Tony didn't like it. This place was isolated and perfect to set him up.

"Just drive to that spot in the road, tell me what you'll be driving and give me what I have come for and that's it." Tony said.

"The place we are going to, where your property is located, is nearby. I can't risk you going to the exact location without me. We just stop on the side of the road and anybody could drive up, even a cop." Trey stopped talking and waited. Then sensing the need to stay aggressive, he spoke again,

"Come on time. Don't be early, don't be late. We don't want to miss each other."

"Hold on a minute," Tony said. He sat on his bed in the motel with the phone to his ear. He started to run the scenario over in his mind. He had plenty of experience dealing in the USA. His experience was that Anglo's will back down to Cartel. He'd even seen an American National Guard unit back away once, down on the Naco line in Arizona. And, if Chalito wanted to kill these guys it would be best to have some privacy anyway.

"Ok, I'll see you Friday at five p.m. At that place you said. Ok?"

"Ok," Trey said and hung up.

Trey sat in his truck after the call and stared out at the hills shining blue against the night sky. It was Wednesday night. He had all day Thursday and part of Friday to get ready. That should give the Sheriff enough time. Now It was up to Clarence to convince the lawman. Then they would reach their moment of truth.

A different truth said that once upon a time Trey would have never gotten into anything like this. Not even close. 'Just ride out with the loot, my ass'...he thought to himself.

Trey drove down to the bunkhouse. His adrenaline had been pumping and he took some shots of Bourbon while standing in the kitchen. Clarence was down in his bunk but he spoke from the darkness.

"Is it ok?" Clarence said.

"Yeah, for Friday evening after five. They still need the rest of the directions, from the intersection."

"We'll figure it out. Get some sleep." Clarence said.

***

Clarence heard Trey get up. With a groan Clarence rose and put the coffee on. When Trey came into the kitchen Clarence had fried a couple of eggs, put them between buttered toast and set the plate out. Clarence served Trey's coffee in a go cup with lid and put a sack of sandwiches on the table. Clarence filled the Thermos with hot coffee while Trey ate his breakfast.

"When are you leaving?" Trey said,

"Six. I meet the Sheriff at eight. It'll take over an hour to get there. I want to be early."

"This timing is tight." Trey said.

"I know Trey, we just have to make it work."

Trey finished eating, gathered a few things for the day and when he was ready he went out and drove off to pick up his crew. He had one stop on the way but that wouldn't take long. He drove out slow and easy on the beat-up, washboard road. Clarence watched him go from the porch. It was still dark out and the headlights bounced off the distance hills.

***

Sheriff Haney was medium height, with a western looking handle bar moustache. He wore a Stetson hat and a gun on his hip. He walked into his office almost the same time Clarence did.

"I know of you Mister Colton. You are a long timer around the Two Ocean country and a top hand on that fine old ranch. Good to finally meet ya'." They shook hands. "How's that business with your Sheriff on the missing Outfitter going?"

"I am not up with it." Clarence said.

"Those wilderness searches can be damn hard." The Sheriff added.

"Now, what's this about rustlers?"

Clarence was ready. He held his plastic bag of hide and his topo map. The Sheriff started to take the piece of hide out of the bag but when he smelled it he closed the bag and said,

"One piece of hide all the evidence you got?"

"I was hoping you'd take my word for it on the rest. We saw remains of six head. I'll show you if you'll find a place for me to open this map. I've marked the locations." Clarence said.

The Sheriff cleared his desk and they both spread the map out. Clarence leaned in and with his pen began to point at the marks he'd made.

"Here our cattle are grazing on BLM lease land."

"Who's cattle?"

"The 2/c Cattle Company."

"Here is an old homestead some miles away from the kills.

Between the two I've marked the kill locations."

"Ok, what else?"

"Here, beside this old house is the barn. In that barn there is a generator operating for a couple of freezers. There is a four-wheeler in there with a trailer for it. Inside the barn is a long butcher's block table and meat wrapping paper and all that you'd need to cut the meat up, wrap it and freeze it. There are several regular coolers to haul the meat around and sell it."

Clarence stepped back while the Sheriff studied the map. After a minute or two the man sat down in his chair and gestured for Clarence to sit in another one by his desk.

"Anything else I need to know?" Haney said.

"They are armed. I think there are four to six of them. I think they are all Mexican. There is nothing in back of the place but open country. We had to ride horseback a good way to get over there. They have all been gone during the day, either selling meat somewhere or harvesting it. I got a good chance to look around. "

"You get license numbers on any vehicles?"

"No," Clarence answered. Sheriff Haney continued to study the map.

"What time are they coming home?" he said,

"Late afternoon maybe, not sure of the time on it."

"Putting together enough lawmen will take time. Two Ocean's Sheriff is busy in the mountains with a crime scene, they can't spare anybody."

"How much time," Clarence said.

"A couple of days."

"It's a little risky to wait. My cow crew is out there and they are armed. If they catch these guys in the act of stealing the cattle there will be a confrontation. My boys are just not going to be able to hold back. If you will I'd like to tell you what I've got worked out."

Clarence stood up, bent over the map again and showed the Sheriff his plan. He pointed to the locations that the 2/c crew could cover. The Sheriff listened to what Clarence had to say and looked closely at the points Clarence had marked on the map.

"Or, to prevent your confrontation you can just order your men off the range until I can get a handle on it." Haney said.

"That can bring me more problems. To let the cattle and horses scatter means a lot of work. We can get around this Rustlers nest and cover the back and sides of the place. It would just leave you to cover the road in. If you came in at six p.m. or so, we could be ready. They'd be boxed in."

The Sheriff leaned back and looked at Clarence with a kind of blank expression and drummed a pencil on the desk. Then he called his Dispatcher in and told her to call the judge and let him know he would need a warrant.

As she went to do that Haney pulled out phone numbers of two other men in the county that had previous law experience. They had used them before as part-time Deputies. He went to his own topo map on the wall and with post-it's in hand he ask Clarence to read off his information again. He then made a note on the post-its and marked each place. Clarence stood by and waited.

"You had any police experience?" Haney said when he finished.

"No, but I was a squad leader in 'Nam and set up blocking actions in combat a few times.

"Thank you for your service." The sheriff said. "I like your plan. You putting a radio relay man on that hill is perfect, if he knows what he's doing."

"He does, he's another veteran and he did it plenty in the Army."

Haney looked at the map and all the miles of country that lay around and behind the homestead. He had long experience with illegals running for the hills. It would take a lot of manpower to search for them out there. And, they would run. They always did. In the most recent years they had started to let illegals get away, just to save the county money. Man-hunts were expensive and he was a small-town sheriff with a small-town budget.

This time, standing there beside him, was a well-respected old time, Wyoming Cowman. This was ranching country and Haney would be judged harshly if he let rustler's escape. This ranch had a crew already out there and already horseback. He thought about the last time he had ask for the States helicopter. The county was still paying the bill for that one.

"I doubt this is going to be particularly dangerous Mr. Colton, but you never know. I shouldn't use civilians. Still, a good show of force can reduce the danger as much as anything can. You make sure your crew stay in their places and don't get mistaken by or interfere with my deputies. Let them know that we will be concentrating on the house and the barn and to communicate with us if they see the suspects move

out and run for it. You do not apprehend, just observe and note locations and directions of flight. Let us apprehend. And, you sure can't
shoot. Not unless you are in grave danger your selves."

"Can't you deputize us?" Clarence said.

"Yes, if you will vouch for all of them. How many again?"

"I can vouch. There will be six of us. Can you lend us radio's? If
I can stay in contact with you."

"Yes, I can."

Haney looked at the map again and at the intersection of the dirt
road and highway. He looked at another dirt track road around a curve
and only a quarter mile or less from the intersection. Haney knew the
place and he could hide the squad cars there until it was time to go.

"We'll park here, just off the highway and keep out of sight." He
said and pointed to it. Then he yelled for his secretary.

"Call and see if we have a deputy anywhere near highway nine,
about midway between eighty-six and fourteen. If so tell him to call
me. I want him to drive out there and check out a spot." Then he
turned back to Clarence.

"Mr. Colton, if you have a man across the road hidden, he'll need
to tell me when the thieves have driven in. I will put a deputy there
with him too."

17

Showdown

Tony had to have a talk with Chalito and Vaca. He knocked on their door and when he entered the room he reached over and turned off the television. They took his news and the plan without comment. When he was finished Chalito said,

"We need a hostage."

Tony did not say a word. He just nodded his head slowly in agreement. He stood there, mind racing at the sight of poor Helena with children or the older white woman at the restaurant, in Chalito's hands when this was all over.

"Take the man, that Mexican that I talked to at the restaurant." Tony said.

***

When Marcos closed up and stepped out to his car, he did not suspect a thing. Then, in minutes he found himself in between two hard looking Mexican men so fresh from the border you could smell it. They placed him between them, in a pickup truck with a gun in his ribs. His thought was that this happened to people in his old country every day with the Cartels. Working in the Rocky Mountains seemed a long way from that. But, his countrymen had brought their scourge with them and it was spreading like a plague.

They drove in silence to the motel, took him into a room and duct taped his hands and feet and laid him on one of the beds. The small, mean looking Mexican took Marcos' car keys and left with the white man. When they returned one said,

"Piece of shit of a car you have." It was the white man that spoke, and in perfect Spanish. He told Marcos no harm would come to him if he cooperated and Marcos began his vigil as a prisoner.

***

Trey drove past the turnoff toward the Camel Humps and followed the road toward Wes's first camp. He stopped, climbed up on his truck bed and glassed the horizon to the South West. The early morning sun played bright on the landscape and Trey could see the ridge behind the rustler's homestead hideaway. This was a good spot to unload the horses and ride from. He got down from the truck, got out the pack with the drug bundles and placed it in a clump of sagebrush just off a little way. He turned the truck and trailer around and pulled up past the clump of sagebrush. He got back out of the truck, picked up a rock and tied a piece of orange survey tape around it. He put that in the middle of the dirt track road, then he got back in his truck and drove off to pick up his men.

***

Clarence got back to the ranch just at lunchtime. When he was walking into the bunkhouse Trey drove in with the crew. They unloaded their horses and tied them at the corral fence. Clarence set out lunch and told Trey what had happened at the Sheriff's office.

"So, it's on tomorrow night.?" Trey said.

"Yes, when we think we have all the suspects in there. I'm thinking two rustler trucks and whatever this Tony will be in."

Trey sat down, Clarence pulled the boiling coffee off the stove and dumped some cold water in it to sink the grounds. Then he poured a cup for Trey. The hands walked in. Clarence had lunch set out. There was a lot to go over. Trey looked at Clarence and said,

"You start."

Clarence was detailed. Roland was to drive out to the highway turnoff. Clarence showed him where, on the map. Wiley was to take a long gun, the 338, scoped, as Clarence recommended. If any-one was coming out, before the sheriff came in, he was to shoot a tire out and nothing more. From Wiley's spot on the Butte he would do the radio relay for everybody. It was up to Wiley and Roland to announce cars or pickups coming in. Wes and Ray would be in the ravine. Clarence showed them their spot on the map and then showed them where he and Trey would be in the grove of trees behind the barn.

Clarence told them about Sheriff Haynes and his instructions. It wasn't received that well. They started asking 'what if' kinds of questions. The kind that if you weren't careful would be answered with, 'yes you can shoot somebody.' Clarence dodged those as long as he could, then in frustration, said...

"Damnit, stay put and don't shoot unless you are threatened. The lawmen will handle this. Can't risk us shooting each other and the

Sheriff was clear about what he expects us to do and not do. When he drives in we got to be in the places he expects us to be. If you can't, for any reason do that, then call Wiley on the hill and tell him where you ended up and he will tell the Sheriff. And, point your rifles down, you know, at the ground. Don't take a chance at pointing it at a cop."

They had their orders. All were soldiers once. It's easier after that to take them. They ate lunch, took showers and in the late afternoon went out to care for the stock.

After lunch Clarence and Roland got in the truck and drove off for the 'last scout', as Clarence put it. Roland would have to go to his place at the intersection by himself on the following day. Clarence wanted to make sure he knew where to go.

Their first stop was the side road the Sheriff would drive in and wait on. Staying back off the road, they parked and walked to a spot in the trees where Roland could sit with his radio and watch the turnoff. While they squatted there talking a pickup, pulling a cargo trailer slowed and then turned off the highway onto that road.

"Well, looky here…" Clarence said. He looked at his watch and it was four thirty in the afternoon.

"Right on time. Hell, this just might work."

"Is that the rustlers?" Roland said.

"I believe so. We're thinking three vehicles total all coming in from four o'clock on. Give Wiley as much detail as you can. The Sheriff will be listening too and will have a Deputy with you.

"What'll I do then?" Roland said.

"Just stay out of it. Keep radio contact, keep listening. Wiley can see a lot from where he will be and if we need you he'll know. I'll want to know if anybody gets back out this way. But, I don't see how that can happen. Wiley's supposed to shoot a tire out if they even try it. You out here with your pickup truck, is a good thing. We might need you to go get something or another."

"Like what?" Roland said. He was feeling a little left out and his tone of voice sounded like he was pissed about it."

"Run the shuttle. Go back and bring the truck and trailer" Clarence said.

That night, just after nine p.m., Trey and Clarence drove up on the hill and called the man, Tony. Clarence had marked the miles from a little crossroads store to the turnoff to make sure the man would not turn on the wrong road. Trey gave Tony those miles and told him to be there no sooner than five-thirty.

"You meet anybody, ignore them. If that doesn't work tell them you are a hunter looking for a place to deer hunt this fall. You will be driving in on that dirt road heading more or less north. Drive slowly until you see me. I'll be in front of a small house. You can't miss it.

"How far?"

"Some ways, eight or ten miles anyway. Stay in the main track, don't turn off anywhere. It's straight in." Trey said.

"Don't disappoint me and I won't disappoint you." Tony said.

"But, if you are fucking with me, if you are planning something, you will cause you and your friends a lot of pain." Then the man hung up. Trey told Clarence what he said.

"I'm not sure what he meant, but…"

"I know what he meant." Clarence said. "He's talking about Marcos, Helena, Casey maybe. We got to get these bastards behind bars and we probably only have one chance to do that."

Trey grimaced, shook his head and knew the truth of what was said. He knew what he had to do.

"I must be stupid to get to this point." Trey said. Clarence looked at him…

"Stupid is not the word I'd use. The word I'd use is 'ballsy'."

"You ought to' know," Trey answered. They had a short laugh and both cut it off at the same split-second. Trey turned to something else and Clarence almost ruined it. He almost said,

'It helps having so little to lose.' But, he didn't say it. He hated thinking it too much to say it.

***

On Friday morning, the day of the raid they ate breakfast, packed lunches and saddled their horses. They would give themselves plenty of time to get ready out there. It was a clear day for it. When they had the horses loaded Wes put his head back and gave out a war hoop, then yelled out…

"It's a good day to die." Clarence and Trey cringed when he yelled it but everybody else just laughed. Nothing like a little gallows humor to start the day.

Wes had experienced disaster more than once in Afghanistan and Iraq. It led him to develop the habit of tracing the steps backward, that is the steps that it took to reach a bad end. He'd come to think of it as a personal de-briefing. It was for that reason he insisted on riding with Clarence. He wanted to talk about this some more.

"How do we know we can reach each other on the radios?" Wes said.

"We don't. But, we will all be able to reach Wiley. He'll relay. That's what he did in the Army. He's up high and nothing between us and him to block the signal."

"How do you know they'll reach?"

"The miles. The radios we use have the distance of thirty miles line of sight. These we got from the Sheriff are the high dollar ones. They'll go further." Clarence said.

"What about Ray?" Ray sat in the back seat of Clarence's truck with his favorite weapon between his knees. It was a mini-14. As usual he was quiet.

"What about him?" Clarence said.

"Well, he likes to shoot. He likes to shoot and ask questions later. He got in a lot of trouble over it in Iraq." Wes answered.

"Oh really?" Clarence thought about that for a minute, hit a bump that lifted them all out of their seats and then he said,

"Ray, you keep the safety on and don't shoot anybody unless you have to defend yourself. Understood?"

"It was one damn time that happened Wes. Sure boss, I'm good." Ray said.

"It's important Ray. We're the good guys in this thing. It's no good to have it look any other way." Clarence said.

"Ten-four." Ray answered. Wes turned in the seat and started to add something to what Clarence said but Ray silenced him.

"Shut the hell up Wes," he said.

"At the first stop Wes and Ray unloaded their mounts and stuffed their sandwiches in the saddle bags. Ray slung his Mini 14 over his shoulder like an old-time guerilla fighter, and Wes did the same with his M-15. Then they rode for the ravine. Clarence watched them go with an entirely new impression of Wes. The kid had been holding out on him. He was smarter than he'd let on.

At the last stop, at the survey ribbon rock, Trey made a tight circle and faced the truck and trailer toward home and parked it. They unloaded their horses.

"Wiley, you go now. Don't wait for us," Trey said. Wiley checked his cinches and put his rifle in the saddle scabbard. He hung a bandoleer of 338 rounds, around his neck and shoulder and clipped his radio to it. Then he rode off. He had the longest ride of all of them so it made perfect sense to send him on.

As Wiley rode away Trey walked over, took the back pack with the drug bundles from the sage and slung it on his back. They tightened cinches. Trey put the fully loaded clips in a pouch hanging from his saddle horn. He put the empty AK 47 in the saddle scabbard. Clarence did the same with his and they mounted up. They rode at an easy clip toward the ridge. Both of them watched and listened for sign or sound of four-wheelers but there was nothing but the wind and the clump of horse's hooves on soft ground. The smell of rain was still in the air when they crossed ground wet from a thunder shower. They could see the cloud moving off to the East. The summer squall had brought the smells of sage out strong and sharpened the senses. Cool air surrounded them and the fresh horses were eager for a faster pace.

***

Trey and Clarence found themselves peering over the ridge watching a barbeque with what was probably 2/c beef cooking on a grill. Trey checked with Wiley on the radio as soon as they were on top of the ridge and got an answer. Wiley acknowledged he had contact with Roland at the highway and Wes in the Ravine. After trying for a few minutes Trey was able to raise Wes as well.

With a good look around Trey and Clarence counted four men and figured the rustlers were all at home. Two trucks were in view. From an ice chest on one tail gate a man pulled out bottles of beer. There was Mariachi music rising up to the ridge in the still air. The time for placing the drugs in the barn had come. Trey called Wiley and told him they would be off the air for a few minutes, then he turned his radio off and handed it to Clarence.

"I think I want to have the horses down in the trees with us." He said to Clarence.

"Me too. If I had to run on foot up this ridge I'd be a dead man."

Clarence looked and pointed further to their right. The ridge they were on was lower to their right and getting lower would help cut the view from the front yard of the house. He tapped Trey on the shoulder and pointed it out.

"Let's go down this way." Clarence said. They mounted and staying out of sight, rode behind the ridge and around the point it made dropping down into the sage. It was just what they needed. The trees blocked the line of sight to the house and they could take advantage of that just like any good hunter would. They led the horses to the trees and tied them up on the back side, out of sight of the house and barn. They pulled out their rifles. Clarence tighten his cinch again just to be ready to move fast. Trey reached in his saddle bags and got his short flat bar and his fence plyers. He put them in his coat pocket. They each put clips in their rifles and a round in the chamber. Clarence took the binoculars now, moved to the other side of the trees and looked for the spot where the loose boards hung on the side of the barn. He also looked carefully about for anyone that might see them. It was all clear. Trey gave the radio to Clarence and started down afoot with the pack on his back and his now loaded rifle in his hands and Clarence watched him go.

"We're crossing the Rubicon now friend." Clarence said to himself.

The barn completely blocked the line of sight from the front of the house now and Trey reached down to test a loose board. When he put the flat bar to it he heard talking inside the barn. It was Spanish and the sounds they made after that sounded like they were moving something. He waited but they seemed to have set in, working at something. Trey could only freeze in place and wait.

Clarence scanned the yard a few times. Only two men were in view. He glassed down and could see Trey squatting down low against the barn wall. When he looked up at Clarence he shook his head and squeezed his fist to say, 'hold up.'

They both sat and waited, the sun sank lower in the western sky. They both checked their watches frequently and finally five pm approached. The time had come slow. Clarence moved up with the binoculars to watch the road beyond the house. Then he would pan back to Trey, keeping an eye on him and anybody approaching his position. They waited.

Then the crackle of a keyed radio came on. It was Wiley. Roland had called him and the message was two vehicles had turned in. Clarence stood up, still behind cover, stretched a little and waited some more. After a short time, the radio crackled on again. Wiley reported the vehicles at his position. He reported a pick-up truck and a little foreign car.

***

Wes and Ray had heard Wiley's message too and picked up their weapons. Wes did a quick "Copy that," on the radio. It made Wes grin to play army again and feel the bushy-tailed excitement run up his spine. They watched the house from the ravine, their heads sticking up like picket pins. Ray turned to Wes and said,

"What's the distance you figure?"

"I'm thinking five hundred yards." Wes answered. They both knew it was too far for them to shoot accurate with the weapons they had. Before Ray could state the obvious Wes said,

"We're blocking, that's all."

The two vehicles stopped below Wiley. Three men got out of the truck and took a leak. One stayed in. Wiley watched through his rifle scope. He put the cross hairs on each of the three. The men were talking. One carried an assault rifle, the thirty-round clip kind.

Wiley watched as the men got back in their vehicles. Three were in the truck. One man got back into the little foreign car and as Wiley scoped it out it started to look familiar. He had never paid attention to little foreign cars but Marty had one the same color and style and the same kind of dent in the rear side panel.

Both vehicles moved off up the road. The car pulled over and let the truck pass. Then the car turned sideways and stopped. It was partially blocking the road. The truck kept going toward the now, very near homestead. The driver of the car got out with his rifle and stood facing back toward the highway. Wiley looked back that way too. Several minutes passed. Then the radio keyed on and it was Roland.

"Law-men coming in."

Wiley saw the squad car coming into view, moving real slow, no lights flashing. His thought was they were to wait for his call, but here they came, two more behind the first one now. They slowed to a creep as the little car across the road came into their view.

Wiley glassed back to the man behind the car and could see him looking hard at what was coming. The man had to be close to seven hundred yards from Wiley's position, maybe more. Wiley calculated the drop in his 225-grain bullet and came up with something like a rainbow trajectory. The radio keyed on and Clarence said,

"Send the Sheriff in." Wiley keyed back "Rodger that."

"Sheriff there is one, armed man, blocking the road with a small car."

"Got it in sight. Is there room to get around it?" Haney said.

"Yes sir. To the West side, to your left. Clarence says come-on."

"Copy," the Sheriff answered, then Wiley saw the patrol cars moving again and as they got closer, the man by the parked car looked to be aiming his rifle. Then the sound of gun fire reached up to Wiley. The Sheriff's cars stopped and the man that stood behind the car kept shooting. Wiley took up the radio, keyed it and said,

"Clarence, a pickup with three men are almost to you, out."

He set the radio down and picked up his rifle to scope the scene. He dialed the scope all the way up to the nine, put the crosshairs about four feet above the man shooting and squeezed off a shot. For a split second he thought he'd actually hit the guy. The man dropped suddenly, down behind the car and out of sight. Then, just as suddenly, he jumped up and started running down the road toward the homestead. Wiley watched him go.

"Scared the shit out of you," Wiley said to himself.

***

Trey could not see anything without exposing himself, so he kept looking up the slope to Clarence for any signals. The music still played and Trey could hear the men in the barn still talking.

Clarence had seen the men in the yard vanish when the truck pulled up. Then, one came back out with a rifle. The truck had stopped out from the house about twenty yards or so. One man got out and approached the man standing in front of the house. The driver stayed put behind the wheel and a third man set beside him in the truck cab.

Trey heard the truck come in too and the men in the barn say something and go quiet. He saw through a board crack that they were standing at the door. Then they stepped out and walked toward the front of the house. Trey looked around the corner and saw them walking away. He moved quickly. He slipped the back pack off his shoulder, and with the rifle in one hand and the pack in the other he moved to the barn door and the pickup truck backed up to it. He put the pack in the bed of the pickup truck turned around and went back to his place behind the barn wall.

Clarence, still watching from the trees, saw the two men in the yard clearly. Then two more men stepped into Clarence's view, both with rifles. For a moment, as they just stood there facing each other, Clarence said to himself,

"Damn Mexican Standoff," Then, the clacking sounds of rapid weapons fire was heard by all. It came from just up the road and just out from the yard the men were standing in.

It had an electrifying effect on the men in the yard. They were pointing guns at each other but not shooting. The Man from the truck, with a pistol showing now, began to move back to the Pickup. He was talking loud and fast to the three men facing him and pointing toward the road. Whatever he said was accented by the palm of his empty hand going up toward the rustlers like it was 'don't shoot'. He held his pistol up toward the sky the same way. He was the only one moving and when he got into the pickup the driver started backing up with tires spinning dirt and gravel everywhere. Clarence saw a man running on foot, coming in from the dirt road. He was shouting and pointing back behind him. He carried an assault weapon and went straight to the pickup and jumped in the back of the truck bed. Then, the first patrol car came in with lights flashing and the siren on. The men that had been standing in the yard disappeared.

The law stopped well off from the front of the house. A second patrol car came tearing in. The officers came out of their vehicles and took positions behind them, ready to shoot. They began firing at the pickup as it moved out of Clarence's view. It backed up fast toward the barn door and Trey's hiding place.

"Spray and pray" boys, Clarence thought, as a few spent rounds sprinkled the ground in front of his tree line. Everybody shoots high at first, he thought. But that was ridiculous.

Trey heard the truck coming his way, heard it thrown in reverse and heard tires spinning. It backed right up to the pickup in front of the barn and crashed into it. The men got out of it and ducked into the barn. Bullets were flying and Trey could only dive down to the ground as rounds hit the truck and the barn door and the wall he lay behind. Then the shooting just stopped.

There was loud conversation inside the barn. Trey, not understanding Spanish, could only think it sounded confrontational. These guys did not know each other. His problem was he couldn't move. He'd be caught in the crossfire between the deputies and the suspects.

Clarence was getting calls from Wes and Wiley, all wanting to know what was happening. Then the Sheriff came on and said to shut them up, it was important that they keep the lines of communication clear of, "Goddamned Bullshit," as Haney put it.

So, they shut up and stayed in place. The Sheriff came on again and ask for Clarence.

"We have how many suspects? how many in the house and how many in the barn?"

"You have three or four in the house and maybe four in the barn. One of our crew are down behind the barn. White guy in a Black Stetson. He is armed." Clarence said.

Just as he ended his call Clarence saw someone opening the back window of the house. Seconds later boards started to come undone from the back wall of the barn. They were being kicked out from inside and it was happening fast.

The location and attention of the Sheriff and his deputies was all to the front of the house, so Clarence made a decision. He keyed the radio and made the call.

"Wes, comeback, Wes…" and Wes came on, "go ahead."

"Wes, get a horseback and come around to the ridge behind me. I think I'm going to need help." Clarence half expected the Sheriff to object but the man did not respond.

Then, from the barn, with a decent size hole kicked open, a Man came out and started running straight toward the open country off a little right of Clarence's position. The man carried a rifle. He was followed by another and that one came up straight toward Clarence. He was followed closely by a man with a pistol and those two ran up the slope toward the trees where Clarence stood.

He had a shot on the front man but that man was un-armed and looked very familiar. The runner in the lead was clearly Marcos. It had been many long years since Clarence was a young soldier. But the shock of seeing American Soldiers shoot each other in panicky combat will stay with a man the rest of his life. Marcos was running directly in the line of sight between Clarence and the man that followed him. Clarence held his fire. As they approached the trees Clarence pulled back further into them for better concealment and to buy some time. But it was already too late. The man with the pistol had seen him and from behind Marcos he fired. Clarence went down without knowing what hit him.

***

Trey had heard the men in the barn kicking out boards. When he looked back through the crack there was one of them with his rifle to his shoulder and he was still at the front firing methodically toward the officers. Trey had no sure shot at him without moving and much of the lawmen's fire was still slapping boards around him. Trey moved to the back and looked around the outside corner of the barn just in time to see two of the men running toward the trees and almost there. Then the four-wheeler started. It came roaring out of the front of the barn and around the far side. Trey had to duck the fire from police officers as bullets tore through the barn's thin planks. He saw the two running men go into the trees where Clarence was and then the four-wheeler was ripping up the slope right behind them. Trey started to move again when more bullets from the police officers ripped through planks and forced him down to the ground again. When Trey crawled back up to the rear of the barn's corner he looked around and saw two more men, running from the back of the house and headed West. One saw him and ducked to cover behind a pile of old fence posts. He fired in Trey's direction. The other disappeared into the landscape. Trey fired at the pile of posts a couple of times but the return fire of the man was accurate enough to hold him behind the corner and the protection of a solid, eight x eight corner post left from the days there was a fence there. Then someone behind him spoke.

"Stand still, don't turn around. Put the gun down." It was clearly an English-speaking voice and Trey did as he was told. He put his rifle against the wall and turned his hands to the side of the barn and placed them against it. Then he looked back over his left shoulder at the Deputy.

"I'm one of the ranch owners helping the Sheriff catch these guys," Trey said. Then he looked back up at the trees. He thought he heard the four-wheeler moving off. He expected Clarence to step out and wave but he did not see him. Then Trey felt a sense of panic start to rise in him.

"Listen Deputy, there is a shooter around the barn in a pile of fence posts and my friend Clarence Colton is up in those trees where two just ran in. The rest have all run off to the West. Can't you see your way to who I am and let's get on with finishing this thing?" Another Deputy came around the barn,

"Everything ok?" He said. "Yes," was the answer and then to Trey, the first deputy said,

"Yeah, go ahead."

Trey picked up his rifle and checked the chamber and the

magazine. He eased up to the corner, leveled his rifle and fired three rounds into the pile of posts. As his own shots still rang in his ear he saw the muzzle flashes of the man firing back at him. Trey aimed beneath those muzzle flashes and continued to fire steadily as he stepped out and walked toward the pile. He fired a steady series of shots as he approached the pile of posts. The two Deputies followed, walking on each side of him and just behind. Another officer stepped out from the far corner of the house and stopped. He seemed to be hurt. Trey reached the wood pile and saw the man lying there, on his back with his eyes open and mouth moving slightly. He had a bloody hole in his neck and his stomach showed blood. Trey reached down, pulled the man's rifle out of reach, then turned, pointed uphill and said,

"Going to need to get help up there now," and he began running for the clump of trees.

***

Wes and Raymond came up and over the ridge on horseback, one hand for the rein and one hand for their weapons. They saw the four-wheeler come out of the trees and head out across the sage brush with one man driving fast, his hands tightly on the handlebars. Ray rode to the trees to meet Clarence. Wes didn't. For him the fight was finally on and he was going after somebody before anybody could stop him. It was Wes's way his entire life. He'd always preferred to beg forgiveness later. To ask permission wasn't his style.

Ray rode into the trees. His horse was so frosted with the hard run that he paced in place and almost stepped on Trey kneeling there beside Clarence. Ray looked down and Trey looked helplessly up and their eyes met. Trey pointed out the way the four-wheeler had gone. Ray sank his spurs and his horse leaped forward and broke through the timber and he was gone with Trey's words ringing in his ears.

"Get that son of a bitch."

Another man stepped out of the trees and spok to Trey in a familiar voice.

"Don't shoot, it's me, Marty."

"What the hell are you doing here?" Trey said in complete surprise.

"They grabbed me when I was closing up last night. Is he ok?" Marty knelt beside Trey and Clarence just as one of the Deputy's ran up, breathing hard. He pointed a pistol at Marcos and Trey yelled again,

"Don't shoot, he's with us." Marcos stood up and raised his hands anyway.

"Are you ok here?" The Deputy said.

"We're going to need an air-Medevac." Trey said. The deputy stepped off a little way and made his call. Trey moved closer to Marcos,

"Stay with Clarence." Trey said. "You are with us. Don't say anything but that. Just keep saying it, ok? You are with the 2/c."

Marty nodded his head and knelt back down beside Clarence. Trey ran to his horse and with his ears buzzing from the shooting and the adrenaline, jerked the tie from the limb and swung up. He rode straight out the way Ray had gone and let his big Chestnut Gelding stretch out across the prairie. In the fading light of the setting sun he saw the silhouette of one rider bearing to the left and the other dropping out of sight behind a low hill, running straight ahead.

When Trey reached that slight rise and saw beyond it, he had gained on Wes and the four-wheeler. The ATV's motor was screaming but there was no speed in it as the driver had to breech sagebrush and shallow washouts. Trey heard shots further to his left and knew Ray had made contact. But, he had the angle on the four-wheeler now, it was making a wide swing back to the right, in a direction that would take it deeper into the wildlands. He rode for the cut-off angle he guessed at. He did not watch the ground growing dark beneath him. He let his horse do that. Gradually he closed the distance.

The four-wheeler was having too much trouble maneuvering the rough ground and Trey could see Wes much closer to it now. Wes's silhouette, against the horizons red glow showed a long legged, lean cowhand upright on a horse that was fully stretched out, making great leaps over unseen hazards. With hat brim blown up by the wind, kerchief stretched out behind, Wes had his short carbine rifle to his shoulder. It looked like a picture of a plainsman of old shooting a buffalo at full gallop and the gun shots came to Trey, pop, pop, pop. The driver slumped from the seat and the four-wheeler twisted, then flipped and it was over. Trey turned back to the shots on his left.

Ray was shooting at something in the brush. Trey saw Ray dismount. Trey came up to him, eased his horse up from the long run and stopped. There were two men at Ray's feet and they weren't moving.

"Damn Ray, I hope they were armed." Trey said. Ray bent down, picked up a rifle and said,

"One was."

"There's one or two more out here." Trey said.

Ray pointed to a rise, a slight hill further over and said,

"I saw movement there, when I was closing in on these two."

Wes rode up then. The growing darkness encouraged the silence as the three paused there, one on the ground and two in the saddle. Trey knew they were waiting for him to say something. He also knew that Clarence would say this needed to be over now while they had a chance to finish it. Trey looked at Ray on the ground and nodded his head.

"Go get 'em." He said. It was all it took. Ray swung up and rode for that rise and Wes spun his horse and went out right beside him.

Trey rode back to the clump of trees where Clarence lay. Marcos stood up and said,

"He's still alive. They've called in a helicopter to get him to the hospital."

All of the patrol car headlights were on now, down in the yard, parked to face and light up the barn and the house. Several officers were moving over the property with flash lights. Roland walked up the hill to them. He had driven in from the road.

"Wiley is riding in right behind me," he said.

"Roland, take Marcos with you and go back to the 2/c. Drive out the road to the Camel humps and pick up my truck and trailer. Bring it back here and pick us up." Trey turned to Marcos,

"You go too and stay there, don't come back with Roland. Fix us all up a good dinner if you feel up to it. We'll be back as soon as we can. I'll pay you."

"Hey, amigo, don't insult me. I will do it gladly." Marcos patted Trey on the shoulder and walked away with Roland.

Ray and Wes rode up to check on Clarence too. They all three stayed with him until the wup, wup of the helicopter, the ground light on, was circling overhead. Seeing the horses panicked Wes and Ray went for them and held on to 'em.

Marcos had tried to make Clarence comfortable. An EMT was lowered from the chopper and he checked Clarence's vitals before they took him. Trey looked down and waited. The old Cowboy's bald head was propped up with a rolled jacket and he was covered with his slicker. Trey touched his cheek and it was cold.

"Nothing for it now," Trey said to his old friend.

"What?" Wes said.

"Nothing,"

In the noise of the chopper and the spotlights beam in the darkness, Clarence was taken away. Just as the noise receded and the horses calmed down Trey drew his crew in close and said,

"You know you are going to need to take the lawmen out to those guys and tell them how it went down."

"I know." Wes said.

"Make sure you say some things to the Sheriff that will keep us out of trouble. Tell him that the men were shooting at you out there. Did they shoot back?"

They were interrupted. It was sudden and it was loud. Everything jumped, men and horses, guns were drawn. Flash lights circled and landed on the source of the commotion. Wes's horse had collapsed to the ground with legs pawing out at thin air. They all had nearly jumped out of their boots. When they looked the animal over they found the blood and a bullet hole in the area of its lungs and heart. But they heard no gunshot. The horse had taken a bullet during the chase and Wes had not realized it. He looked at the hole, turned to Trey and said,

"How's that for shootin' back? Damnit to hell. That was a good horse."

Wes bent down and as the horse gave its last breath he began to remove his saddle. Ray stood by with a light to help him. Trey bent to help too.

***

In the wee hours of morning the Sheriff released them and they headed for home. Trey thought about Clarence. The man had a pretty good life. Better than most maybe. And, all through this deal he had been sharp and dependable. Ever since Trey had sat in the bed of his truck, on that cold day and showed the money to Clarence, the man had stepped up. Clarence was maybe dying now, from an honest to God shootout. It was one he was on the right side of the whole way. Trey thought that Clarence would have explained it that way and, in fact he already had. There were worse ways to go.

Trey had that moment when he felt things would work out. He never could understand where these intuitions came from, but getting one now was sure a welcomed feeling. He took the time to stop and listen to it. Trey could see the 2/c surviving. It would not be backed down, never cower to Cartel or thieves. That was just proven a fact.

Bankers, lawyers and real estate developers might be another thing. But, they were not the problem just now. Clarence would say they had established a precedent. It made Trey laugh just to visualize his friend talking like that. They'd heard it all before from him. Once upon a time they would not have known what Clarence was talking about. Trey knew now.

It seemed impossible in the modern world to re-create anything close to the great historic ranches that came to be in the days of the old west, least way from scratch. There are big ranches of course, most turned into game ranches now, wildlife refuges, retreats, spas and all sorts of things that the wealth of city men and their wives brought out to the big country. This was different. They were different. Not a one of the 2/c crew had come from a city or from money. All of them had roots in the soil of a country their kind had settled, worked and defended for generations. They were small town boys and proud of it. There was possibility for more now. A chance to work for more than wages, a chance to own it themselves, to live on land with elbow room and call it their own. This had happened to them for one reason and one reason only. It's because they had some luck and were willing to fight to keep it.

Epilogue

As the days and weeks followed that dangerous night the crew of the 2/c searched for scattered cattle and horses that had grazed off in all directions. The crew rode out to each herder's range, found his horses first then pushed his cattle and world back together in a way he could manage. Then they left him to it and went to the next one. In the end it was just Wiley and Trey on Wiley's herd and the two Cowboys with a string of seven horses each all worn the hell out. They talked about the days when each had twelve or fifteen mounts to stagger out the work load. A man can feel worn out himself and a fresh horse can revive him. But when both man and beast are worn down it's a hard way to go.

When you use a good horse too much he can go sour on you and learn to hate the work. And sour was a real tough thing to reverse in man or beast. Sitting at the fire one night they came to the conclusion that this was called 'burn out' in the cities and towns and a malady of urban dwellers that they largely avoided in the world they lived in. Oh, well. So much for feeling superior.

"Denial is not just a river in Africa." Trey said. Wiley, after a considerable pause answered with,

"I thought that the Nile was in Egypt?" Trey laughed and it took a minute for Wiley to see his error, that the Nile River was in both, one and the same damn places.

They did really good on not talking about the shootout. But, they did talk around it. One was the way they had gotten Marty out of there before he was questioned.

Trey had a long talk with Marty and they came to some conclusions about his story and place in the nights events. With Marcos's old arrest record, he wanted no part in being included in any of it. The 2/c had solved that by saying Marcos was with them, and by the quick action that got him out of there. By the following morning they had his story down pat and they were sticking to it.

It had been easy to get Marty 's car back. He just told the Sheriff it must have been stolen at the restaurant when he was not there and since he wasn't there he didn't know it was stolen. If the Sheriff thought that was too coincidental he never said so. He just gave it back to Marty after they searched it and found nothing they could use to make anything out of.

Trey wanted Marty 's opinion on how it had all gone down. Trey was feeling a little bothered about the rustlers receiving a death sentence out on the range, one they might not deserve. Marty 's reply said much about the differences between how an Anglo sees a thing and how a Mexican migrant sees the same thing.

"Trey, in Mexico our great ranches are owned by very important people. The Vaqueros that ride herd on the cattle of these ranches were born there on those same ranches. They are very proud men and extremely loyal to their Patrons and to each other. It is a code and they grow up with it firmly in their blood. If these men that took your cattle had been caught stealing cattle from one of these ranches in Mexico he would have disappeared. No questions would be asked. But everyone would know. I say your rustlers knew the risk back where they came from and I say they should have known these risks might exist here, in the USA as well."

***

The Sheriff had all the evidence he needed for the rustling and the drug dealing charge. The fact that no one was alive to be charged was a concern but solid evidence helped explain that. It was a good haul for a small-town Sheriff. The street value on the drugs was reported as something like one million dollars. That seemed an exaggeration but nobody would challenge it. The amount of cash found was seized and reported, no amount given.

When Wes and Ray talked to the Sheriff they came off ok. It had seemed they could have captured somebody, but the fact that Wes's horse was shot out from under him and each of the men killed had been armed and their weapons had been discharged, that makes them fair game for law enforcement most anywhere. So, without further ado, the Sheriff's department went back to its daily business of busting huge drug rings for Wilford County and the people of Wyoming. Keeping it simple helps you get re-elected and the Sheriff was not going to muddy those waters. Haney was a happy man.

Weismann, now back from his trip, contacted Trey to find out how things were going. Trey took the drive into Two Ocean and met with him. It was late morning on a Friday when he arrived there and

Weismann had the newspaper accounts of the big shootout on his desk. His secretary had saved them for him and he had been reading about it in detail. It was quite a story and had made the local and national news for some time. Trey sat with him and told his guarded version of events like he'd given to the Sheriff and subsequent investigators. Trey didn't give the reporters one damn thing. He had sensed quickly that it was best to let the Sheriff's office shine on this and the 2/c crew understood it too. They talked about it long enough that night and Trey would not let them quit and go to sleep until he was convinced they understood it. Before he and Weismann were finished it was lunch time. Weismann was buying and they went across the street to eat.

Trey was recognized by more than a few patrons. His picture had been seen in the news and anybody in town that did not know him from his Dagger Ranch days knew him now for what was billed as, "The Shootout in Conant Valley." It had not happened in the Conant Valley, but a full two drainages West of it. But, that did not matter to news people. Now the 2/c headquarters, barn and bunkhouse were billed as the scene of the battle.

At the lunch Jen walked up and sat down beside them completely un-announced. It seems she just wanted to say hello. It was a brief exchange, friendly, concerned, so good to see you are ok kind of thing. But, she touched Trey's arm several times, her knee was against his knee the whole time and when she got up she ducked under the brim of his hat and kissed him quickly on the lips. He smelled her and he felt the blood rush, the one so long neglected now that he almost set there and let her walk away. Then nature reminded him of his needs and he jumped up, excused himself and stepped out onto the street just before she got in her car.

"Jen, can I see you?" He said and wondered if his voice sounded too much like he was begging.

"When?" She answered, and boy did she smile when she said it. She looked at him in such an intense way that he knew she was ready for him too.

"This afternoon, this evening at your place, before I leave town." He said.

She stood quietly in front of him, she looked down and then she stepped closer. She reached for his vest and shirt collar and straightened it.

"I'll be home about four," She said and turned quickly away. She walked away moving so fluid and sexy that he could barely stand to wait at all.

When Trey sat down again with Weismann and the blood stopped rushing in his head, he tried to talk a little business. The 2/c had made only a little profit for their effort. That would have been nice to make more but then again, they'd never really counted on it. The summer rains had come in a timely way and the grass was always good ahead of them. That gave them respectable weight gains on the cattle. Now they had the money sitting in the account. When Weismann saw the business direction of the conversation he called for the check and they adjourned to his office and its privacy.

Weismann wanted to know how this gunfight had gone down, so once seated at his desk, he asked Trey about it.

"What happened out there Trey? Seven dead men, deputy wounded, Clarence shot."

"Well, they were shooting at us and when Clarence took a bullet, that got our blood up."

"I'll say," Weismann answered. "Surprising the Sheriff let his deputies loose like that. They're being investigated for it but with the money found and the bundles of cocaine, he's coming up justified. Have they asked you a lot of questions?"

"No, not really," Trey answered. "We all had to give a statement and sign off on it. Thing is, me and my crew had time to talk it over with each other later that night and the next morning. With all of us in the same bunkhouse we were able to get our stories together."

"So, the paper said you were all deputized?" Weismann said,

"Well, kind of. Sheriff had us make that statement but it was after the fact."

"Who did the shooting?"

"We did. They came out the back at us. The Sheriff and his boys were in the front of the place."

Weismann was trying to be careful and not push. But he had some reasons for it.

"All the dead were out back and said to have been run down by deputies on horseback. That's you and your 2/c crew?"

Trey nodded his head, "Yes, it was us."

"Damn man, damn bold I'd say."

"This whole thing has been bold for me," Trey said.

"I guess it has." Weismann nodded his head slowly and continued watching Trey's expression closely.

"So, you've got options now Trey, what will you do next."

"What would you suggest?"

"For you, Real Estate. It's been consistent out here. I would help you find the right thing if you want."

"Clarence would say that we don't have enough money to buy land and the cattle too. There would have to be loan money on one or the other and then we're at risk. We lost my family's farm and ranch that way, back when I was a kid."

"What do you want to do then?" Weismann voice was low and understanding.

"In a perfect world, put a big ranch back together. One like the Dagger. Keep good horses, breed our own, raise fine cattle. Hold to traditions, make ourselves proud I guess,"

"Like you're feeling now?" Weismann said.

"Does it show?" Trey answered.

"Oh yeah, and you got good reason. Why don't you get out of here and go see that beauty. We'll talk again soon. You guys get up to the hunting camp and put some work into it. This winter we'll advertise, get some hunters in the draw for next year and get that business going. As far as your ranch idea, let me study on it. There might be a way," Weismann said.

Trey left the office. Weismann sat back in his chair and watched from the window until Trey had driven away. Charles Weismann had been having some fun, traveling worldwide the entire summer. But, in some places, like South America and Mexico, he had stopped to see old business acquaintances. They had asked for some numbers from him and it was best to see that they got that paperwork. It's how Weismann covered himself, keeping good records. And, some of it was complicated enough that it helped to explain it in person. That way he was able to ensure that they did not come up with the wrong conclusions, the kind that is guesswork and void of facts.

In the course of these visits Weismann was asked to get back into his old line of work. He did not say 'no', but he did not particularly want to do it. The business had been, at one time, an almost gentlemanly one. At least for the bosses and their professional level help, the lawyers and accountants. But, that had changed. It had become a game of dangerous venture for all involved, even those at the top. Weismann and Fenwick had never had a structure for that. They were protecting themselves from the law but no way to protect themselves from that kind of bottom up danger. And, with the Dagger Ranch gone, no way to cover the movement of money now either.

The 2/c crew could change that. They'd proven themselves. All Weismann had to do now was let a little time go by and if none of the ranch crew broke ranks for brief notoriety, fame, money or just plain carelessness, Weismann would start thinking he had a potential gang of action-oriented men, ones he could trust and that could trust each other. Real Cowboys were a click-ish bunch anyway. That was a combination to base a solid business on. Then, maybe he'd finally be able to afford that retirement property in the exotic and exclusive land of his dreams.

***

Trey drove straight from Weismann's office to Casey's little townhouse. When he knocked he heard a voice loud and clear say,

"It's open," from inside.

Trey walked in and there the man was, spread out on his back like an old Walrus on the beach of some far North seashore, with one fin taped up chest to shoulder. But this was no beach. Clarence had the biggest recliner Trey had ever seen. It was huge. It had pockets for remotes and two cup holders. One cup holder held a can of beer and one had a paper cup, spittoon. Clarence's gut had been growing in that chair and now it was too prominent to ignore. Trey walked over and petted it and said,

"When's it due? There can't be just one baby in there." Even more amazing was how huge the TV screen was. But, even so, Clarence sat real close to it.

"Your eyes getting weak?" Trey said.

"Shut the hell up, what do you want?" Clarence said. Trey grabbed the remote, flopped on the couch and said,

"Nothing, I just stopped by to change channels for you. Don't want you to strain yourself."

"Well, you can take the bullet next time." Clarence croaked out.

"What brings you to town?"

"Weismann's back. He wanted to get caught up." Trey looked at his watch, then got up again and put the remote out of reach of Clarence on a corner table.

"Give me that..." Clarence said.

"Naaa, you need the exercise. Maybe you can work off a quarter ounce of fat walking over here. Course then you got to get back. Bring the phone with you so you can call 911 if you can't. I'll see you later, I got to go."

"Where you going? Casey will be home directly and she'll cook." Clarence said.

"Can't, got a date."

"Oh, who is she?"

"Jen" Trey answered.

Clarence paused, thought for a second and then started to hum and sing...

"Jen-gin-miney Jen-gin-miney, gin-gin – jer-roo...I like you, do you like me too."

"Where'd you get that?" Trey said.

"A movie on TV. Something about Chimney sweeps." Clarence answered, then turned around to say more but Trey took off and the door slammed shut behind him. Clarence straightened up his recliner and slowly pulled himself out of the deep chair. He moved to retrieve the remote, went back to the chair, sat down and reclined again.

"Lucky man " He said to himself.

Then he started flipping channels. And, he had a lot of channels to flip. Casey had seen to that. She got him cable TV. He had the whole package. Clarence figured in a couple of more weeks of convalescence he'd be an expert on politics, the economy, current events and religion. As the Bard said, 'The world is a stage'. Clarence would add that everybody didn't necessarily want to be on it. But, the talking TV heads sure did want it. They competed hard for the attention just like politicians and preachers. They were beginning to look like one and the same to Clarence and his 'bull-shit' meter was starting to run overtime.

At first, he thought he would enjoy teaching and preaching all that stuff to the crew back at the ranch. Clarence sat and stared at the screen and could see himself pacing about the bunkhouse lecturing on all of these issues, his newfound knowledge shared unselfishly with the 2/c crew. They, being his only audience outside of a barroom.

But, it might not be welcome. It might be received like a voluminous fart in the bed tent on a roundup. It might be like bringing in outside contaminants to a place free of such nonsense as he had been seeing on that big TV screen. You could only take so much of it.

At that, a sense of satisfaction settled over him. He had survived another gun-battle in his life. All were in the service of his country, save one. Many of his countrymen had vilified that war, way back then. But the isolation of the Cowboy life had helped him to distance himself from the hand-wringing over it, the second guessing, the division, the pain it caused, and finally the absolute rejection of war for practically any reason. It was sad to him that his country's warrior ethos became so damn despised that even the nations heroes seemed to have given up on it.

But those heroes were still out there, growing up beneath it all. And, after 9/11 they showed up. The spike in volunteer enlistments after the attack on the World Trade Centers proved that we still have it in us, to defend ourselves as a nation. It was so damn good a thing for an old veteran to see and to know those young men recognized that a good country was still worth fighting for. Clarence had plenty of time to think about these things while he lay in intensive care in the Veterans Hospital in Cheyenne.

If you go to the VA Hospital today you walk among them, the old and the new veterans. The ones just back in the world with the weight on their shoulders now. To Clarence they looked like kids. But then again, so did the Doctors. Clarence could not help wondering if either of them really knew what they were doing. If not, then they sure would need to learn together. Like pairing up a green horse with somebody that had never ridden before. Clarence no-longer wanted to see the results that sort of thing could produce. He exhaled a long breath and said,

"Don't go there," to himself. He had his life, he had a good woman, he had a job. There was money in the bank, beer in the fridge and whiskey in the bottle. The cook was headed home and she was amazing to watch in a kitchen. He had a fine old classic western movie on the TV and at his age he still had a future. The 2/c had another season coming and money to do it with. His thought was,

"We got our own stage and we can be our own hero's, right where we are."

Clarence started the movie and sank deeper in his chair. He knew he was over-thinking it. Better to stay with what worked, that old status quo. Being informed on current events was starting to wear him out.

End

www.ingramcontent.com/pod-product-compliance
Lightning Source LLC
Chambersburg PA
CBHW031327170626
46807CB00002B/599